M000210578

BRING
HIM
HOME

BOOKS BY NICOLE TROPE

My Daughter's Secret
The Boy in the Photo
The Nowhere Girl
The Life She Left Behind
The Girl Who Never Came Home

BRING HIM HOME

NICOLE TROPE

bookouture

Published by Bookouture in 2021

An imprint of Storyfire Ltd.
Carmelite House
50 Victoria Embankment
London EC4Y 0DZ

www.bookouture.com

ISBN: 978-1-83888-975-3
eBook ISBN: 978-1-83888-974-6

For D.M.I.J.

CHAPTER ONE

Saturday afternoon

It was not Amber's intention to get lost.

It was not her intention to find herself surrounded by gnarled, scribbly gum trees, their twisted, knotted branches reaching out to catch her hair and clothes. It is after 3 p.m. and black clouds are beginning to gather in the autumn sky. A storm is predicted. 'One month's rain in three days,' the news site warned. Amber shivers in her hoodie. She should have a coat and a hat and a backpack carrying everything she could need should she get lost. But she really didn't mean to get lost.

She was just going to walk in the forest, leaving the beautiful, perfectly named Dream cabin with its sandstone floors and soft leather couches for twenty minutes so she could at least see some of the surrounding bush before the rain set in.

She intended to walk for ten minutes one way and ten minutes back, and then, returning to the cabin, she would open the very expensive bottle of wine she had brought, fire up the spa and watch the rain come down over the gorge, where the trees bristled with the bright oranges and reds of autumn, creating a multicoloured quilt of beauty that would soon be obscured by water. It is the second-to-last week of autumn and she knows that soon the trees that celebrate the changing seasons will be bare, leaving only the evergreen trees standing proudly. The winter cold has, however, already arrived. She pulls the arms of her hoodie over her numb hands, realising how silly it was to have come for a walk like this.

When she returned to the cabin, she was also going to make herself a plate with the pricey Brie and wafer-thin water crackers she'd brought along. And when she was tired of the view, she was going to get out of the spa and binge-watch a season of something funny on Netflix.

And all of that would make up for the fact that she wasn't supposed to be here alone. She was supposed to be with Finn, celebrating their two-year anniversary and maybe, just maybe, getting proposed to.

She feels ridiculously naïve when she thinks about this now.

Finn – blonde-haired, blue-eyed, funny and fabulous Finn – is now with Melody. Melody, who works in IT at the advertising firm where they are all employed. Melody, the quiet, sensitive boyfriend-stealer.

As Amber tramps over the thick green and brown layer of damp leaves, she wishes on them both winter colds that linger. She stops and looks around her again but cannot see any evidence of life, although she can hear rustling leaves and movement in the undergrowth. She feels bad about wishing a cold on Finn but only for a moment. He has completely and thoroughly broken her heart, and she only left the cabin because she thought the chilly air would help her stop crying. It did, at first, but now she's lost and she feels tears spilling and her nose starting to run.

'Why go to the cabin alone?' her best friend, Martha, asked. 'It will only upset you.'

But Amber insisted on going. It was her birthday present to him and she'd already paid for it. She thought it would do her good to get out of the flat and just be somewhere else for a bit. But now she is not so sure.

Walking forward a few paces, she pushes aside the tree ferns with her knees and lifts her phone into the air where a small gap in the canopy of fig trees appears, but she cannot get a bar of service.

She had stepped off what appeared to be a well-trodden path to look at the leaves on a Japanese maple that seemed more pink than red in the afternoon light, but somehow she couldn't find her way back. It happened so quickly it was almost as if the bush had closed in behind her, hiding the path and forcing her to turn in circles as she tried to judge a way out.

She knows that she can't be far from the cabins that make up her resort or from another collection of cabins. They are scattered all over the place here on Mount Watson in the Australian Blue Mountains.

She looks down at her phone again as the wind whips up, blowing a few strands of loose hair across her face and into her mouth. She spits them out, irritated.

'Help,' she says. She doesn't shout it, feeling too embarrassed.

She walks for another minute as the clouds sink lower and the noises of the bush taunt her. She knows there are snakes around, and who knows what else – although there may not be snakes out in the cold, in which case she has no idea what could be making the noises she's hearing. She starts walking a little faster, making more sound than the creatures around her, and suddenly she turns right, just to go in a different direction.

As she steps around a giant fig tree, she sees the edge of a roof. Her relief makes her giggle. She hopes that whoever is there will help. They may have a landline inside so she can contact the sour-faced owner of her cabin and beg to be fetched.

Once she gets to the cabin, she realises that it is part of her resort. It was one of the cabins she considered renting for a couple of days but it was already booked.

'We have regulars in there,' Irene, the owner, told her, sounding annoyed that she had even asked. 'Anyway, it's got three bedrooms and you said this was for a couple.' Irene had finished her sentence

with a sucking noise that Amber now knows was the inhalation
of a cigarette. She's seen Irene twice since she got here and both
times she was sucking deeply on a cigarette. Amber is glad the
woman left her post at the front office to go away for a few days.
'Just put the keys in the box out the front of the office when you
leave. I won't be here. Make sure the place is tidy or you'll be
charged an extra fifty dollars on top of the cleaning fee.' Irene
is definitely in the wrong profession. She seems to hate tourists.
Amber shakes her head – Irene won't be there to come and fetch
her even if she does get hold of the office. Hopefully someone
will answer her call or perhaps the occupants can point her in
the right direction.

She steps over a large fallen branch as she makes her way to
the cabin.

It's a lovely timber-clad building with two levels and a small
window in the triangle roof. There are flower boxes out the front
filled with banksias in pink and red and orange. The timber is
painted in a deep red that catches the last rays of the sun, reminding Amber disconcertingly of blood. Outside the cottage, a black
Mercedes station wagon waits to be driven.

Amber steps up onto the timber porch and knocks on the
front door. As she hits her knuckles against the scarred wood,
she is surprised to feel it swing open a little. 'Excuse me,' she calls
through the partially open door, 'I'm sorry to bother you but I'm
lost and not sure how to get back to my cabin.'

She waits but only silence and warm air from a cedar-smelling
log fire come from the cabin. Amber chews on her lip. She could
just leave and find another cabin. She is sure to stumble across
another one soon. But then she looks behind her and sees that
the light is disappearing fast, a far-off rumble of ominous thunder
alerting her to the incoming storm. It will be here soon. She doesn't
want to be walking through the bush at night, in the darkness and

the pouring rain. She doesn't even have a torch on her and she is already shivering in the cold air.

She knocks again, causing the door to swing open further. 'Maybe they've gone for a walk,' she mutters. She supposes she could wait or she could just dart in and use the landline, which she knows they probably have as her cabin has one.

Looking at her phone again, she sees it seems to have a tiny bit of a signal, though not enough to place a call. The wind scatters some dead leaves at her feet as she pushes open the door and walks into the living area of the cabin.

She focuses on the fire first, where the wood has burned down to grey-white logs, and then she looks at the leather couches, studded with brass buttons and softly moulded by many comfortable nights. And then, as she searches for where the phone might be, she finally sees the tableaux behind the sofa.

On the red and cream rug – which she will later understand was only cream to begin with – is a woman.

Her eyes are wide and nearly black with dilated pupils as she stares at Amber. Her skin is pale and her hair is an unnatural-looking inky-black. She is crouched next to a man who is lying on the floor. In her hand is a large kitchen knife, the blade smooth and suitable for easily slicing through meat and vegetables. The knife the woman is holding is covered in deep red blood. The man is wearing a pale blue shirt, blood spreading across his chest. His eyes are closed.

Amber feels her mouth open and close. She cannot quite believe what she is seeing. Taking a step back, she gets ready to run. Her heart rate has ramped up and her skin is tingling, her breath coming in pants as though she is already running. Instinctively, her body knows she needs to move.

She looks back at the woman, who is absolutely still, as though she has been posed in that position. 'Are you… what… he-hello,'

Amber attempts, her voice trembling, but the woman doesn't move. Amber understands quickly that this is not a game or a joke, that what is happening here is so far beyond what she can deal with that she cannot even begin to think about what to do. She needs help.

Taking a step closer to the open door where the cold wind is drifting in, Amber lifts her phone, relieved to see that it has finally found signal. Her hands shake as she dials 000. The woman on the floor is unmoving, a staring statue. She is holding the knife up, as if to show Amber, but she doesn't even seem to be breathing.

Stepping outside, Amber trips clumsily down the stairs, meaning to put as much space between her and the stone woman as possible but knowing she needs to maintain a signal on her phone. 'Help,' she croaks when a man answers, and she falls to her knees, mud splattering. 'Help.'

Around her the wind whistles, disturbing small piles of damp brown leaves. Their rotting smell catches Amber at the back of her throat and she swallows to avoid throwing up. Above her, a giant fig tree creaks and groans.

Amber knows that she will never be able to rid her mind of the image of the woman, deep red blood glistening on the knife she held over the man's body. It will change her forever.

'Stay away,' the man on the phone tells her, not that she has any intention of going back into the cabin. 'Don't touch anything.'

'But the woman, she's holding a knife,' she replies breathlessly.

'Stay away,' the man instructs again. 'Help is coming. Are you safe? Is she threatening you?'

'No, she hasn't moved. She's not moving at all.'

'Help is coming,' he repeats.

It is only minutes until Amber hears the screech of police and ambulance sirens, and the whirring roar of a helicopter that competes with the rolling thunder that foreshadows the rainstorm to come. It is only minutes until someone wraps her in a blanket and there are police everywhere, moving quickly and shouting with guns drawn. Then Amber watches as the woman, her gaze fixed on something only she can see, is led out to a waiting car, followed closely by a policewoman with a large brown bag that Amber imagines contains the bloody knife.

CHAPTER TWO

Theo, 11 years old

I run, I run, I run. Cold air, cold air. I run, I run, I run.

I can run. I can always run. 'He likes to run,' Mum always says. 'He likes to run more than anything.' I use my body to run but running takes me away from my body as well. Running takes me away from everything. My brain wants my body to run. My brain is autistic. My brain is different. My brain is me and I can run.

I run in the cold air, the wind rushing past my ears, louder than my breath.

I step on leaves and in dirt and on sticks. Leaves, dirt, sticks, leaves, dirt, sticks, leaves, dirt, sticks. Sometimes I feel something under my foot but I still run.

I had to run. I couldn't stay. 'Run,' said Dad. 'Run!'

The sky rumbles. There is no sun.

There are leaves and trees and noise and pain. Pain when I run. No shoes. No shoes. 'Where are your shoes, Theo?' Mum always says. 'Please put on your shoes. You like your blue shoes, don't you?' Mum doesn't understand about shoes. Shoes itch and hurt and squeeze. I can't wear shoes.

'It's not safe to be outside in the bush alone, Theo. Stay inside. Stay safe.' Mum wants me to be safe. But I wasn't safe with her. I had to run.

'Run,' said Dad. 'Get help.'

I stop. I breathe in and out, in and out, slowly. I can't run anymore. *Boom, boom, boom* goes my heartbeat in my ear. I can see the sky. I can feel my breath. Cold. I stop. Scrunch, wisp, growl. Scrunch, wisp, growl. There is something here in the bush, something alive, something that will bite or scratch. Snakes and rats and wallabies live in the bush. Spiders crawl and insects sting. Too much. Too much. I run.

But here is a cabin. Is help here? I don't know help. *Boom, boom, boom.* Too much noise. Too much.

Here. Here I can hide under, crawl under. Wait. I can't run anymore. I should wait. Dad will come. I wait.

'Shelter in place, Theo – do you know what that means? It means that when we are at the cabin, if you ever get lost, you just wait. Find somewhere safe and wait and we will come and find you. Shelter in place, Theo. If you get lost, you must shelter in place.' Mum said shelter in place and Dad said shelter in place but then Dad said run. I didn't know what to do. I did run but now I can shelter in place.

This is a place. This is a place where I can shelter. Old wood, cracked and broken, piles of bricks and the smell of smoke. A small cabin with space underneath. Leaves and dirt and sticks and stones. I can shelter here.

I crawl under. I move my feet and a spider runs away. I make lots of noise with my body to scare away the biting, stinging things.

Cold, cold, cold. My jumper stretches, itchy, itchy. 'Theo, don't put your jumper over your knees, it will stretch out.' My jumper stretches.

Above my head there is a *thump, thump, thump.* 'Quiet, you creatures,' shouts a cross voice. I am scared of the cross voice. I stay still so it cannot find me and get me.

I rock, I rock, I rock. Darkness creeps into my safe place. It is night. 'It's night-time now, Theo, time for sleep. Here's your blanket.'

My blanket is soft, soft, soft. Where is my blanket? Where is my bed? Where is Mum? Where is Dad? Dad said, 'Run, Theo, get help.'

I cannot close my eyes. I am scared of the noises, scared of the dark, scared of the cross voice.

I rock in the dark and I cover my ears. But then I hear singing. I let go of my ears and listen to the words. I hear the song, my song, our song, Mum's song: 'This little light of mine, I'm going to let it shine...'

Mum sings to me. I am her little light. I am this little light. But that's not Mum. Mum's voice is soft and low and quiet. Mum's voice is peace and calm. This voice crackles. This voice is high. Not Mum. But it is our song.

My eyes get heavier and heavier. I am small, I am a ball. I am a ball in my bubble. I am round and safe under here. I cover my ears, but I still hear the song. Everything else is silent. My eyes close, close. I am in a bubble now, my bubble. No one can touch me in my bubble. No sound can get to me, only our song is in my ears. I am bubble-safe and I am a little light. I am...

CHAPTER THREE

Rose, 85 years old

'And another thing,' mutters Rose to the picture of her sister, Mary, sitting on the polished wood buffet. 'I am sick of these city people tramping all over my land. I found two of 'em just this morning. "Private property," I said, and the one fella, the little one wearing a blue beanie, he just laughed at me. "Gosh, sorry," he said, "we thought this cabin was abandoned. There isn't a fence or anything!" Cheeky bastard. I saw them off quick enough, waved my rake at them and they just ran.'

She puts her cup of tea down on the large oak table and picks up the hand mirror she keeps there. The table used to sit in the house she grew up in, right in the centre of town, with a large kitchen and three small bedrooms. The table was the only thing her family took when they had to move here to this cabin, where the rent was affordable for a woman on her own with three kids. The table fills the whole living area but Rose doesn't want anything smaller. It's full of burns from the cooking pot and scratches and some gouges from her brother, Lionel. Lionel got angry sometimes, anger he couldn't control, and if no one stopped him, he would grab a knife and go at the table. The wood was strong enough to take his anger, anger at everything he didn't understand and couldn't control because of the way his brain worked.

Rose touches a deep gouge, her brother's face coming to her. She misses him and Mary every day. There are parts of the table that she has worn smooth with her cloth because she always sits in the same spot to eat, the spot she has sat at since she was a little thing, barely able to see over the top. It is the table where they gathered to eat and where she and Mary did their homework. Its large turned legs are strong and still beautiful even though the varnish has worn away.

Rose remembers the first time she and her family saw this cabin. She was eight, Mary was thirteen and Lionel was only four. Their mother had hung on to the house in town for as long as she could, but the rent was far beyond what she could manage on her own. Their father had fled to Sydney, finding a son with problems too much to deal with. Rose's mother, Dorothy – or Dot as she was called by those who knew and loved her – had brought the three of them up here on a sunny afternoon in the December summer, just before Christmas.

Rose remembers the way her mother smiled sadly as she showed them the run-down little cabin in the mountains, as though she understood that it was nothing at all like her children had expected.

It was essentially only one room with a small bedroom off to the side. The stove was old and blackened but at least there was a bathroom close enough to almost feel inside. The floorboards were rotting and there were gaps where the winter chill would creep in.

'Now, chickens,' her mother said, using her pet word for her children, 'I'll make it nice. You'll see. Vincent from town is coming up to do all the repairs so we'll have a good strong roof and the floor will be fixed.' Vincent was the town handyman, able to repair or build almost anything. He's long gone now. Most of the people Rose knew when she was a young girl are long gone. The worst losses were her brother and sister.

'I can sew some curtains, Mum,' Mary said, ever the peacemaker, as Rose ran her hands along a panelled wall, finding splinters and chipped paint. 'I'll make a little room for me and Rose, and you can have your own space. Lionel can sleep in the middle. We'll be just fine.'

Rose tried to smile through her tears but she knew she would miss the little room with pink gingham curtains that she shared with her sister. She would miss simply turning on the light and not having to worry if the generator had petrol, and she would miss water gushing out of the tap because the water for the cabin came from a tank that needed to be kept full, and it had been a dry, dry year.

They made the cabin a nice place to be. Vincent had worked virtually for free, knowing of the family's troubles, and the floor was fixed, the roof made strong, and he even sectioned off a room for Rose and Mary. The bathroom was enclosed and made part of the house, and between Mary and her mother, they turned the cabin into home. Before she knew it, Rose couldn't imagine living anywhere else.

Now, Rose rubs her hand over the back of the hand mirror, loving the cool, gleaming surface. The mirror with its mother-of-pearl backing, flashing its multicoloured sheen, is the most beautiful thing Rose has ever owned. It was a gift from Mary for her twenty-first birthday. She looks in the mirror and chuckles. She can imagine that the young men she scared off earlier today thought she was a witch, with her white hair hanging down her back in a messy plait and her crooked teeth. She's never been one for creams and fancy stuff. But her pale blue eyes still sparkle when she smiles, so there's life in her yet. She pushes a piece of hair behind her ear and lifts her head, straightening her neck. 'I was a beauty once, Mary, wasn't I?'

Under the cabin a rustling sound alerts her to the possums waking up for the night. A rumbling in the sky tells her that rain will be here any moment, soaking into the ground and making it difficult for her to go outside. But she wouldn't begrudge the farmers what they need.

There is more noise under the house, rustling and crunching. 'Better get out and about before the rain comes,' she calls to the possums. Any minute now they'll be scampering over her roof and running down the drainpipes as they go out looking for food and fun. More crackling irritates her and she stands up and grabs her broom. 'Quiet, you creatures!' she shouts, more to let them know that this is her house than anything else, using her broom to thump on the floor a few times. 'Humph.' She nods. 'That's better,' she says when they go quiet.

'Silly possums,' she laughs. 'And don't tell me that I should have been polite to those boys on my land earlier, Mary. It's not my fault that all those cabins just grew up here overnight and now the city people wander in, no matter the time of year.' Rose nods her head as she speaks, occasionally glancing at the picture of her sister as though the serene expression on Mary's face may change in reaction to what she's saying. It's a picture of Mary and her husband, Bart, and their children, William and Nancy. It was taken when Mary turned sixty and is one of those posed studio images which Rose doesn't love as much as the candid photos of her sister laughing or busy in her garden. But it is in a lovely frame and Rose likes to look at it and remember Mary, with her neatly coiled brown hair and kind smile.

'I miss you, love,' she whispers as she does every day and has done every day for the last five years since Mary left this earth. When she passed away, she was surrounded by her children and grandchildren, just as she wanted to be. Rose held her sister's hand as her breathing rattled down to the last breath in the big, metal-framed bed she had shared with Bart her whole married life. Rose had felt a chill settle over her shoulders, knowing it was Mary's last touch goodbye.

There were a lot of tears from the children but Rose kept her tears to herself. The pain was too big for tears, so big it took her breath away. She sat for an hour holding her sister's hand, and bless those two kids, they left Rose in the room alone for those last precious moments.

It had been quick in the end, which was how Mary would have wanted it. She had got up in the night, gone to the bathroom and had a stroke. They'd taken her off to the hospital, but it seemed as though as soon as they'd got her there, her body had decided it was done. She'd drifted in and out of sleep but roused herself to whisper to William, 'Take me home, love.' And so, they had. She only lay in her bed for a day before she was gone; and Rose was pleased that her sister got to hear a kookaburra call out to the world and feel the summer breeze on her face. It was as good a way as any to go.

Rose looks forward to death herself now – not in a maudlin way, just in a kind of peaceful acceptance. She likes being alive, but death is not a scary thought. Especially now that her beloved Mary is gone. She looks down at the mirror again. When she was young and her hair was a chestnut-brown, her skin smooth and her blue eyes wide and clear, it never did her any good. It just brought her sadness and pain, so she doesn't mind looking like an old crone now. People tend to leave an old crone alone.

Rose shivers and goes over to the fire, throwing another log on. She's wearing her warm underwear already underneath her baggy grey pants as she knows it's going to be a cold winter this year.

'Please come and live with me in town, Auntie Rose,' William begged after Mary had passed on. He's a good one, is William. When he was about twenty-five, he moved in with his lovely friend Graham. At least Mary had called him a 'friend', but Rose wasn't a bit surprised when two years ago she got invited to their wedding. They had it in the pub and the whole town came. It was a real 'knees-up', as her mother would have said, and Rose tried not to be sad that Mary had missed the special day.

'I felt you there with us, didn't I, Mary, especially when William and I had a dance,' she says to the picture of her sister.

She likes visiting William and Graham, and they make a good roast chicken when she goes over for dinner. She usually stays the night in the special room that they say is just for her, but she is always glad to come home. Home is where the memories float in the air. She doesn't like to think of giving that up.

'I don't like town, William,' Rose said as she does every time he asks her to come and live with him. 'All I need is my groceries brought up to me and I'm good.'

'You've got no proper electricity, Rose, just a generator, and you won't even get a mobile phone. You're all alone out there and we all worry about you. The landline goes out far too often.'

'I'll stay as long as I'm able, William,' she always tells him.

Rose rubs at her hip, which complains something terrible in the cold. Truthfully, Rose stays away from town if she can. Town is not a good place. Town holds bad memories and people she doesn't want to see. Bad winds its way down the generations – that's just what happens. She's heard things, things she never wants to think about if she can help it.

After holding her hands up to the fire, she switches on a light, hearing the generator fire up. She's glad of the new generator, to be honest, even though William said he had to 'bend her arm' to convince her. It's nice to have the lights and stove working in the colder months. In summer she's happy to cook outside with her little pot but autumn nights get chilly in the mountains. Winter is fierce and vengeful, and some weeks she doesn't even make it outside for her usual tramp around the bush.

'Might have a bit of that leftover stew William sent, Mary,' she says now to the empty cabin. She busies herself getting the stew from the fridge and putting it into a pot, stirring until it starts to simmer, filling the room with its warm, meaty smell. The chunks of meat are tender and the gravy rich with wine so it's an enjoyable dinner. But once she's cleaned up and the darkness has closed in, she feels the sadness settle on her. She does what she always does when her heart aches – she starts to sing. 'This little light of mine, I'm going to let it shine, this little light of mine…' A favourite hymn from childhood, one that her mother sang to her, and when she was gone, taken too soon, one that Mary sang to her after that.

Rose remembers church when she was a young lady, exciting and special on a Sunday because of all the boys from the surrounding farms that attended. She remembers herself and Mary next to each other on the slick, wooden pews, rubbed smooth by many hands over the years, whispering to each other about this boy or that boy. She misses church but she can sing to the Lord and he hears her just as well up here in her little home. She feels the presence of her sister in the cabin as she sings, and joyful memories appear, crowding out the awful ones. 'This little light of mine, I'm going to let it shine…'

CHAPTER FOUR
Cecelia, 46 years old

She keeps her eyes closed, just feeling the motion of the police car as they drive.

'I've never seen anything like it,' she hears the female constable say to her companion.

'Humph,' he replies.

There is a smell in the car, a slight tang of body odour exacerbated by the blasting heat from the air vents. Cecelia is shivering anyway. They didn't let her change, simply giving her a blue paper jumpsuit to pull on over her clothes. 'You need to put this on. It's to protect the evidence,' the policewoman told her, her light brown eyes filled with suspicion, one hand resting on the gun at her side as if daring Cecelia to make a move.

The officer had shouted the instructions, bothered by Cecelia's silence, by her inability to make any words emerge from her mouth. And then she had mimed that Cecelia should put on the jumpsuit, as though she thought she might be deaf. Cecelia had complied, pulling on the jumpsuit. The knife had gone in a brown paper bag while Cecelia watched, wide-eyed.

What happened? Nick? Theo? What happened? The questions repeat themselves in her mind. She would like to open her mouth and ask but she seems unable to do that. Despite her best efforts, she cannot make a single sound.

She splays her fingers, looks down at her hands. They are sticky with blood, the metal smell mixing with the body odour in the car, making her stomach lurch. *Whose blood is this? Is it mine?*

They are taking her to the hospital. They have told her this twice. There was an ambulance but someone else went in the ambulance, she thinks. *Nick went in the ambulance*, she tells herself. *This is Nick's blood. Why am I covered in Nick's blood?*

Nick was angry. 'Why does it always have to be like this, Cecelia?'

Nick was frustrated. 'Why is everything about him? When will there ever be time for us?'

Nick didn't understand. 'It's your choice, you know. I'm completely sick of it. You wouldn't even care if I left. The only thing that would worry you is that there would be no more money. That's all I am to you now! Just a pay cheque. But I'm not going to live the rest of my life like this. I can't and I won't. We can't work this out. I need time away from you and all this.'

She remembers her husband's deep blue eyes, narrowed and furious, his hand moving through his thick brown hair, his voice getting louder and louder. *It's Nick's blood.*

Lifting her hands to her cheeks, she feels that they are wet with tears. He was so angry with her, so frustrated. And she understood that he meant it this time. This time he was really going to leave. He was right about her fear over not having enough money to take care of Theo. He was right but he is still more than just a pay cheque. Is he more than just a pay cheque? *What happened then? What happened?* Her head spins with it all.

She feels the car stop. They are at the hospital and the police-woman takes her arm, helping her climb out. She's grateful. Her legs are weak. She doesn't look at the other police officer, instead looking at her blue-bootied feet. *Nick's blood is evidence. I am covered in evidence – but what happened?*

In a hospital room she is taken apart, one item of clothing at a time, as everything is swabbed and tested. They only stop when she is down to her underwear. *There's something you're missing*, she wants to say but speech is impossible. She cannot speak because she's not allowed to speak. Instinctively, somehow, she feels that. She wants to tell the nurse to look at where she is looking, to notice the damaged skin. *Do you see that scratch across my stomach? Can you see it? It wasn't there this morning.* The cold air in the hospital room makes it sting, but only a little. There is more than the scratch to see but it could have been so much worse. She doesn't know how she knows this, but she does.

Where is Nick? And where is Theo? Where is my little boy with his father's blue eyes and a halo of curls?

'Run,' Nick told Theo, she recalls, and so their son ran. But where is he now? She wants to tell them they need to look for her child but what if they find him? What then? Theo has seen too much. Standing in her underwear in the hospital room, she shivers so hard her teeth chatter. There is a small mirror on the wall, and she takes a few steps towards it but immediately turns away. There is blood on her chin and on her lips. *I am Snow White. Black hair, pale skin, red lips.*

She has a vision of herself touching her face, her hand covering her mouth to hold in her scream. It is Nick's blood on her lips, she realises with a sickening thud.

Where is Nick?

Where is Theo?

Is he safer out in the bush, out in the mountains? She wants to whimper with the fear and despair of it all, but no sound emerges from her.

On Friday morning, only yesterday, they loaded up the car, the excitement of a winter holiday making eleven-year-old Theo scattered and jumpy. Change isn't easy for him but he likes the cabin, loves going there on vacation. He was looking forward to it. 'Get your cars, Theo. Find your blanket,' she kept repeating as he hopped on one leg and then jumped on the trampoline to rid himself of excess energy. They all like the cabin. There would be boardgames and bushwalks and peace. No phone calls, no interruptions, and she and Nick could work it out. They were supposed to work it out.

Where is Theo?

Please keep him safe, she silently begs, *please, please just keep him safe*. Her little boy is out there on his own.

'Let's get you into a shower,' says the nurse gently, bringing Cecelia back to the cold, square, white room where there is only a bed, a plastic chair and a two-drawer metal side table. She looks outside the window at the fiery red leaves of the maple trees in the garden surrounding the hospital. It's autumn and it's cold. Theo is out there wearing only his jumper. He must be afraid and panicking. He must be cold and so confused. She shivers.

'Come on, love,' says the nurse. She is older, probably in her sixties, her grey hair wound in a bun and her red lipstick seeping into the cracks around her lips, but her emerald-green eyes are calm and filled with sympathy. Cecelia thinks that she could probably talk to her, could probably explain what happened or, at least, what she remembers. She opens her mouth but nothing comes out. The nurse watches her, waits and then says softly, 'You need to have a shower and a rest and then things will be… easier.'

What will be easier?

There is something there, inside Cecelia, something pushing against a barrier. The truth is trying to get out. She knows that this morning she made pancakes for Theo, made at least ten pancakes so that she could give him four perfectly round ones, because her little boy will only eat perfectly round pancakes. She knows that she and Nick ate the rest with bacon. Theo and Nick were at the cabin for breakfast and then they went for a walk. There is a storm coming and they wanted to walk before the storm hit.

They returned with cheeks kissed red by the cold air. Theo was holding a large stick that she had to convince him to leave outside, and she made him peanut butter sandwiches for lunch. 'Eat now,' she knows she said, and then she waited while he inspected his plate. He smiled when he saw how perfect the triangles were and that the carrot sticks were uniform, placed correctly. And then her husband and son went fishing and she went shopping and... Outside, night has arrived swiftly as though a light has just been switched off. She knows that the last few hours of the day are the problem. She cannot think what happened in the last few hours.

She glances at the window again. There is a rumble of thunder threatening its fury. It will be a big storm. 'The biggest this year,' they said on the news that played on the cabin's television this morning.

The nurse takes Cecelia by the elbow, steering her towards the bathroom. 'Come on, then. In you get. Do you need help? Shall I help you?'

Cecelia doesn't know. *Do I need help?* She thinks she may need help.

Turning on the shower, the nurse checks the temperature, points out soap and a washcloth wrapped in a packet. 'I'll wait for you out here,' she says, closing the bathroom door.

Cecelia's gaze lands on her face in the mirror over the white basin, and she instantly looks away. She discards her underwear and steps into the water, quickly tearing open the washcloth and adding soap. And then she rubs at the skin on her face and her body, rubs hard at the scratch on her stomach, hard enough to make the sting burn. She rubs and rubs and rubs.

Lifting her face to the warm water, she feels the spray hit her lips. It's not hot enough and she feels like she needs heat, as much heat as possible, to cleanse her body. She fiddles with the taps, turning up the hot water, turning down the cold, but it's still not hot enough.

If she can just find Nick and Theo, then what happened will return and she will not have this large gap in her memory. She remembers giving Theo lunch, the feel of the bread underneath her hands, the large knife she used to cut the carrots. She must have eaten something herself but she has no idea what. But later, something happened in the cabin, something awful. It must have been awful or Nick would never have told Theo to run. 'Run, Theo,' she heard him say. She remembers that. 'Run, Theo,' he shouted. But what was her son supposed to be running from?

CHAPTER FIVE

Kaycee, 19 years old

Kaycee snorts and giggles. 'Do another one, Kace!' shouts her boyfriend, Adam, and Kaycee obligingly fills up the glass with apple-flavoured vodka and downs it, no coughing, no choking. Her throat is already lubricated by all the shots she has taken tonight.

'I think that may be enough,' she says as she feels her stomach roll and twist, and Adam laughs, patting her on the back. 'It's never enough with you,' he says, and then he looks around the university bar and shouts, 'Kaycee says she's had enough.' There is general laughter and shouts of, 'Rubbish,' and, 'Not Kaycee,' and, 'Kaycee's never had enough.'

Smiling, Kaycee bites down on her lip, which is numb. She knows that if she gets up now and goes back to her dorm, she can get some sleep, and then when she wakes up hungover with a dry mouth at three in the morning, she can use that time to finish her assignment that's due on Monday. It's warm in the university bar, almost too warm, with the heaters blasting from their stations on the wall. It's seven o'clock, and she told Adam that she only wanted to stop at the bar for a couple of drinks before they went for dinner.

'Sure, sure,' he said, giving her his best cheeky smile, his deep dimples distracting her as they always did. He knew that she would never stay for just one drink. They were supposed to try the new Italian restaurant in Newtown – a trendy part of Sydney filled with interesting restaurants and stores. They were going to catch a train and stand in line because you can't book. She looked at the menu online, already planned to order the spaghetti alla Calabrese, rich and salty with olives and chorizo. For once they were actually going to do something with their Saturday night instead of just getting drunk and stumbling home to the dorm for a cheap takeaway and bad sex. She knows Adam isn't going anywhere now. He is holding court, telling a story, his voice booming over the music that blasts from the speakers. He is surrounded by his fans, by pretty girls attracted to his blonde hair and big brown eyes, by boys who think he's smart and funny. He's not leaving this bar tonight and Kaycee knows she should just leave him to it, just walk out and go back to her room.

But she taps her glass instead and smiles at the cute, curly red-haired barman. He doesn't live on campus like she and Adam and most of those hanging out in the bar do. She knows he already told her his name twice tonight but she can't remember it. She touches her anaesthetised lips again, hating the way they feel. She needs to stop doing this, she tells herself, she really does, as the barman fills up her glass.

'Maybe this should be the last one,' he says. He has a square jaw sprouting a three-day growth and sea-green eyes that she can't help staring into.

'Don't police her drinking,' Adam snaps, his eyes darkening with anger. Kaycee looks at him, wondering when he walked away from the crowd he was talking to. How much time has passed? She squints at the clock on the wall with its cracked glass face. It's after eight. When did that happen? They got here at five.

'Somebody has to,' says the barman. He stands up straight and squares his shoulders, letting Adam see how much bigger than him he is.

'Whatever,' says Adam and he drifts off down the bar again to another group of people. Adam is supposed to be her boyfriend but Kaycee knows that he's not actually all that interested in her. He likes to watch her get drunk, likes to have drunken sex with her, but they've never really spent any time together beyond that. He's not a nice guy. She knows that, knows that he cheated on his last two girlfriends, and she's pretty sure he's cheated on her. But he's so good-looking and very charming, and when he asked her out the first time, she found herself saying yes. She's not sure why they're still together after five months but fears it may just be apathy on her part. Truthfully, she doesn't have the energy to have a conversation with him, doesn't care enough to. Mostly, she doesn't care enough to do anything except get to 5 p.m. and devour her first drink of the night.

She runs her finger through a spilled drop of vodka on the peeling wood veneer bar, spreading it into the scratches and flaking off some more of the varnish. Her parents would be utterly and completely horrified at how she is behaving. *Whatever.* She taps the glass again so that the barman will pour her another drink.

Turning, she looks around the bar, at the small round wooden tables and the peeling fake leather chairs, and sighs. This is not how she imagined her university years would be when she started nearly two years ago. She thought that she would party, yes, but she also imagined that there would be deep friendships formed and a lifelong partner met and a whole new world of information and ideas opened up to her.

Instead, she has somehow found herself the campus joke. She is barely scraping by in all her courses. She is meant to be on her way to a world-class science degree. She is meant to be one step away from working for the Garvan Institute, researching brain cancer. She is meant to be a lot of things but she has somehow managed to be none of those. She is mostly drunk and sad.

Kaycee moved out of home in the hope that she could finally begin her life without her parents interfering when it suited them and without having to think about her brother first, last and before everything else. She wanted to just be; that was the plan anyhow.

She looks at the drink the red-haired barman has poured her and then she turns away from it. *Just get up and walk out now*, she tells herself. *Just do it. Leave Adam, leave them all and go back to your room and get some sleep.*

She sighs. She has no idea what tethers her to this bar and these people who don't care about her. Not for the first time, she wishes that she had not been so insistent about moving out.

'But we only live forty minutes away from the university,' her mother said. 'You can commute.'

'You promised I could stay on campus if I wanted to,' she replied.

'When I thought you were going to go to Melbourne, not when you're staying in Sydney.'

'It's fine, Cecelia,' her father said, stepping in. 'We can afford it and we did promise. It will be good for Kaycee to get away, to have some time to spread her wings.'

'Fine – I give up,' her mother said. She helped Kaycee pack and bought her everything she needed, but she never, not once, said she was happy about it. 'We'll miss you,' she said the day Kaycee loaded up her car to move to the dorm. But even then, her mother's eyes strayed to where Theo was crouched in the driveway, studying a collection of ants hauling a dead beetle.

'Bye, Theo,' she called.

He looked up, his hands signing the word 'goodbye', and then he returned to his study of the ants.

'He's going to miss you so much,' her mother said, her attention on her son.

'I'll be home for dinner on Friday, Mum,' Kaycee said with a sigh, annoyed and desperate to get away, to be free. She just didn't imagine freedom would look like this.

She should have gone with her family to the cabin they rent in the autumn school holidays every year, but she had no desire to spend two weeks at the arse end of the Blue Mountains near the small, nowhere town of Mount Watson. She couldn't imagine anything more boring. 'I have assignments to get done,' she lied to her mother. Assignments could be done anywhere and submitted online. Anywhere but in the university bar.

'Well, you got your wish,' she mutters to herself now.

'What did you say?'

Kaycee swivels her stool back to look into the barman's green eyes. 'Oh, nothing.'

'Your phone's ringing,' he says, pointing at her mobile lying on the bar, covered in splashes of vodka.

Kaycee wipes her hand across the screen, not recognising the number. She answers it anyway. 'Yeah?'

'Is this Kaycee Somerton?' The man's voice has an official edge, and without thinking she sits up straight.

'Yeah…' she says warily but then she remembers it's Saturday night. There is no way one of her tutors or professors would call her on a Saturday night.

'My name is Constable Emmerson. I'm with the Mount Watson police. I'm afraid your parents have been involved in an incident.'

Kaycee feels her stomach churn and her head feels light enough to float right off her neck. She puts her hand in front of her mouth, scared she's going to throw up. 'An in-incident?' she stutters. 'What does that mean?'

'It's difficult to explain, but—'

'And Theo?'

'Theo?' questions the man on the other end of the phone.

'Theo's my brother, he's eleven. He was with them at the cabin. Is he okay?'

'Oh… we didn't know he was supposed to be there. We haven't seen him. I forgot about Theo.'

'What?' She gives her head a shake, hoping this will help her focus, but all it does is make everything in the room ripple and sway. She is going to be sick very soon.

'I think you should come here so that…' the constable says. 'You should come here. Your mother and father are in the hospital.'

Kaycee bites down hard on her frozen lips, dropping her phone. She makes it to the bathroom just in time.

CHAPTER SIX

Sunday

Theo

Light. I open my eyes. Grey light. Grey rain light. *Shoosh, shoosh.* Grey rain sound. The rain is a waterfall. There is no sun. The ground is hard and wet and I have no soft blanket but I still slept. Now my skin is cold and my bones are cold. I am cold, cold, cold. 'Theo, put on your jumper, please,' Mum always says. 'It's cold. Theo, you have to wear a different jumper, the blue one is in the wash. Theo, please don't do that. Theo, stop, wait, I'll get it, I'll get it, Theo, please calm down.'

Where is Dad? Where is Mum? It is morning. In the morning I have breakfast. The toast must be crunchy. It must be equal triangles. The peanut butter must come to the edges or it tastes wrong. It must be smooth, smooth or it looks wrong and I can't eat it. I like the crunch of toast in my ears. All the other noise goes away. *Crunch, crunch, crunch.* It is morning and I need breakfast.

There is a noise. A slither and a sniff. Too much noise. Something runs over my foot, something running out of the rain. I don't know what it is. Brown fur, teeth. I am scared. It's in my bubble and I can't make it stay out. I close my eyes and cover my ears with my hands. I make a sound to make the other sounds go away. I make a sound in my throat that fills my ears. 'Eeeee,' I say and I rock. I will wait until all the sounds go away. I will wait until the something with fur goes away. I wait and I rock and then there is a change in the air. I feel it. Something is different. I open my eyes and I see what's different. A person is here. A person has come. Not Mum. Not Dad. Not Kaycee. A person I don't know. A stranger. The stranger has crawled under this cabin and come into my bubble. I stare at the stranger and the stranger shouts.

'Oi, you! What are you doing? Come out from under there!'

White hair, saggy face, angry. I can hear angry. I know angry. I see the face. My eyes see the face again and again, like a million pictures at once. White hair, saggy face, angry. White hair, saggy face, angry. Too many pictures so I close my eyes. I want it to go away. I want the angry to go away. Sometimes Mum is angry with me. Sometimes my hands do things that make Mum angry.

'Mum is angry with you, Theo. You broke all the crayons. Why would you do that?' That's what Kaycee said.

I couldn't tell Mum about the smell of the crayons. The smell made me break them. I like the smell from inside. *Click, crack* went the crayons and the smell was light and blue.

I shut my eyes tight, tight to make the angry stranger go away. But that doesn't happen.

I open my eyes. Still there, still there. Too many pictures. I want to run. I try to run but the jumper has caught my legs. I put my hands over my ears. I rock, I rock and I watch the stranger.

'Run,' said Dad. But Dad hasn't come. I don't understand. Where is Dad? Where is Mum? I take my hands off my ears because the stranger is speaking to me.

'Ah,' says the voice, the high, crackly voice. I see her face, not angry now, softer. The stranger is a she. *Shoosh, shoosh* is the rain sound. The voice comes closer, closer – too close. I want to run. But I have to rock. I need my bubble. I need my bubble. I shut my eyes, cover my ears.

'Hey, hey, look at me, open your eyes and look at me.' She is shouting, and I hear that. I hear that even with my hands over my ears.

I open my eyes and I look, taking my hands from my ears.

'Do you want to eat?' she asks in a soft voice. She moves her hand and makes a sign. I see the sign and I understand. She can talk to me. 'Eat,' she signs. 'Eat.'

I nod my head and I sign back, 'Eat. I want to eat.'

'Come, come,' she signs. Her hand moves. I understand come. I understand eat. I will come. I will eat.

I take my jumper off my knees. I watch her crawl away, slow, slow. White hair, saggy skin, crooked teeth can speak to me. *Swoosh, swoosh* and I am in the rain and I am wet and she is wet. Up the stairs, into the house. This is not our cabin. We stay at the cabin for two weeks every year. Two weeks is fourteen days. Fourteen days is three hundred and thirty-six hours. But this is not our cabin. This is not Mum or Dad, but white hair, saggy skin, crooked teeth looks at me and she makes the sign, 'Eat,' and I nod. She can sign. I will eat. In the morning I eat.

The sky is grey, the rain is watering the mud and trees outside.

'Here,' she says, 'dry yourself,' and she gives me a towel. It is old and scratchy but it can make my skin dry. At home my towel is blue and thick. At home is Mum and Dad but this is not home. There is no Mum here because Dad said, 'Run.' I ran from the knife. I ran from the blood. I had to run.

CHAPTER SEVEN

Rose

'Up with the sun, Mary,' says Rose as she wakes. There is not even a sliver of light coming in through the threadbare white lace curtains, but her body instinctively knows the time. It's six and the light will come soon enough although there will not be the brightness of a sunny autumn day. The rain set in last night, rumbling in and staying. Everything is grey, and Rose remembers rainy days with Mary and Lionel, remembers bread toasted over the fire, dripping with butter, and thick hot chocolate made in the pot. Such a special treat. Mary would only have a little so that her siblings could have more. Lionel would hold his cup in both hands, sipping slowly, knowing there would be no more if he spilled. He understood some things. Hot chocolate was precious; he understood that.

'Takes me a while these days,' she says to herself, and she moves her arms and legs, checking that everything is still working before she clicks on her bedside lamp. She is layered underneath the heavy quilt William gave her for Christmas last year. It is warmth itself and she knows it would have cost him a lot of money. He is good that way, William, practical with gifts, and he seems to always know what she needs.

Finally, she sits up and rests on the edge of the bed, shivering a little despite the layers of warm underwear and the fluffy gown her niece sent for her last birthday. It must have cost a fortune and Rose had a mind to send it back, but the purple fluff was so soft and the gown so warm she kept it. 'Purple is such a ridiculous colour,' she says to Mary. 'I never was one for purple, was I, love? I liked blue. Nancy said right away she would change it but I don't like to offend, not me.'

She hugs the gown around her and stands up – the first step of the day is always the hardest. Muscles and bones protest against the cold and movement but she keeps going. Filling the kettle and stoking up the nearly burnt-out fire, putting some bread in to toast and generally getting the day going.

As she sits down to sip at her strong black tea, sweetened with four teaspoons of sugar – none of that fake rubbish for her that William and Graham use – she tries to listen out for the morning sounds of the mountains, but the rain drowns everything out. She usually listens for the *peter-peter* call of the little Jacky Winter birds that are everywhere around her small home, but there's nothing to hear today but the pounding of the rain on the tin roof.

It eases up for a moment before returning full force, but in that brief hiatus there's another noise that catches her ear.

It's a rustling sound, a movement coming from under the cabin. The possums must be returning from their night-time shenanigans. But the noise is repeated, the same sound over and over again, and that's a bit unusual. More than a bit unusual. She's never heard something like that before. And then, as there is a roll of thunder and the rain returns, a kind of keening starts up, high and distressed. It's possible to hear it even above the rain.

She stops sipping her tea and listens.

'There's definitely something under there, Mary.' Something trapped and scared. She stands up, taking her rake from where it stands next to the front door. 'I'll see whatever it is off, love – don't you worry.' She pulls on her father's old raincoat, left behind when he went off looking for a new life. It reaches down to her toes and she slips her feet into her sturdy brown boots. She's as covered up as she can be. The coat is heavy but it will keep her dry.

She doesn't like to think of some poor creature suffering. Maybe it needs to be put out of its misery if it's hurt. A rabbit caught by a fox might manage an escape after being bitten but then the poor thing has to die in pain. Rose doesn't like to think of something small and harmless in agony, though it doesn't sound like a rabbit – in fact, it doesn't sound like any animal she's ever heard. 'Well, no use just standing here, Mary.'

The rain dribbles and plinks onto her porch as she takes a deep breath of the frigid early-morning air. Puddles are everywhere as the saturated ground gives up trying to drain the water away, the trees weighed down by the continuous onslaught. It takes her a bit of time to manoeuvre herself down to see under the house and she's glad that there's a little bit of light by the time she gets there.

Later she will think that it's lucky she has a strong heart or she's sure it would have stopped dead right then when she saw what was under the cabin. Instead, her heart runs a mile a minute before she gets angry and starts shouting, 'Get out of there!'

It's the way he is sitting that calms her down, the way he has his jumper stretched over his knees and his hands clamped over his ears. He rocks back and forth and shakes his head like he is trying to blot it all out, to make it all stop. She remembers then, remembers what that means, and she talks to him the same way she talked to Lionel all those years ago. 'Look at me! Look at me!' And then when he does, she shows him the sign for 'eat'. That's how she used to talk to Lionel after all, just with signs.

She smiles when he responds. He's obviously not deaf or he wouldn't be covering his ears, but she knows about kids like him. 'Come,' she gestures, and then she does the sign for 'eat' again and he silently follows her up into her cabin.

The rain pummels him but he moves up the worn steps and onto the shelter of the porch quickly enough. Rose takes longer, but finally they are both inside with the door shut tight against the force of nature. She shrugs off the coat, leaving it in a sodden puddle by the door, and pulls off the boots, glad to return her feet to her slippers. Taking a towel, she hands it to the boy and then she points at a chair.

He watches her, wary, afraid. She can read his confusion and would like to throw a thousand questions his way, but somehow, as though she is being guided by something else, she knows to keep quiet.

Sitting down slowly on the chair, he rubs himself with the green towel, frowning at how rough it is.

He looks, she thinks, like an angel, and for a moment she wonders if that's what he is. The Lord works in mysterious ways and it would not be all that surprising if an angel turned up on her doorstep with white-blonde hair and saucer-like blue eyes, his rosebud lips blue with cold.

If this is a test, Lord, I hope I pass.

She hears Mary's words in response as though her sister is standing right next to her, whispering in her ear: 'Don't be ridiculous, Rose. He's a lost child. Just be kind and help him.'

She has no idea what to give him but she starts with water. He looks at the glass and then sticks his finger into it before gulping it down like he's never had a drop to drink before.

Taking the toast she's made for herself, she puts it onto a plate in front of him. She puts the butter near him, along with a knife and some peanut butter, and she sits down. His blue eyes are wide and filled with incomprehension but she makes the sign for 'eat' again, pointing to the toast. He picks up the knife and puts it down again. He is soaking wet and shivering but it doesn't seem to be bothering him, and she realises that they need to establish a little trust first before they can do anything else.

'Eat,' she signs again.

He taps the jar of peanut butter and looks at her. Rose understands, so she spreads the creamy-smooth spread across the toast and then thinks for a moment before finally cutting it into two perfect triangles. She puts the toast back on the plate and waits. Eyeing her suspiciously, the boy picks up the piece of toast, takes a bite and, finding it to his liking, gobbles it down in two ticks.

Rose quickly places another piece of bread under the griller while he finishes up and then drinks another glass of water.

She has never seen hair quite so white before, not the kind that doesn't come out of a bottle at least. Emily in town has hair that colour but Rose knows for sure that it's not her natural shade. Emily is the local hairdresser and her hair colour changes with the wind.

The boy has a heart-shaped face and a little pointed chin. He is, she thinks, a touch taller than her, but then she was never very big to begin with and she knows that with each passing year she gets smaller and smaller. His skin is baby-smooth though so he can't have reached puberty. He could be ten or eleven, maybe even twelve. He is dressed in thick tracksuit pants and what looks like a hand-knitted blue jumper, although Rose is sure it must have been made to look like that in a factory somewhere. His feet, she notices when she peeks under the table, are bare and filthy and there is blood on one of them. But the clothes he is wearing look expensive enough and she knows that he might just not like shoes. Lionel never did. He would scream bloody murder each time they put them on him. By the time he was seven his feet were as tough as old boots and he could walk over thorns and not feel them. Their mother worried he wouldn't know he was hurt so she and Mary took it in turns to inspect his feet every night as they cleaned them, making sure there were no cuts. He was a difficult one for keeping still, hating the feel of the cloth on his feet.

She would like to look at this boy's feet more closely, clean them and make sure there's nothing stuck inside, but she knows not to touch him. He has that look, that 'don't touch' look. She has to tread carefully. Once her aunt came from Melbourne for a visit and she grabbed Lionel in a hug. He was only six then but he kicked and screamed so hard, her aunt was in tears and she had a bruise on her side that shocked Rose with its blue-black colours. Kids like Lionel don't like to be touched. He may be nothing like Lionel but something tells her that he is. Maybe the Lord sent him her way because he knew she would understand. She won't touch.

'So, who are you, little one?' Rose asks, not expecting an answer and not getting one. 'Better see who's looking for you because I bet someone is,' she says, standing up and turning on the radio, finding the ABC station. Those are the folks who'll know if a child is missing. She has no idea what she will do then. Presumably if he is missing, then there will be searchers out soon. She could lead him to the road and hope to meet up with some of them. As she thinks about it, a burst of thunder fills the sky. The rain is not going anywhere and she knows it's only meant to get worse.

For the first time in her whole life, Rose wishes for a mobile phone.

'Please let me just get you a simple one, Auntie Rose,' William has said at least once a month, but Rose prefers the silence, prefers not having anyone contact her unless they call on the landline. 'Of course,' she says, going to her old black landline phone and picking it up, her heart beating with the relief of being able to call her nephew or the police. She'll call William first and then the police. She knows his home number as well as she knows her own, and even if he's not there, he has a machine to take her message. But as she gets ready to ring him, she realises that she can't hear the dial tone and she remembers the fierce wind from last week, the tremendous cracking sound of a falling tree and the loss of her phone line.

Five days later the phone is still dead, and now there is the rain and this boy. Rose sighs. She's never been bothered about being up here all alone before.

There was an article in the *Blue Mountain Daily* about her once. 'Solitary Rose', they called her. She's read the article many times now. She liked to read about herself from the perspective of the young journalist who huffed and puffed as she made her way into Rose's cabin. She was a chubby little thing with a big smile and brown curls everywhere.

The reporter was happy to taste Rose's special chocolate cake and she had a few scones with jam and cream, so Rose was pleased that her baking efforts hadn't been wasted. They'd talked all afternoon and Rose felt like a real celebrity after the article came out.

Rose Wilson has been a resident of Mount Watson her whole life. Born at home in 1936, she left school early and stayed at home to help her mother raise her disabled younger brother. 'We didn't know what was different about him then,' Rose explained, 'but now I know he was autistic.'

For the last seventy-seven years, Rose has lived in the small cabin off Bell Road. She speaks fondly of the early days of Mount Watson when she and her sister used to help with the picking of apples and the whole family had picnics in the bush. Electricity came to Mount Watson in the early 1940s, but Rose still remembers the smell of kerosene lamps and the presence of horses and carts in the streets. Despite all roads in Mount Watson now being tarred, Rose only has a dirt road to her cabin. She also relies on electricity from a generator and tank water. She claims she would never want to live anywhere else.

Sometimes, when she is feeling a little down about how her life turned out, Rose will reread the article, remembering that she won't be forgotten. William said it will be up on the internet forever, so Rose likes to think that she will be around forever, really. Things may have changed in Mount Watson but a big rainstorm like the one drumming on the roof right now still knocks out the power in town, and the giant gum trees and triangle pines still get in the way of mobile phone signals, so Rose believes that here, in her little corner of the world, nature is winning. And she still has her cabin and her privacy, and whatever the world is doing out there is no business of hers. Unless the world comes right to her door, demanding to be let in.

She turns to look at the boy as she waits for the news. 'The world has come knocking, Mary,' she says, and she is answered with the rain coming down harder. The world has come knocking indeed.

CHAPTER EIGHT

Cecelia

Cecelia sits up in the bed, her heart racing as she smells blood, sees the knife. 'Run,' she hears Nick say. She looks frantically around the room and then out of the window, placing her hand over her heart. *Where is Theo?* The rain washes against her window. The occasional flash of wavering red leaves, the trees being battered by the storm, is the only indication something exists outside the square room with white walls. There is a lamp on beside her bed, chasing away some of the grey from the sky, but she knows that without it the room would be shadowed and dull. It's warm inside, but she knows that outside the air will be sharp and biting.

Theo is out there, alone and cold. Shivering, she feels what he would feel. Or maybe not. Sometimes he doesn't seem to register if it's too hot or too cold. She prays he's not feeling it.

What happened? Why did Nick tell him to run? The questions spin through her head.

She is sure that the memory of what happened is there, somewhere. If she closes her eyes, she can almost see it, but it is stuck behind an opaque wall of tinted glass. She cannot see through, cannot see in.

Trying to get out of the bed, she realises that her hand is tethered to a drip. She needs to find Theo. As she goes to pull out the drip, the door swings open and the nurse from yesterday walks in. 'Now, now, you're not going to do that,' she says as though speaking to a recalcitrant child. 'You need your fluids. You haven't had anything to eat or drink since yesterday afternoon. Are you feeling better?'

Cecelia opens her mouth to tell the nurse about Theo but she cannot make her voice work. *Theo is missing. Why is he missing? Why did he have to run? What happened?*

She wants to scream with frustration but she can't even scream. There is a memory there. Something big and dark, something suffocating her words, something terrible. She lifts her hand as if to rub at the glass and then realises that the wall of glass is inside her own head. She cannot speak because she is not allowed to speak. Something is stopping her.

The nurse, whose name is Annie according to her tag, pats her hand. 'They are looking for your little boy but the rain is really going to slow down the search. They can't use the helicopter or the dogs. Do you know where he might have gone?'

Cecelia shakes her head. She has no idea. It is not possible to know what Theo may be thinking. His lack of speech makes everything harder to explain. And he's only eleven.

Nick told him to run because of what happened and he would have been scared, she knows that. Their son will have run until he ran out of energy. Theo likes to run more than anything; he can run for hours if he needs to. He will not have shoes. He hates shoes. She once asked him to explain why and he painstakingly used his iPad to tell her that they suffocated his feet. She couldn't argue with that. It's fine in summer when he's home, and his school allows him to be barefoot for most of the day. But in winter and when she needs to take him to the dentist or to the doctor or something equally important, she has to reward him with endless treats just to get the shoes and socks on, and then she has to keep rewarding him. She knows it's not what Benjamin, his teacher, believes is good for him, but sometimes she's tired and she cannot summon the energy to engage in yet another battle over shoes.

Annie sits down on the bed. She is a large woman and the mattress dips a little, pitching Cecelia sideways. She rights herself and looks at the nurse.

'Here,' says Annie, pulling a pad and pencil out of her pocket. 'Can you write down what happened? Can you tell me?'

Her voice is kind and soft and Cecelia takes the pencil and holds it against the page but she cannot make the words come. The fear of the truth holds the story tight. There is just the darkness, the opaque glass, when she tries to think about it.

'Never mind,' says Annie comfortingly. 'Listen, I know that sometimes these things can be hard to discuss. I saw your husband before he was taken up to get ready for surgery. From what Dr Greenblatt told me – he's our resident doctor who you'll see some-time today – your husband has one deep wound to his chest, from the knife.' Annie stops speaking and looks at Cecelia as if waiting to gauge her reaction to this statement. Cecelia keeps her gaze fixed on the nurse's face as she thinks about her surgeon husband going in for surgery. Supposedly, doctors make the worst patients.

When Cecelia doesn't do anything except return Annie's stare, the nurse sighs and pats her hand again before continuing to speak. 'He's a big man and you're just, well, you're just a slip of a thing. I know that marriage can be a complicated and difficult thing sometimes. I know that there are men who take their anger at the world out on those they are supposed to love. I know this happens because it happened to me. I'm not small but I let my ex get away with hurting me for years.' Annie turns her head away, looking at the wall instead of at Cecelia, and her thoughts focus on the past as she speaks. 'It was alcohol that turned him into a monster. Every time he sobered up, he would apologise and cry, and just like a lot of women, I thought I could change him. I thought if I could forgive him enough and love him enough, then he would be a better man. But that wasn't possible. I stayed with him for years. Too many years. It can feel impossible – escape, I mean.

I understand that and sometimes it's just too much.' The nurse shakes her head. 'I stayed too long and I sometimes wonder what would have happened if things had got too much and he'd pushed me too far and… I got hold of something to protect myself.' She turns and looks at Cecelia. 'Is that what happened? Did he push you too far? I saw the scratch on your stomach and the bruise on your side and the fingerprints on your arm.'

Cecelia looks down at her hands as her body grows hot. She touches her side and feels the slight throb of the bruise Annie has mentioned. *Did he push me too far? Nick said he wasn't going to do this anymore. That he was sick of it all. Is that what pushed me too far? What happened then? What happened after he got so angry, after he told me he was going to leave me? Did he actually say the words or did he use the phrase 'we need to talk', that all-encompassing phrase that means someone has made a decision, one person has made a decision?*

Cecelia takes a deep breath and realises that this is what happened. It's the last thing she remembers. Nick basically told her their marriage was over. He didn't need to say the actual words. Twenty-two years, two children and he was done. But she has no idea what happened after that. She clenches her fists, fights the urge to lift her hands to smash at the dark glass hiding the truth.

Annie waits, her focus burning into Cecelia, but Cecelia cannot speak, cannot explain. There is something to explain, she knows that, but she has no idea what.

'Ah, well,' says the nurse after a few silent minutes, 'let's get you up and showered.' She pulls back the sheets, exposing Cecelia's legs to the air of the hospital room. 'Come on,' she says, and Cecelia does as she's told. 'The police need to speak to you, when you're… when you're able,' she says as Cecelia leans on her.

The thought of the police and their questions, their suspicions, their accusations, makes Cecelia want to throw up.

Standing in the shower under the weak gush of warm water, Cecelia allows herself deep breaths of relief at being alone and unwatched for a few minutes. She is still tethered to the drip so it's difficult to move, and her hand feels heavy and strange. The bruise on her side is large and spreading, purple with yellow edges. She doesn't remember being hit there but it must have happened. She probes her memory, pushing against the glass, but as she does this, her heart races and the bruise on her side pulses with pain, pinpricks of fear dancing on her skin even as the water pours over it. Last year a filling in her tooth fell out and each time she put her tongue into the space she felt a small shock of pain and cold that rippled through her body, making her squirm, so she kept reminding herself to leave it alone. Her body wants her to leave this alone as well. She feels herself retreat from the glass in her mind. She doesn't know what she will find if she pushes against it hard enough, if she shatters it. For some reason, that scares her.

Is Nick going to live?

How will I exist if they don't find my son? What will happen when they do? Is he safer out there in the rain and the cold than if they find him?

The last thought makes her heart stutter. Why does she think that? Why does she believe that her son is safer out in this weather, alone and afraid and lost, than he would be here with his mother or found by one of the searchers?

She wants to talk, to scream, to shout, but she feels stuck right where she is. If Annie doesn't return, she knows she will not be able to get out of the shower. She will just stand here forever.

'Out you come,' says Annie finally, opening the door. She holds out a towel, and Cecelia tries to smile at her, to let her know she's grateful for her kindness, but she feels her cheeks wet with tears. Something inside her rises up and she knows that there is fear and pain there. Her body sags against Annie's strong arms as she rubs Cecelia's back through the towel.

'Now, now, love, it's okay, it will be okay,' the nurse soothes as she helps her into her hospital gown and some paper underwear.

Cecelia wishes for her pyjamas, soft flannel pants and a patterned top with small purple flowers all over. 'Mum's garden pyjamas,' Theo calls them. She climbs into bed, taking a tissue from the box beside her to blow her nose.

'Now I'm not going to push,' says Annie, 'but I got you these.' She takes some pamphlets out of a wide pocket in her uniform, handing them to Cecelia.

Cecelia looks down at the first one, purple in colour: *Violence against women is never acceptable, never excusable, never tolerable*, she reads, the white letters large and almost threatening.

The next pamphlet has a picture of a smiling woman and purple letters that read: *A life free of violence is possible.* Cecelia wonders why the colour purple features so strongly in all the pamphlets.

Closing her eyes briefly, she sees Nick's face, his mouth wide open, anger pouring out in harsh words. She has always believed that domestic violence can only be claimed when you are physically hurt, battered and bruised, but lately she has read things on the internet, seen things on television. Domestic violence comes in many forms. She opens her eyes and stares down at the pamphlets. Did Nick go further than just harsh words? Is that what she can't remember?

'I'll leave you to it. Your breakfast will be along any minute. I'll let you know what happens with your husband's surgery but I want you to know you're safe here and no one can hurt you. The police are going to be by later to speak to you.'

Feeling her breath catch in her throat, Cecelia grabs Annie's hand.

'Don't worry if you can't tell them anything. That nice Constable Emmerson will understand. His wife is a nurse here as well so he knows how difficult domestic violence situations can be.'

Cecelia's heart thrums in her ear. She remembers Constable Emmerson and his wife from a dinner party they had years ago. They invited a few couples from town, enjoying the idea of meeting new people. He has dark hair and dark eyes and a mole above his lip. She remembers him. She doesn't want to speak to him, cannot speak to him, but the words won't come so that she can explain this to Annie.

She would like to tell Annie that she is not safe here. Somehow, she knows that she is not safe here but she has no idea why.

She is not safe here and Theo is probably safer out there. And Nick? What about Nick? She has no idea what happened to Nick.

'That's it, Cecelia, I'm done. I can't do this anymore.'

Nick was angry. Nick was frustrated. Nick was done.

CHAPTER NINE

Kaycee

Kaycee opens her eyes, squinting at the beige curtains of the room she is in. She's not entirely sure where she is. It still seems dark outside but it feels like it must be morning, like she has slept for a long time. The thread of a dream pulls at her, Theo running in the wind, almost flying with the force of it. She was chasing him but he was getting further and further away and she couldn't catch him. In the dream her heart raced and her lungs burned but she couldn't make her legs move fast enough. Theo is missing. The knowledge of this is a sledgehammer inside her already pounding head.

Her father has been stabbed. Her mother is in hospital. Theo is missing. These facts have swirled through her mind all night, waking thoughts as she moved between light and deep sleep. She swallows, her mouth dry and horrible-tasting. Her stomach is calm for now but she knows that if she moves even a tiny bit, it will fight back with overwhelming nausea.

She registers the sound of forceful, gushing rain. Rain will make it harder to find Theo.

Her mouth is so dry that she can feel her lips are cracked. She closes her eyes again.

'I see you're up,' says a voice and Kaycee sits up in the bed, her head immediately ramping up its drumbeat as she coughs. Her stomach punishes her for moving, and she swallows hard.

'Here,' says the man sitting on the bed next to her. He hands her a small glass of water that tastes of chlorine but which she gulps down gratefully. 'And here,' he says when she's done that. He gives her a large coffee and two Panadol. 'Take this and then we'll talk.'

Kaycee nods, doing as she's told. In her mind images form and merge. Last night. The bar. The call. The drive. The hospital. The police. The questions. The coffee slams into her stomach but she manages to swallow a couple of times until it settles.

She looks at the man, noting his red hair, green eyes and square shoulders. 'You're the barman,' she says.

'I'm Jonah,' he snorts. 'Last night you got a call about your parents being in an accident and you downed three more vodka shots before asking me to drive you to the Blue Mountains District Hospital.' There is a light red-orange stubble along his pronounced jawline. His voice is tight with anger.

'Oh,' says Kaycee. She keeps sipping her coffee even though it has no milk or sugar in it. The bitterness helps her focus, although as the memories of last night force their way out of her hungover fuzziness, she wishes she didn't have to focus.

She can see herself lying across the bar, her face down on its sticky surface. 'Someone has to help me get to my parents, my parents are dying!' She had been crying, whining loudly, but she knows that people kept laughing at her. Adam kept laughing at her. 'You're so funny when you're drunk!' They thought she was joking, and because she kept drinking, they ignored her. Why did she do that? Who does a thing like that? Who gets a call to say that their family are in trouble and puts more alcohol into their system? What kind of a person has she become? The agony of regret is a sharp pain behind her eyes. She is used to her morning hangover curses at herself. It is a rare morning these days when she does not wake up to a dry mouth and flashbacks of horrible, stupid behaviour from the night before. But today is different.

Today is worse. Today she would like to wish away the Kaycee she is now, wish her away forever.

A flush of shame colours her cheeks, making her shift in the bed. She is wearing the same thing she wore last night: jeans and a black top, 'The Folklore Album' in red letters on her chest. She notices Jonah staring at the words. 'Taylor Swift,' she says.

'I know.' His jaw twitches as though he is biting down hard.

'Thanks for driving me…' she says softly.

'Yeah, well. No one else volunteered. I have no idea why you're with that guy Adam. He's a complete dick.'

Kaycee opens her mouth to defend her boyfriend, to tell Jonah that he has no right to comment on her relationship, and then she closes it again. He's right. Adam is a dick.

'Oh God, babe, who cares? Your family only think about them-selves anyway,' Adam said last night when she stopped drinking, stumbling over to him at the table where he was sitting with his arm casually draped around some girl's shoulders. 'I really need to get to the Blue Mountains,' she begged. The memory is sharp and clear and appalling but Kaycee still wonders if she made it up. She hopes she made it up but thinks she probably didn't. She wonders who the girl was but realises in the same instant that she doesn't care.

'I had to pull over three times so you could throw up,' Jonah carries on, 'and then when we got to the hospital, the police wouldn't let you see your parents because you couldn't even string a sentence together. They told me to take you to a motel, which I did. I slept next to you because I honestly thought it was possible that you were going to choke on your own vomit.' He stares at her, waiting for a response.

'Oh, God,' moans Kaycee, humiliation flooding her body.

'You are not a big person – you get that, right? You're small and thin and last night you consumed the best part of a whole bottle of vodka. Your system can't stand that much. You could have died. And that's not the first time I've watched you do that.'

'I don't need a lecture,' whispers Kaycee, glancing away.

'Yeah, well, you need something. I'm studying medicine and I'm telling you that you're only one binge away from killing yourself.'

Kaycee holds up her hands. 'Enough, okay, I get it, I get it.'

'Good.'

She sips her coffee as they sit in silence for a minute.

'The constable, um, Constable Emmerson told me to bring you to the hospital in the morning,' says Jonah.

'Did he say what happened? Did he say if they've found my brother?'

'I don't know what happened but they've begun searching for him. They had the dogs out last night when there was a small break in the rain but that came back pretty quickly. They won't be able to use them today. They need you to try and speak to your mother to see if she knows where he might be.' He looks down at his hands and she follows his gaze, noting he has a cut on one of them. He has large hands, capable-looking hands. 'Your mother can't speak. That's why they needed you. They're hoping you can get her to speak.'

'But why can't she speak?' Kaycee rubs her brow, confusion taking over. Her mother is always talking. She keeps up a running commentary to Theo on everything she's doing. How can she have lost the ability to speak? It doesn't seem possible.

'No one knows. Something happened and your dad… I don't know all the details yet but it's important that you get her to talk. They think she'll be able to tell them where your brother might have gone.'

Kaycee stands up. 'I can't… Oh, God,' she says, running for the bathroom, where she throws up a stomach full of bile and black coffee.

'Are you okay?' Jonah calls.

'Fine,' snaps Kaycee as she rests her head on the rim of the toilet. After a minute she stands up and confronts herself in the bathroom mirror. The sight of her pale face, stringy, vomit-filled, white-blonde hair and sunken blue eyes shocks her. 'What have you done?' she whispers to herself. 'What have you done to your life?'

'We really should get to the hospital,' calls Jonah.

'You can go,' she shouts through the bathroom door, unwilling to even look at him ever again. 'I'll get myself there. I can sort myself out from here! But thank you for driving me.' She wants him out of this room. She needs to be alone so she can pull herself together. She doesn't even know Jonah's second name, and he's right in the middle of this nightmare. 'Oh,' she gasps as she remembers some of what the police officer tried to tell her at the hospital last night: *An incident at the cabin. Your father was stabbed. Your mother won't speak.*

There is silence from Jonah and she hopes he has just left. Pulling off her clothes, her nose twitches at the smell of sweat and vomit, and she jumps into the shower. A strong jet of hot water soothes her a little as she tries to remember everything from last night. There is a vague memory of going back to her dorm room and stuffing some clothes in a bag so she hopes she actually did that. She stands in the hot water until she feels her stomach settle, using the floral-scented motel shampoo to wash her hair.

When she opens the bathroom door, wrapped in a towel, she finds Jonah sitting on the bed.

'That's better,' he says.

'I told you to just go. I can manage from here. Thanks for driving me.' She knows she sounds like a petulant child but she is resentful of his judgemental presence. She is judging herself enough. Looking around the room, she's tearfully relieved when she spots her black backpack.

'I'm not the kind of guy who would leave someone in your situation.'

'I'll be fine.' She grits her teeth.

'I'll leave when I know that's the case.'

'Fine!'

'Fine,' he agrees.

Kaycee takes the backpack into the bathroom, putting on clean underwear, some jeans, a shirt and a warm jumper. She brushes her teeth, relieved that she thought to bring that as well, and then she wonders if maybe Jonah packed for her. She has no memory of thinking about what she might need, or even being capable enough of that in last night's state. She's grateful that there are warm clothes in the backpack because outside the rain showers down and that means it will feel like winter outside despite it being autumn.

Using the emergency stash of make-up that's always in the backpack, she does her best to conceal the blue shadows under her eyes and give her cheeks a little colour. She blow-dries her hair, letting it hang straight down her back even though she usually curls it or ties it up. She's been meaning to cut it or dye it a different colour like her mother does. Her mother's white-blonde hair washed out her skin and made her brown eyes always seem dull. Black hair suits her better, but she and Theo both have blue eyes from their father. 'They look like beautiful dolls,' Kaycee remembers her grandmother saying a few years ago when the family had a studio portrait done. She shakes her head. She will have to call both her grandmothers and tell them what's happened. Sue-Anne – her mother's mother – won't understand much because her early-stage dementia causes her to become easily confused, but Kaycee will explain to the head of the residential home where she lives. Hilda – her father's mother – will probably be in her car and on her way here five minutes after Kaycee calls. *At least I'll have her. I can stay with her and send Jonah home and pretend last night never happened.*

'Right,' says Jonah when she comes out of the bathroom, 'that's a lot better.' He shakes his head. 'I know that you got a scholarship for your science degree. You talk a lot when you're... drinking.

I have no idea why you're washing everything away with vodka.'
His green eyes are wide and filled with concern. Kaycee realises
that she has spent quite a few Saturday nights looking at him. She
can only imagine all the things she's told him.

'I don't need another lecture, Jonah.'

'Sorry. I'll take you to the hospital. Here.' He hands her a bag
containing a large flaky croissant, which she devours as they drive.
The falling rain obscures everything so Kaycee doesn't bother
searching for the reds and golds of autumn in the trees. Instead, she
plays a game she always played as a child when she found herself
in a car in the rain. She picks one single droplet and watches as it
starts at the top of her passenger window and then rolls down to
the bottom. The quicker the drop moves, the worse the rainstorm
is. She doesn't even have time to start counting before the droplet
she chooses is at the bottom.

Her stomach settles a little and she calls her grandmother,
explaining quickly.

'I'm booking a ticket home right now,' Hilda says, 'but the
cruise only gets into port in a few days.'

'I forgot you were on holiday,' replies Kaycee, frustration at
how far away her grandmother is gnawing at her.

'I'll be there soon, darling.'

Hilda doesn't ask any questions, knowing that the most
important thing is to get to where her family are. Kaycee's father
has the same pragmatic approach to life: first assess the situation,
then start asking questions that may not have any answers.

'So many questions,' Kaycee whispers to the cold windowpane,
her breath fogging up a small circle.

Jonah is quiet although Kaycee knows he must have heard her
speak. The roads are dangerous in the fierce rainstorm, filled with
potholes and washed away at the side in some places. His eyes are
narrowed as he peers through the windscreen, the wipers rushing
across but failing to make everything clear.

When they pull into the car park outside the hospital, with its beautiful sandstone façade, Kaycee begins to regret eating at all.

'Just breathe,' says Jonah as though he understands exactly how she's feeling. He grabs her hands, squeezing, and Kaycee nods. She wants to tell him she's a big girl and that she's fine and she certainly doesn't need a man taking care of her, especially one who seems way too judgemental for the man who actually served her the alcohol last night, but she needs someone here or she's afraid she might crumple into a heap on the ground. She has no idea what could have happened to her parents, how badly hurt they are. She doesn't know what could have happened to Theo. They are searching for him, but do they know the kind of kid they are searching for? A wave of pure hatred for herself and her behaviour sweeps over her. Her family needed her last night and she chose alcohol over them. She vows silently that her drinking days are over.

She lifts her chin. Her family need her and whatever has happened between them before this, she needs to keep it together for them now.

'It's coming down pretty hard. I don't have an umbrella. Ready to make a run for it?' Jonah asks and Kaycee nods her head, hoping her stomach can manage a quick sprint. The raindrops are not gentle on Kaycee's head and face but instead slam into her with cold force.

As they enter the building, Kaycee finds that she knows exactly how to get to reception. Her family have rented the cottage from Irene for the last seven years, every autumn for two weeks, and in that time, they have visited the hospital at least a dozen times. Theo likes to run and he has no concept of fear. He doesn't wear shoes, and if something bothers him or scares him or there is too much noise and he goes into sensory overload, he will climb a tree or run away. Once he even climbed up onto the roof of the cabin, terrifying them all.

As a family they have attended the hospital for his cut feet, for a broken wrist, for a deep scratch on his face, for an ankle that they thought was broken but was just badly bruised, for a cut on his thigh that required stitches and for numerous ear infections. Each time her family entered this hospital, her parents wore the same look of worried concern over Theo. Each time they left with medicine or a plaster cast or a few stitches, her parents smiled with relief. Kaycee has no idea what will happen today. *If they cannot find Theo…* She swallows hard because that thought cannot be allowed to form.

As she gets to reception, she looks at the nurse sitting behind the white melamine counter and opens her mouth, an explanation ready. But there is no need for her to say anything.

The nurse is Phyllis and she knows Kaycee and her family well. 'Oh, Kaycee, love,' she says, tearful with concern. 'I'm so glad you're here. They need to know how to find Theo. We don't know enough about what does and doesn't bother him.'

'My mum and dad,' says Kaycee, and the tears that fall cannot be stopped.

'All right, all right,' says Phyllis, coming from behind the desk and wrapping Kaycee in a hug. Jonah stands next to them, looking slightly awkward.

'Excuse me, Kaycee,' says a man in a police uniform, coming towards them. Kaycee lets go of Phyllis and nods her head. The constable has thick black hair and nearly black eyes. She knows that they spoke last night because she remembers his face and the small mole above his lip. She remembers trying to concentrate on that so she wouldn't throw up again.

'Yes,' she says, taking a tissue that Phyllis hands her. Jonah stands right next to her, so close that Kaycee can feel the heat from his body. She turns to him to tell him he can go but instead, 'Don't go yet,' comes out of her mouth.

'I'm not leaving until you say so, okay?' he replies, grabbing her hand.

Kaycee holds on tight, as though letting go will mean she'll sink under heavy black water.

'I think it's best if Kaycee sees her mother alone,' says Constable Emmerson.

'It's okay,' Kaycee says to Jonah, and she lets go of him. In an effort to stop her hands trembling, she folds her arms, pushes her hands beneath them, hugging herself.

Jonah nods. 'I'll get a coffee in the café. I'm guessing there is one. I won't leave. Don't worry, I have all day.'

'There is one,' says Phyllis, 'I'll show you.'

'Thank you,' mumbles Kaycee because she is crying again.

'I'll take you to see your mother,' says the constable.

'I'm sorry I couldn't help last night,' she says quietly as they walk. She lets her arms hang down by her side, her fists clenched. She steps around a trolley filled with covered trays; the smell of toast and eggs coming from the slightly steaming trays seeps into her nose, her stomach rebelling against the idea of food. An old man in a wheelchair smiles up at her as he is pushed past by a nurse. It's relatively quiet in this part of the hospital. Kaycee is used to the hustle and bustle of the emergency section.

'You were very drunk,' says the constable quietly. 'We sent you to a motel with your boyfriend because you were almost incoherent. He said he would watch you. I believe he is a medical student and he spoke to the resident on call and she seemed satisfied that he knew what to do.'

'Oh,' gasps Kaycee, 'I'm so sorry, I... I don't know...'

'Never mind now,' says the constable. He has stopped outside a pale grey door. 'Your mother is in here.'

'And my dad?'

'Your father is getting prepped for surgery on the second floor. We have surgeons coming up from Sydney to operate because we don't have someone qualified here at the moment. They should be here soon. We wanted to fly them in but the rain stopped that so they are being driven over.'

Kaycee feels her knees give way and she spots a grey plastic chair that she sinks into. 'Can you please just explain it all before I see her?'

'I did last night…' begins the constable and then he stops, realising that Kaycee has forgotten most of what he said. 'A lost tourist stumbled across the cottage your family rent. She found your mother in there hunched over your father. She was holding a knife and your father had been stabbed. We didn't know Theo had run off until you asked about him because Irene is staying with friends in Sydney and we couldn't get hold of her. She would have checked them in, of course, so she would have known. It was quite chaotic, and until you told me, I'd forgotten about Theo. I've only met him a couple of times and… well, I guess no one was thinking straight last night. Phyllis asked about him as well when she started her shift, but by that time, I'd spoken to you already. Sergeant Peterson – you know Peterson – he was with a sick friend last night so his phone was turned off until really late. He would have told us about Theo but at least when we called you, you informed us. We have had a search party out all night looking for your brother but the rain has made this very, very difficult. There were only a handful of people out last night but we expect many more to join the search today. They are calling his name through bullhorns and hoping he responds.'

The constable stops speaking and Kaycee looks up at him, reading silent judgement on his face. Maybe if she had been able to help them last night, before the rain had really set in, Theo would be here and safe. She accepts the look with a nod. She deserves to be judged.

'Theo won't respond to his name,' she says.

'Yes, you did try to explain that last night but you weren't very clear. We think your mother may be able to help us find Theo.'

'Okay… What did she say?'

'That's the thing. She hasn't said anything. That's why we got hold of you. She hasn't said a word since she was found.'

'Not a word? She hasn't even asked for Theo?'

'Not a word.'

'What happened to them? What could have happened?' Kaycee hears her voice rising, feels the panic setting in.

'Listen to me, Kaycee,' says Constable Emmerson, crouching down and looking up at her. 'You need to try and get your mother to speak. We have no idea what happened in that cabin and we don't know if your father will survive. He will go into surgery soon but the knife wound was very deep and they are keeping him sedated at the moment. We need to find your brother. I know that this is overwhelming. It can't be anything but overwhelming, but I need you to be strong for me so we can find your brother and work out what happened. Right now your mother is going to be charged with attempted murder if your father survives, and if he doesn't…'

Kaycee takes a deep breath as she listens and then she is silent, chewing on her cracked lips while she digests what he's just said. *Knife wound. Deep. Sedated. Theo is missing.*

There is a scent in the corridor of antiseptic on top of old cooked food. Every hospital Kaycee has ever been in smells the same way and she has no idea why. She has been in a lot of hospital corridors and waiting rooms since Theo was born. She is ashamed of her younger self now as she thinks about this. She was always so difficult, so resentful at having to spend yet another night waiting for yet another doctor to see Theo because he jumped off the couch or threw himself down the stairs or stood on something sharp or caught a cold and wouldn't take medicine to bring his temperature down. When she was old enough to be left alone at home, she almost relished that time, rare moments when she didn't have to think about anyone but herself. In the last two years she knows she has not given much thought to Theo and her parents. And if she has, she has swamped those thoughts with alcohol. When she moved into the dorm at university, she promised to be home every weekend, but she has found one excuse after another to stay away, and she lets the terrible shame and pain of that hit with its full force. She is a bad person, a bad sister, a bad daughter.

'It would be nice for all of us to see you more,' her father told her in a phone call last week. He rings her at odd times during the day if he gets the chance in between surgery and rounds. Sometimes he won't call her for days, sometimes he calls three days in a row. His schedule is unpredictable. Heart surgery is unpredictable.

'I'll try, Dad.'

'I know you will, and we're always here no matter what.' His love for her is unconditional. She has always understood that. Things are more complicated with her mother but she has never doubted her parents love her. She looks down the hospital corridor as a nurse pushing a trolley with a squeaky wheel comes towards them. Holding tightly to the plastic arms of the chair, she fights the urge to run down the corridor and out into the rain, where the air is icy-cold.

You don't get to fall apart now, she tells herself. *You don't get to whine about it all being about Theo. You don't get to be a kid now. You need to grow up and be the adult your family needs you to be.*

'Okay, I better see her,' she says finally, standing up. She has to focus. She must think about Theo and her parents, and she needs to stop feeling sorry for herself.

'Let's go,' she says to the constable, and he nods his head, pushing the door to her mother's hospital room open.

CHAPTER TEN

Theo

Toast is loud in my ears. *Crunch, crunch, crunch.* I like toast. No more noise, just *crunch, crunch.* Peanut butter is soft and a bit salty. Soft. Salty. *Crunch.* Soft, salty, *crunch.*

The old eyes look at me and look at me. 'What's your name?' she asks.

I eat my toast.

'Do you know where you're from? Do you know where you live? Where are you staying?'

I listen to the crunch inside my head so I can't hear her words. There are too many words. I don't look at her old face, white hair, small smile, blue eyes. I don't look because I see too many things at once. I look at the toast, triangle, brown, flat. I am in my bubble. In my bubble I can only hear the crunch. I can only see the light brown middle, dark brown edges of the toast. In my bubble I am safe. I only have to listen to one thing. I only have to see one thing.

She reaches for my arm, her hand coming through my bubble, breaking it open, letting in all the things to hear and things to see. I jerk back. Don't touch me. My head gets full and I want to bang it, to bang it on the ground to make it stop feeling so full. I look around, my body itches. There are ants all over me. I fall off the chair and I lie on the wooden floor and I kick and I bang my head. I bang it once, twice, I bang and bang until the full feeling goes away. And then I am still.

I turn over and lie on my back. I look at the ceiling and the big wooden planks up there.

She stands above me, her face moving too much. I close my eyes, but when I open them, she is still there and she makes a sign. A sign I know. A sign I can answer. She moves her fist forward and then she puts two fingers up near her head and then she moves her finger and I know that she is asking my name.

I stand up and I spell it out for her: 'T. H. E. O.'

'Theo?' she says and I nod.

'You're Theo?' she asks and I nod again and my body is calm and I have the feeling of ice cream inside me because she knows my name and she can sign and that means she can help. Ice cream is a taste. It is the taste that Mum gives me after dinner. I like it when it is mint-flavoured with pieces of chocolate inside. The chocolate is a bitter taste but it is made sweet by the mint ice cream. My teacher Benjamin and I talk about taste at school. We sign about and write about sweet and sour and bitter and spicy. I like sweet more than anything. 'You've got a real sweet tooth, dude,' Benjamin told me.

Benjamin can sign. Mum can sign and Dad can sign and Kaycee can sign. I miss Kaycee. Kaycee lives at university. Kaycee is going to be a scientist. Kaycee read me a book about all the greatest scientists in the world. I liked the part about Albert Einstein. Kaycee said he was autistic like me. 'See, Theo – it doesn't matter if your brain works differently, the most famous scientist in the world was just like you.' I remember everything Kaycee says to me. I remember lots of things but I also forget. I forget how to tie my shoes. My brain isn't interested in tying my shoes.

'Run,' said Dad. 'Get help,' said Dad. 'Run. Get help.'

Grey hair, saggy skin, blue eyes can sign. If she can sign, she can help. Can she help?

'I am,' she says and then she signs, 'R. O. S. E.' She is Rose. A rose is a flower. A rose can be pink or red or yellow or white. This rose is old and small and grey. I nod my head and I sign her name and I see her smile but I look away. Too much. I sit down at the table again and I eat my toast. *Crunch, crunch, crunch.* The room is warm and I am not cold. I have to tell Rose about help. 'Run,' said Dad. 'Get help.' I must tell Rose about help. But there are too many words to explain. When there are too many words to explain my head feels full up and my skin itches and then I have to bang my head to make it all go away.

A lady came to my school one day. She had yellow hair and too many teeth but she could sign. 'I'm doing my doctorate in Autism Spectrum Disorder,' she told me with her hands and her mouth. 'I wanted to ask you how you experience the world. I would like to know how you think and feel, and Benjamin said that you are the best speller in class so I wanted to talk to you.' But all her words got stuck inside me and there were too many words. 'ImdoingmydoctorateinAutismSpectrumDisorderIwantedtoaskyouhowyouexperiencetheworldIwouldliketoknowhowyouthinkandfeelandBenjaminsaidthatyouarethebestspellerinclasssoIwantedtotalktoyou.'

The words went round and round in my head, faster and faster, and it was too full and I had to lie down on the floor and bang my head until they went out, but they are still there, just not going around and around anymore. All the words I hear stay in my head forever. The words are always there.

'Hey now,' Benjamin said to her. 'You should know that he needs to hear one thing at a time.'

The lady went away after that.

Rose can help. She can help but I can't tell her what happened. I can't tell her about help because there are too many words. I don't have my iPad and Dad said, 'Run.'

I remember it all. I remember the knife. I remember the blood. I remember everything.

CHAPTER ELEVEN

Rose

She shouldn't have grabbed for his arm, but she got frustrated and she wanted his attention. 'I know better, Mary,' she mutters as she watches him. Now she doesn't move, doesn't go near him. She doesn't do anything at all except wait for him to wear himself out.

That's what they used to do with Lionel. That was the only thing they could do. It was a frightening thing to watch, to see him bang his head against the wall or the floor as though he were trying to split open his skull. He was always calm afterwards, perfectly quiet. 'Why?' she asked him once using signs. 'Why do you hurt yourself?'

'It itches,' he told her. She was never really sure what that meant. If something itched, you scratched. 'Maybe he means it itches inside his head,' said Mary, and that made some sense to Rose. If there was a feeling inside your head that you couldn't get at, that you couldn't resolve, then probably giving it a bang would help. Rose knows that there are moments when thoughts of the past pop up, just pop up and demand to be paid attention to. But they bring with them the pain of a terrible memory, and so Rose drinks more than one glass of whisky, trying to make it fade. If she couldn't drink, perhaps she would also feel the need to bang her head to make the thoughts disappear.

It feels like it took them almost the whole of Lionel's life to work out how to take care of him and they never got it right.

Obviously, they never got it right or they wouldn't have had to send him away in the end. Rose takes a deep breath because this thought makes her want to scream. It has always made her want to scream out loud at the unfairness of it all. She shrugs. Perhaps she should give her head a bang.

But he was so difficult to take care of. She remembers that if they took him out for the day into town, he would be jittery and jumpy and inevitably there would be a fit in the middle of the street or in a store. He would start out fine but eventually he would struggle, trying to look everywhere at once, and he would cover his ears and then he would fall to the ground and everyone who was around would stare down at him, shocked and horrified. It wasn't so bad when he was little but when he was about this boy's age, people couldn't help their distaste. It wasn't a nice thing to see. Sometimes he hit his head so hard on the floor he drew blood and then he wouldn't let anyone touch him to clean it off. Rose knows that her mother held her head highest when Lionel threw a fit in town. She would look around and catch the eyes of the staring people, just daring them with her own steel-grey gaze to say anything. But Rose and Mary knew she suffered from the looks like they all did. Everyone was ashamed of Lionel. They didn't understand him.

Eventually it was easier to just keep him at home.

'That boy should be locked up,' Rose remembers Elsie who ran the local store saying. Rose watched her mother set her face and bite down on her lip. Elsie had the only store in town and Dot, their mother, knew not to upset her. The shopkeeper had been known to ban people from coming in if she felt like it. But Dot's silence only lasted until they were out of the store. All the way home she muttered to the Lord about the need for him to punish those who showed no compassion. Dot believed firmly that the Lord was on her side because he was the one who had made Lionel, and everything he made was perfect so he must have had his reasons.

Rose doubted that Elsie would be punished. She never said it out loud but sometimes she thought that perhaps the Lord was looking elsewhere on the day Lionel came to be.

Elsie wasn't the only one who thought Lionel should be locked away. It was disturbing to watch him twirl and flap when he was excited or bang his head against a wall when something bothered him. Rose understood that and sometimes she could see that her mother was growing weary of taking care of him. He never liked to bathe, and even when he was becoming a man, his sisters and mother had to force him into the tub, tempting him with biscuits and cake. After Dot died, sometimes a whole week would go by without him having a bath until Mary and Rose felt they had enough energy to do it. He didn't seem that unhappy once he was in the warm water; it was more the air hitting his skin as he took off his clothes that seemed to bother him.

'You need to put it into an institution,' their father used to say when he was still around. 'We can't be dealing with this shit all the time.'

'He's your son, Aubrey,' their mother hissed at her husband. 'Don't you call him "it". He's our son and no son of mine is going into an institution!'

Rose remembers her father sighing, only his bushy eyebrows moving up and down giving any clue to his concern. 'He's nearly four years old and he doesn't speak. You've only just got him out of nappies. He's not like a real child at all.'

'He's my real child.'

The biggest arguments her parents had were over Lionel. He was the last baby, a late baby, born when their mother thought she was well and truly done. Rose remembers her mother that summer before Lionel was born, waddling up and down the orchard rows, picking apples even though her great big belly got in the way.

Her dad was so proud when Lionel had arrived. 'Finally a son,' he crowed, 'not that I don't love my girls.' He winked at Rose and

Mary, who were hopping up and down with excitement to see the new baby. He went off to the Arms Hotel to have the traditional many rounds of free drinks a new father got, and Rose and Mary sat with their mother in the clean hospital room where her doctor had advised she have the baby.

'Dad stopped being proud when all of Lionel's nonsense started, didn't he, Mary?' says Rose softly now as she watches the boy kicking and banging on the floor. He spent a lot of time at the pub in those first few years getting 'a bit of peace for meself'.

Rose knows, from listening to the radio, that things have changed a lot over the years. The ABC has had some good programmes about kids like Lionel and Theo, and Rose knows there are special schools for them all over the place now, schools where they are taught and helped with compassion and love.

She looks out of the window at the pouring rain and sighs. The past is never a good place to visit. She needs to focus on what's happening here right now so she can figure out what to do. She shakes her head, letting go of the memories.

'He's a bit loud, isn't he, Mary?' she says now and she's glad of her isolation, for the lack of people around her. She wouldn't want anyone to think she was hurting the child if they could hear him through the rain, but on the other hand if someone did hear, then they would come. Rose is relieved when he finally subsides into silence and turns on his back, breathing deeply as he relaxes.

The boy looks exhausted and her instinct is to simply stay away but instead she stands over him and looks down. 'What's your name?' she signs. For a moment she thinks she may have signed it wrong or that he hasn't understood, but then he stands up and his hands begin to move.

'Theo,' he tells her and Rose smiles because now they're making progress.

She tells him her name, and he signs back so she knows he understands.

It surprises and pleases her that she remembers so much of how to sign.

It was her mother who hit on the idea of signing to Lionel. He could hear – there was no doubt about that. In fact, it seemed as though he could almost hear too well.

In town there was a little deaf girl and much was made of the fact that she could communicate with signs. 'Retarded,' people had whispered about her until her mother started teaching her to sign, and soon she could hold a whole conversation. Rose remembers watching the girl's hands fly as she chattered away to her mother without making a sound.

'Don't be ridiculous, he's not deaf,' Aubrey said when Dot told him what she wanted to do.

'Maybe he just can't find the words,' she replied, never one to be defeated by her husband's pessimism.

Mary and Rose learned as well, watching their mother as she worked from a book a lady in the big city had sent up to them.

'Eat,' was the first sign they all learned. It's easy enough: you just bring your hand to your mouth. They did it to Lionel every time they sat down for dinner, and every time he was given some food. Rose thought her mother would faint with joy the first time he signed back. He was nine years old.

Soon Lionel had a whole host of signs and he could even spell out his name. He never got much further than that but he could make himself understood and that meant somewhat fewer fits. His sisters noticed that there were different kinds of fits. There was the 'I need something and you don't get it' fit, and then there was the 'this is all too much' fit and the 'don't touch' fit. Every time they thought they understood all the things that bothered him, there seemed to be more. They don't call them 'fits' these days. They call them 'meltdowns'. Rose thinks that's a good word because sometimes it did seem like Lionel just dissolved into kicking and screaming.

'All right, Theo,' she says softly, 'now we're getting somewhere.'

Just then the news comes on the radio and she sits down right next to the old rectangular box that William says shouldn't even be working still.

'A shocking crime has rocked the small town of Mount Watson,' the smooth-voiced newsreader says. 'Late on Saturday afternoon, a lost tourist came across a cabin and found a horrifying scene inside. Police are still at the very beginning of their enquiries but it is believed that an altercation took place between a man and a woman who are known to each other, leading to the man being in critical condition. A young boy who was in the cabin with the couple has disappeared and police are appealing for help to find him. Theo Somerton is eleven years old and is autistic. He is non-verbal and may not know he is lost. He will not respond to his name being called. He has blonde hair and blue eyes and will probably be dressed warmly, although this has not been confirmed. He is one hundred and fifty-five centimetres tall and approximately forty kilos. All citizens of the Mount Watson area are asked to be on the lookout. People are being asked to gather at the Mount Watson village hall if they are able to aid in the search. PolAir and the dog squad have been enlisted to help but resources are being hampered because of the rain. More to come as news comes to hand.'

'Well, well, lad,' says Rose. 'Looks like you've caused a bit of a ruckus. I don't know what's happened to your parents but it doesn't sound good, you poor thing.'

A large clap of thunder makes Rose jump and Theo drops to his knees and crawls under the table, his hands over his ears. Another clap leads to a keening sound from the boy. Rose bends down to see his white-faced fear as he rocks under her table. Lionel hated storms as well and would hide in their mother's cupboard. Once, when the rain went sideways, hail bouncing off the tin roof of their little home, thunder and lightning screaming and flashing through the air, Rose could hear Lionel inside, moaning with terror. She did the only thing she could think of then, climbing in with him, wrapping her arms around him and holding him tight. Lionel didn't like to be touched but sometimes he didn't mind a tight hug. Most people would think it too tight, but the tighter she held on, the more Lionel relaxed.

'I'm too old to get under the table, lad,' says Rose now but the boy's keening grows louder with each thunderous boom.

'All right, all right,' mutters Rose and she bends her old knees, gritting her teeth at the shooting pains as they protest, crawling underneath the old kitchen table. As she edges closer to the boy, she sees him trying to move away. 'Now, I know just how to make it better,' she yells over the noise and, perhaps in desperation, the child stops moving away, allowing Rose to place her arms around his skinny shoulders. She tightens her hold on the child, even though it hurts her arms to do so. She squeezes and squeezes until the wailing stops and she feels his body relax.

'They'll suspend the search while this is on, lad. We'll wait here and we'll be fine. This place is older than I am but it's got a good solid roof. Don't worry. We'll be fine here,' whispers Rose as she holds on to him.

His body grows looser, and even through the ruckus of the storm, Rose feels that he has succumbed to sleep. She's sure he was under the cabin all night so he is probably exhausted. Once he's fully relaxed, she lets go and crawls out from under the table. She finds some blankets and drapes them over him, making a heavy warmth for him to sleep in. He'll like that. She knows he will.

Lowering her old body onto a kitchen chair, she is grateful that the whisky and the Panadol are close by. She doesn't bother with a glass, sipping straight out of the bottle as she swallows down a couple of pills.

She wants to help – more than anything she wants to – but she's too old to be mothering a boy like this. Autistic is what they call it now. William gave her a couple of books from the library because he knew she was interested. It was amazing to read the descriptions, to be able to finally understand what had been going on in her brother's head. 'It's like a wire in my head has short-circuited,' one woman reported. 'I can't look at people because I don't just see a face, I see a thousand faces,' a young boy was quoted as saying. What Rose grew to understand is that there is a spectrum and that everyone with autism is somewhere on that spectrum. Some are just a little bit uncomfortable in public and have to be taught to respond to people's facial expressions. But some won't speak and some may struggle to function in society. Every autistic person is different and she wishes that she had known some of it when Lionel was a young man. 'When you've met one autistic person, you need to know you've only met one autistic person,' a doctor with many, many letters after his name wrote.

They might not have made the decision they did in the end if they had understood.

'Retarded,' they called Lionel back then but he wasn't. The ugly, spitting word isn't used anymore and much for the better, thinks Rose. The world was simply just a bit too much for her brother. He was as smart as anyone at the stuff he was interested in. When they first got the generator working so they had power, he was fascinated, pulling out wires on the radio and anything else with a power cord and putting them back again. Things always worked when he was done and, in another life, Rose thought he could have gone to work for the electric company, fixing things in people's houses.

After reading the books, Rose felt a deep sadness that she and her sister had not known how to take care of Lionel. People know so much these days. William is forever tapping on his phone, asking it questions. All the answers in the world are out there now, just a few clicks away.

But some things can't be answered. How a boy came to hide under her house is something that she might never know the answer to.

'What could have happened in the cabin, Mary?' she says to her smiling sister. 'What could have happened?'

Theo sleeps on, his light snoring telling Rose he is deeply asleep. She hopes he is warm enough because he was still damp. The fire flickers a little, reminding Rose that it needs another log. They are warm and safe in the cabin as they wait for the rain to ease but Rose knows that things could get very difficult. She is not strong enough to stop him if he really tries to hurt himself. She remembers holding Lionel away from the wall when he wouldn't stop the banging. He was fierce in his need to hurt himself. The boy is calm and asleep now but he may not be for long, and who knows what he saw, what trauma it might lead to.

'I'll need you and the good Lord to lend me a helping hand with all this, Mary,' says Rose as outside the rain comes down harder, intent on staying.

Getting up, Rose makes herself a piece of toast, realising that she's not had any breakfast yet. The boy sleeps on, and she relaxes as she eats, pondering what to do. William visited only two days ago, loaded up with food and anything else she might need, so he likely won't stop by again for another couple of days. He may decide to check on her. He thinks this cabin is just about ready to fall down but Rose knows her home. It's not going anywhere. It's braved worse storms than this. The Australian weather is a mercurial thing. One moment it sends a flood to drown you, and as soon as you get over that, the sun bakes the earth and fires flare, rushing through the bush to eat up everything in their path. Rose knows she is safe here. There is enough space between her and the thick undergrowth to stop the flames, and she has sat through many storms listening to the rain dancing on the roof. But it's only been her, only ever her, for decades – just how she likes it. What if the boy turns violent? What if he runs away into the bush, where it's cold and wet? What then?

It's not even lunchtime but Rose takes another sip of her whisky. 'The good Lord will forgive me, Mary. It's all a bit much at the moment.' She looks at the old round clock on the wall, ticking away. It's nearly time for another news bulletin. She hopes there will be more news. That's all she's got right now: hope and whisky.

'You've got me and the good Lord too, Rose,' she hears her sister reply.

'I know, love,' she says. 'I know.'

CHAPTER TWELVE

Cecelia

When the door to her hospital room opens, Cecelia is staring down at her congealing breakfast. The pile of scrambled egg looks almost solid and the toast is burnt around the edges but soggy in the middle, the coffee bitter and lukewarm. She cannot imagine how she is supposed to eat the food but it doesn't matter anyway since her throat refuses to swallow anything other than liquid.

'Hello, Cecelia,' says a woman and Cecelia looks up from her tray. The woman is older, her brown hair artfully streaked with grey and cut into a shoulder-length bob. She is wearing jeans and a red jumper but an official-looking badge hangs around her neck.

'My name is Ellen, I'm the psychiatrist here. I thought we could have a chat.'

The woman waits patiently for Cecelia to answer, but when she doesn't do or say anything, she drags the plastic chair from the corner of the room to the side of Cecelia's bed.

'Constable Emmerson has asked me to speak to you before he talks to you again. He wanted to see if we could find a way to help you speak.'

Cecelia shrugs her shoulders. The woman's voice is even-toned and deep. Cecelia can imagine that she can calm a patient quite easily.

'Annie, your nurse, told me that you weren't able to write down what happened? Is that right?'

Cecelia opens her mouth, allowing her breath to emerge into the silence.

'Perhaps you'd like to speak to me? I can help. I really can. I've been told about your little boy. I'm sure you'd like him to be found. Perhaps you can help with that. Can you tell me what happened so that we can work out where he might be? Can you tell me how you happened to be holding the knife? Can you remember anything?'

The woman is asking too many questions. Cecelia doesn't have the answers for her. She doesn't have the answers for herself.

'Selective mutism is a choice, Cecelia...' begins the woman, and Cecelia starts shaking her head. This is not her choice. It was not her choice. She shakes her head back and forth, making herself giddy, and all she can think is that this was not her choice. She had no choice.

'Okay, okay, it's fine, it's fine,' says the psychiatrist. 'I mean it's a subconscious choice. Your mind is protecting you.'

Cecelia stops shaking her head and then she pushes the trolley holding her breakfast tray away from her. This woman cannot help her. If she speaks, if the words are allowed to come, then Theo... what? She doesn't know, she simply doesn't know, and she fights the urge to bang her head so that the truth is released.

The psychiatrist studies her closely. 'Perhaps we could do some relaxation exercises together? It may help to release the memory.'

Cecelia turns her head away from the woman, stares out at the interminable rain.

You don't understand. You don't know me or what my life is like. You can't help me.

Cecelia knows that this woman can do nothing for her. She slides down in her bed and pulls the covers up to her chin, closes her eyes. She cannot speak. She cannot tell this woman what happened. She has no idea how to shatter the glass wall in her memory, and if it does break, if she pushes through, she is filled with fear at what she will find.

The woman waits in the silence for a few minutes. 'I'll come back later,' she says softly. 'We can try again.'

Cecelia keeps her eyes shut as she listens for the door to her room to be opened and closed so that she is once again alone with her secretive thoughts.

They will have called Kaycee. Cecelia knows this. Their daughter will be here soon. She may not want to be here but she will come.

Kaycee had not been able to leave their home fast enough, her car packed full with her bags, duvet and pillows, the blanket she likes and the worn yellow teddy bear she's had since she was a baby. Cecelia had felt her daughter's need to be free of her as a pain in her heart, and when Nick had slid the last box into the back of her small red hatchback, the look of relief on her elder child's face was too much for Cecelia.

'I'm sorry you've been so unhappy,' she whispered in her daughter's ear as she hugged her goodbye.

'Oh, Mum,' Kaycee said, letting go and shaking her head, and Cecelia understood that those words encompassed so many things that Kaycee wanted to say.

Oh, Mum, it's too late now.

Oh, Mum, why must you make things so difficult?

Oh, Mum, you'll forget about me. You'll be thinking about Theo five minutes after I leave.

Oh, Mum, you don't get to turn back time.

After that, Cecelia kept reaching out to her daughter despite knowing that her daughter didn't want her to.

'You need to stop calling me, Mum,' she said, her voice soft with disappointment in Cecelia's belated mothering. 'Now that you have all the time in the world for Theo, you've decided to question how I'm spending my days?' Her tone was more strident with those words. 'You can stop pretending to be mother of the year, you know – I'm fine without your input.' A final, furious stab.

No one can be angrier with you than your teenage daughter, and no one knows how to skewer you with barbed comments like she does.

'I love you, Kaycee. Can't you understand that no matter what has happened I will always love you?' Cecelia said when she had called, asking her to join them at the cabin this year.

'But it's not enough, is it, Mum? You love me, I know that, I've never questioned that, but you don't really have room in your life for me and you haven't since Theo was born. And that's fine. I understand, but don't keep trying to drag me back into things. Give me a little time and space. Anyway, I have loads of assignments due after semester break.'

'Just leave her be,' Nick said after that.

It is Cecelia's fault, she knows that. In taking care of Theo, she has lost sight of everything and now… what has happened?

Why can't I remember? I know Nick is hurt. I know Theo is gone. But I don't know what happened.

Her brain is protecting her as the psychiatrist said, she is sure. Whatever happened, it is not something she wants to know. Her brain is doing the equivalent of what Theo does when he covers his ears with his hands, closes his eyes and rocks. Consciously or subconsciously, she doesn't want to know.

Was she the one who hurt Nick? An image appears of a face, not one she'd seen before. Who is it? A young woman. She was wearing a green hoodie, Cecelia remembers now. She simply walked into the cabin and then she screamed or kind of yelped in fright. She screamed because Cecelia was holding a knife. She remembers the knife now, its smooth steel blade and the brushed silver handle. She used it on Friday night to cut the chicken into strips. Theo will only eat chicken if it is cut into strips, crumbed and fried and then laid out on his plate in a neat row. The blade went through the chicken easily. 'I could use a knife like this at home,' Cecelia hears herself say at the time.

Did I hurt Nick? I was holding the knife so I must have hurt him. But how is that possible? I would never hurt Nick.

Cecelia sighs as snatches of a conversation come back to her. She is sure the conversation happened this weekend but she is also sure that it's a conversation she and Nick have had many, many times.

'You have no idea how hard this is for me and Kaycee,' her husband said. 'Since the moment he was diagnosed, he's all you've thought about.' So much judgement in his words, so little understanding.

'That's not true, Nick. I have to work with him. I have to try and make sure that he can function, that he's okay.'

'I don't doubt that,' he replied, 'but why do we have to lose you for him to be okay? Why can't you still need us, still want to be with us?' he almost pleaded. He was running out of hope for them and she has known that for some time.

I did hurt Nick, she realises with a sickening jolt. *I hurt Nick and I hurt Kaycee and now they are angry with me all the time. But that gets tiring. Being everyone's punching bag gets exhausting. They all need me but there isn't enough of me to go around.*

Cecelia opens her eyes and pulls the covers down as she watches the rain. It spatters against the window, blown sideways by the wind and hitting the glass as though trying to push through. She imagines the windowpane shattering and knows that the rain would be ice-cold. She cannot hear much through the thick glass but she knows the rushing rain will be drowning out all other sounds outside.

Would Theo know to seek shelter? Every year that they have come to the cabin, she has gone over the plan with him, the plan if he becomes lost. He must find somewhere safe and wait, just wait. Theo is a runner. He runs when he is filled with joy, when he is angry, when he is sad and when he's scared.

Every time Cecelia thinks she has a handle on her son's triggers, there is another one. Loud noises, too many people talking at once, storms, strange smells, cats but not dogs, orange-coloured food like pumpkin but not carrots, a corner of his duvet being crumpled, new people, his grandmother's camel-coloured coat, washing liquid that smells like the ocean. And when something triggers him, he runs. Fear triggered him yesterday, terrible, strong fear. *Was he afraid of me?*

They have a watch for him, a smartwatch with a GPS function so that they can always locate him. But he wasn't wearing it in the cabin. There was something about the band that had started to bother him and she knows that Nick was going to look at it after their son went to sleep. Theo refused to wear it and he couldn't explain why.

'Maybe a piece of the rubber band is torn or something. I'll get him a new one if I can't figure it out.' Cecelia knows she felt a spark of worry that he would be without the watch in the cabin but she reasoned that the coming rainstorm would keep them all inside. *It's not like he's going to go running in the rain*, she thought.

But he did run, because he had to run. *Why did he have to run? What scared him enough to send him out into the bush?*

It was a gamble to come to this cabin the first time all those years ago. Theo was only four years old and Cecelia worried about the lack of baby-proofing in a rented cottage in a small town in the Blue Mountains, even though he wasn't a baby anymore. They wanted somewhere away from people. The loud static noise they had managed to recreate on an iPhone would bother other hotel guests. They hadn't had more than a couple of nights out by the time Theo was four. Cecelia had felt her life shrink, becoming smaller and smaller. She had gone from being a working mother of one child, fitting in her marketing job around Kaycee's schedule, to being a stay-at-home mother of a child with special needs. Her days were taken up with managing Theo and his therapies – speech therapy and occupational therapy and physiotherapy and visits with a psychologist. And when Theo was at his special school three days a week, she was reading about autism, going to lectures and connecting with other parents who had children on the spectrum.

'Let's get away,' Nick said when school holidays were coming up.

'Where on earth would we go?' Cecelia asked him, as exhausted as she had been since the day Theo was born. The idea seemed preposterous.

'We could go to the mountains. We can rent a cabin somewhere out of the way.'

Cecelia stared down at the carrot she was chopping up, making sure to cut it into perfect strips so that Theo would eat it, knowing that although he had eaten carrots every day this week, there was no guarantee that he would do so again.

She was terrified of changing things where Theo was concerned. But then she looked up from what she was doing and saw something in Nick's eyes when he asked. It wasn't often in those days that she really looked at anyone except her son, but she really looked at her husband then, and she saw defeat or perhaps resignation. He assumed she would say no. He expected it and all she needed to do was to confirm his suspicions. In a sudden mad longing for her former life, she found herself saying yes.

He worked hard at the hospital and he deserved a break as much as any of them did.

Nick was a heart surgeon who spent his days saving lives and then came home to find his wife overwhelmed by the task of caring for Theo and Kaycee, who she knew was basically taking care of herself. Sometimes, Cecelia lay in bed at night and listed all the ways she had failed that day. She knew that if she told anyone that she did this, they would be horrified. The psychologist she saw occasionally, when she felt she might go insane, would certainly be unhappy. But she felt the list to be almost soothing. If she acknowledged how she had messed up, then maybe she would not make those mistakes again.

Today I tried to rush Theo so we could get to school on time, leading to a meltdown. Today there were no carrots for Kaycee's school lunch. Today I forgot that Kaycee had to take her favourite book into school for a talk. Today I yelled at Theo when he wouldn't go to the bathroom and then messed in his pants. Today I was late to pick up Kaycee and she was one of the last children standing outside school with Mrs Anderson, who was angry at being held up. Today I forgot to ask Nick how the surgery on that little boy went. Today I didn't call my mother's residential home to plan a visit.

She knew that Nick wanted more from her, and that Kaycee wanted more from her as well. That everyone wanted more from her, but Theo took everything she had, including a love so deep and so complete that sometimes she couldn't breathe when she looked at his angelic face.

Outside the hospital window, rain rolls on relentlessly. It wasn't raining when they arrived at the cabin on Friday. It was cold, the bite of the coming winter in the air, but the sky was clear. The weather changed so quickly. Everything has changed so quickly and she can't make sense of it.

'I've had enough, Cecelia. I can't do this anymore.' Did he say that on Friday when they arrived, or was that on Saturday morning? The hours at the cabin have blended into one another. She remembers her husband moving his hands around as he said the words, indicating the cabin and Theo and her – most of all her.

'What about me?' she wanted to scream at him. Did she scream that? How angry had she become? Because even now as she lies in this bed, she can feel anger rising up from her toes. She was so angry. He was angry too.

Their anger swirled around that cabin, filling the air with its poison until… *What happened then?*

They never used to argue that way, she knows that. She can feel it. They are very far from the people they used to be.

She had been so completely in control of her life when they met. He was a newly minted doctor, still studying all the hours he was not working in the hospital in his chosen speciality of cardiac surgery.

Cecelia was working in marketing, was in charge of the five people in her division. She met Nick at a gathering at the hospital to which she and her firm were invited because they had been hired to do some marketing for the hospital's new research facility that was in need of millions of dollars in donations. 'See if you think any of those attending could be the face of the hospital,' Cecelia's boss, Geoff, had said. 'Nothing wrong with a good- and trustworthy-looking doctor to help pull in some big dollars.'

Cecelia had been drifting around the conference room with half a glass of acidic red wine in her hand when she spotted Nick standing morosely in the corner, a plate piled high with tasteless sausage rolls and mini quiches in his hand. He was shoving them into his mouth, one after the other. 'You don't have to eat all the party food, you know,' Cecelia had said. A brown curl of hair had fallen onto his forehead and his blue eyes could not be concealed by the glasses he was wearing.

He swallowed. 'I have surgery – well, not me but I'm helping – and I won't get to eat for hours and hours.'

'But it's six in the evening. Surely you don't operate at night?'

'We do if we get a heart, and it should be coming in,' he glanced at his watch, 'in half an hour. It's for a fifteen-year-old boy and it's going to change his life.'

His whole face changed, colour livening his pale cheeks, his eyes lighting up, and Cecelia fell instantly into infatuation.

'How long does it take?' she asked.

'Around six hours, give or take. But I have to go and prep him as well so… hours and hours.'

'Want to meet for a drink afterwards?' The words had tripped out of her.

'Ha,' he snorted, 'that could be around two in the morning.'

'I'll wait up. And here,' she said, taking a business card out of her bag and writing on the back of it, 'is my home address as well.'

Nick laughed and Cecelia noted a nice smile and broad shoulders.

She handed him the card and got back to working the room, introducing herself to hospital board members.

At 3 a.m., a banging on her front door roused her from sleep, and when she opened the door Nick was standing there, his face pale, his eyes red. 'We lost him,' he said and all Cecelia could do was open her arms.

Kaycee came along quickly and easily after they married, but Theo took longer. Cecelia had almost given up hope when she finally fell pregnant with him.

He was perfect with white-blonde hair and grey eyes that turned an iridescent blue after a couple of weeks. He was so beautiful that Cecelia found herself taking twice as long to get around the supermarket as people stopped to admire her baby boy. Unless he was crying. And once he started crying, he just wouldn't stop. By the time he was three months old, she knew that he would not be soothed out of his crying fits. If he became fussy while they were out, she knew that she needed to get home as soon as possible. Babies are supposed to become easier as they get older. Kaycee had settled herself into a manageable routine by the time she was six months old. If she was tired, she napped in the car or her pram. Nick and Cecelia took her out to restaurants, enjoying being out with their well-behaved baby girl. But Theo simply got more difficult. They only tried taking him to a restaurant a couple of times before they gave up; the stares from other diners as he screamed as though in pain was too much for them.

Cecelia watches one single raindrop trace its way down the windowpane. Kaycee used to do that in the car, and if Cecelia wasn't driving, she and Kaycee would each pick a droplet and see which one would win the race to the bottom of the window. She had never been able to play that simple game with Theo.

Theo will be hiding somewhere, she tells herself. *He will be sheltering in place.* She has taught him that over the years at the cabin. She only agreed to the vacation the first year in the hope that she and Nick could find a way back to each other. There have been moments when that has felt possible, moments of harmony. She can remember the first time they made love in the big wooden bed, can still feel her surprise at her husband's advances when they had both been completely exhausted and uninterested for years.

The cabin was a rest from their reality, from her reality of taking care of Theo alone. Now, she feels a tear snake its way down her cheek, matching the progression of the droplet of rain she is watching. Theo will be sheltering in place. *Please let him be sheltering in place.*

Over the years of being his mother she has had moments of struggling in her role as Theo's mother, terrible dark moments when she has wished she had the space and time to simply breathe and not worry. She works harder with him after those moments, loves him more deeply, commits more time to him. The magic of the cabin has faded but they have still come back every year, even as she and her husband have grown further and further apart.

But she never imagined they would be so far apart that she would do what she did, what she is supposed to have done. She closes her eyes and searches the blank space in her memory, sees an image of the knife, of blood, a smile, a sneer. 'Run,' Nick told Theo. And so, he ran. But Nick couldn't run. It was too late for him to run. It was too late.

The door to her room begins to swing open and Cecelia keeps her eyes shut, blocking out whoever it is, blocking out everything.

'Mum,' she hears, and even though it is Kaycee and she has been waiting for her to arrive, has longed for her to arrive, Cecelia doesn't open her eyes. She finds that she cannot face her nineteen-year-old daughter. She cannot explain what happened. Her child will look to her for an explanation, for a reason. But Cecelia doesn't have either of those and her heart feels as though it is swelling inside her chest at all the things she does not – cannot – know. She would like to open her arms and enclose this child, this beautiful now distant young woman, in a tight hug and tell her that it will be fine, that everything will be fine. But she can't because of everything she does not know.

CHAPTER THIRTEEN

Kaycee

Kaycee finds herself clenching her fists as she looks at her mother lying still in the hospital bed, her eyes closed. She wants to grab her and shake what happened out of her. Constable Emmerson has remained outside for a moment, having a whispered conversation with the psychiatrist who has just walked out of Cecelia's room. The woman nodded at Kaycee, offering a small smile of sympathy. Kaycee would have liked to speak to her but she needs to speak to her mother first.

Walking over to the bed, she takes her mother's warm hand in her own. Her mum looks pale, her black hair a stark contrast to her face, but somehow, she also looks younger. When her mother's eyes are open, they are forever filled with worry, her brows furrowed, and it's always about one person and one person only: Theo. It's been that way since he was born.

She can see her mother's eyes moving rapidly under her eyelids.

'Mum,' she says softly. 'I know you're awake and I know you can hear me. Please talk to me. Please tell me what happened. Please help us find Theo. Do you know where Theo is?'

At that, her mother opens her eyes and looks at her. For a moment it seems as though she doesn't recognise Kaycee but then tears spill over, running down her cheeks and neck. She blinks rapidly.

Constable Emmerson comes into the room and her mother shifts in the bed, moving away from his presence. Kaycee thinks she seems afraid of the policeman who stands quietly, waiting to see what Kaycee is able to achieve with her mother.

'Oh, Mum,' says Kaycee, her eyes filling as well, 'what happened?'

But her mother just shakes her head.

'Look,' says Kaycee, sniffing and using a hand to wipe away her tears, 'where is Theo? I know he was with you but they can't find him.'

Her mother opens her mouth, moving her lips as though she is trying to speak, but no sound comes out. She pulls her hand away from Kaycee, shoots the policeman another fearful glance and then turns onto her side, curling up into a ball.

'Mum, you have to tell me what happened,' says Kaycee forcefully.

But her mother is small and silent in the bed.

'Maybe she'll write it down,' says Kaycee to Constable Emmerson.

'We tried that. She won't even hold a pen.'

'I don't know what to do,' says Kaycee. 'When can I see my father? Maybe he can tell me what happened?'

'I'm afraid you can't see him until after his surgery.'

'But why?'

Constable Emmerson offers Kaycee another sigh. 'He's badly injured, Kaycee.'

'Please?' she asks, her voice small. She's begging. If she can just see him, maybe touch his large hand, sit near him, then perhaps she will be able to see a way through this. Her father has always made her and Theo feel safe and protected. What will happen if he is not around to do that anymore?

'I'm afraid not. They need to keep him safe from infection.'

Kaycee has studied the infections that run rampant in hospitals in one of her courses. She has seen the damage they can cause. Terror creeps up her spine. Her father might die. She cannot be without her father. When they speak, he doesn't ask questions about what she's eating or whether she's getting enough sleep. He tells her about his patients, encourages her to discuss things she's learning. After they speak Kaycee always finds herself resolving to give up the drinking and dedicate herself to her studies. But something always draws her back to the bar.

There is a sudden flare of anger inside her, a dread-driven anger over the possible loss of her father, over her mother's silence and the fate of her missing brother.

'Can I talk to a doctor? Can I do anything at all except have you sigh at me?' she snaps at Constable Emmerson. 'I know I was drunk, okay. It was wrong but I didn't exactly expect my Saturday night to end with my parents in hospital and my brother missing.' Kaycee's voice has risen and she feels frustration bubbling inside her. She has no idea what she's supposed to do. Her mother does not move but her stony silence does not stop Kaycee from understanding her mum's disappointment at her being drunk. She has always been able to read her mother's despair at less-than-perfect behaviour from her.

Behind Constable Emmerson, the door to the hospital room opens and another policeman looks in. 'Is everything okay in here?' he asks.

'Fine, sir,' says the constable, looking at his feet.

'Hey, Kaycee, how are you?' says the policeman.

Kaycee looks at the officer, slightly disturbed by his familiar tone, although she quickly realises that she has seen him before. He is a large man, his belly straining at the buttons on his shirt. His grey hair is cut short and his green eyes sag at the corners. He rubs his hand over his chin, where a grey beard has appeared.

'Look,' the man says, 'we need to ask you some things about your brother, about Theo. I don't know if you remember me but I'm Sergeant Peterson. We've met a few times. My wife, Monica, and I came to dinner at the cabin a few years back. I go fishing with your dad sometimes. Do you remember?'

Kaycee studies the officer, trying to place him. It's been two years since she has been back to Mount Watson with her parents for their annual autumn holiday.

'I think so,' she settles on because she only vaguely remembers him. She never paid much attention to her parents' dinner guests. 'Mixing with the locals is important,' her father liked to say, but for Kaycee, a dinner party meant that she had to try and keep her brother amused in a small space where the Wi-Fi kept dropping out.

She knows that she used to love the cabin. It was her favourite time of year and her favourite place to be. The walls are made of timber and the fireplace is surrounded by stone and her bedroom is small and up in the attic with only a little window to look out at the bush. Each year she would rush upstairs as they arrived and open that window, letting in the crisp autumn air and noting the trees in varying shades of red and green as they prepared for a bare-branched winter. The cabin provided sanctuary from the real world. It was the only time of year that her father was really not on call. It usually took him a day or two to switch off his phone and stop calling to ask for updates on his patients, but Kaycee could see that the cabin would work its magic as the hours passed, and finally, he would put the phone in a drawer and forget that it was there.

He and Kaycee would go on long walks together in the mountains, and he would take Theo fishing even though Theo wouldn't hold a rod. Her father would put on a silly khaki hat that made him look older but also symbolised a letting-go of his everyday worries. She and her mother would sit on the couch together at night, each stuck in their own novel, munching on homemade popcorn while Theo played on his iPad. It wasn't always perfect. If Theo had a meltdown, she would see her mother's face change, could see the thousands of questions she was asking herself about why it had happened, and if her parents had people over for dinner, she would have to amuse her brother, which she had grown to hate. She could have come to the cabin last year. She could have come this year as well, and a tiny finger of guilt nudges at her. If she had been here, none of what happened would have happened.

But over the years she began to resent the cabin and its break from real life. It felt like her family were acting in a play. Her parents had more and more hours of not speaking to each other, and the peace that they had found at first seemed like only a dream. Kaycee began to hate the cabin and everything it represented.

'Look, I've met your young man in the café,' says the sergeant, dragging Kaycee away from her reflection as her stomach jolts a little at the idea of Jonah being her 'young man'. 'Let's go and have a coffee and maybe a bite to eat and we can try and figure out how to find Theo. I know it's raining now and the search has been scaled down until it clears, but there are still people out looking. Anything you can tell me about him would help. We know he's autistic but I don't know much beyond that.'

Kaycee nods and takes one last look at her mother, curled up small and pretending she is not where she is. Kaycee doesn't blame her. What could have possibly happened in that cabin?

In the café she offers Jonah a weak smile as she sits down, realising that it would be nice to have someone who was actually hers. Adam has never felt like hers and she's aware that right now he is probably in some other girl's bed. He's not hers and she finds that she doesn't even care. She's unsure how she has managed to spend the last five months with him. She doesn't even like him. She swallows. The alcohol has helped. Everything changes after a few drinks, and while when she's sober she is irritated by Adam's arrogance and disinterest in anyone but himself, drunk Kaycee is blind to all that. Drunk Kaycee finds the nasty things he says about other people and even about her own family, about herself, hilarious. She experiences a hot flash of hate for drunk Kaycee.

The café is small and cosy with only three sets of tables and chairs, and walls painted in lilac. A large coffee machine takes up nearly the whole counter and the continual hiss and spit of coffee being made is comforting as the café fills with the freshly made scent. One wall is taken up with racks filled with teddy bears and flowers and boxes of chocolates. Kaycee wonders if her mother would like something sweet to eat.

'Have they found your brother?' asks Jonah.

'No, but they'll find him. I mean, they have to find him, don't they?'

Jonah squeezes her shoulder. 'They've got a lot of people looking.' He cannot give her the reply she is looking for. Kaycee chews on her bottom lip. Theo could be anywhere. He's been gone a whole night and she knows without a shadow of a doubt that he would not have been wearing shoes. Even if he started out with shoes on, he would have discarded them. There is nothing he hates more than shoes. 'They make my feet feel too many things,' he told her when she asked him last year. He was pretty good with his iPad by then and sometimes, if she caught him at the right moment, it actually felt like they were having a conversation.

Sergeant Peterson places a cup of coffee in front of her and a packet of two shortbread biscuits. 'Wasn't sure what you wanted,' he says. He sits down at the small, square, plastic table and rubs his eyes. It looks like he's been up all night.

'I know that we have a lot of questions and no answers, but I think that perhaps the first thing we need to do is find Theo. Is there anything you can tell us that can help?'

Kaycee takes a sip of her coffee. It's sweet and milky and she takes another sip, craving the caffeine hit. 'Okay,' she says, and the sergeant nods as though she is speaking to him but she's actually speaking to herself. She needs to get it together now. She needs to do whatever it takes to find her brother. She banishes all thoughts of drunk Kaycee, of how badly she behaved last night, from her mind.

'Theo is eleven. He's autistic and non-verbal. I know that he wouldn't be wearing shoes. He hates shoes. He won't come if you call him because he doesn't respond to his name, and even if he gets hungry, he won't approach any people he sees. His favourite television show is still *Bob the Builder*. He doesn't watch it anymore but he likes to have it playing in the background. And if he's having some sort of a meltdown, it calms him down – the music and the song, you know… "Can we fix it?"'

Sergeant Peterson chuckles a little. 'Yeah, I know it.'

'Okay,' says Kaycee, feeling irritated. It's not a joke. 'I know that he's eleven and too old for it but it's comforting to him when things feel out of control. He's actually really smart and he watches a lot of science programmes and other stuff but this is what my mum uses when he's really bad. If he's run off, he must be really scared and confused. Although he really does like to run. He can run for… for ages.'

'Of course, of course,' soothes Sergeant Peterson. 'I'll tell the searchers to get a recording of the song and play it through some loudspeakers. Maybe that will bring him out.'

'That's good,' says Kaycee. 'Oh, and he really likes that hymn called "This Little Light of Mine". My mum sings it to him when he's going to sleep and she has done since he was a baby.' *To both of you, Kaycee, I've always sung it to both of you.* Kaycee hears her mother's hurt tone, a tone she has become familiar with over the years every time she has accused her mother of only raising Theo when she actually has two children. In her rush to distance herself from her mother and from her family, she has perhaps forgotten the things her mother did do for her.

'Righto,' says Sergeant Peterson. 'I'll get all this information to the searchers and then I need to speak to you again so we can work out what might have happened.'

'But why would I have any idea?'

Sergeant Peterson stands up and looks down at her kindly. 'Something must have been going on between your parents for your mother to do what she did. We need to see if we can find a motive. Maybe your dad is… maybe he… has a temper.'

'What?' says Kaycee, standing up, her hands burning to the tips of her fingers with the desire to shove the sergeant away from her. 'My dad does not have a temper. He doesn't hurt my mum. Don't you even suggest it! Neither of my parents would hurt each other. Theo and I never got so much as a light smack. You don't understand, that's not who they are.'

'Okay, okay,' says the sergeant, holding his hands up. 'But something happened and we need to find out what.'

Kaycee looks down into her caramel-coloured coffee. She doesn't want to be here with this man, speculating about her family. She wants to do that alone, wants to try and figure it out without being watched. Exhaustion creeps over her.

'Do you think they'll find him?' she asks, looking up at the sergeant.

Her rubs his hand over his eyes again. 'We've never lost a tourist, and we've had a few go missing. Your family has been coming here for years so I think that Theo may be kind of familiar with the terrain. I'm hoping he will find somewhere safe to wait out the storm, and we have virtually the whole town looking, with more people arriving every hour. The woman who found them in the cabin – the tourist – is helping as well. Everyone wants to find him. It's strange that your mother won't speak. I can't help but think…'

'Can't help but think what?' snaps Kaycee.

'Look, don't worry about it. Constable Emmerson will contact me if and when she speaks so I can talk to her about what happened. Right now, I would prefer you to only discuss Theo with her. If she starts talking, tell her she needs to wait and speak to me. I think it would be better if I got her side of the story first. I know how to talk to people who've gone through this kind of thing.'

'What kind of thing? My mother didn't hurt my father. My father isn't violent. I know that. I promise you that.' Kaycee sighs. 'Look, can I go and stay with her? Can I sit with my mum?'

'Yes, that's fine.' He offers her a slight smile.

'Maybe I can come and help look for Theo,' says Jonah, and Kaycee turns to him, shocked at the suggestion.

'Don't you want to go home? I mean, you've already done so much. He's not… I mean, don't you have to get back to go to uni tomorrow?'

'It'll be fine,' says Jonah. 'I have a couple of lectures that I can listen to online while I walk.' Kaycee is sure this is not true. The one course that would require attendance at uni would be medicine.

'We need all the help we can get,' says the sergeant.

'It's decided then,' replies Jonah.

Kaycee nods and it's only when she is sitting next to her mother's hospital bed that she realises that she should probably be helping look for Theo as well. They haven't seen much of each other over the last two years but he would still respond to her before he would respond to a stranger.

She could have spoken to him more, even without being home. She has an app on her phone that lets her talk to him on the computer.

'He misses you,' her mother has said in virtually every conversation they have had since she moved out.

'He's fine, Mum,' Kaycee has always replied, dismissing her brother the same way the world dismisses autistic people who don't seem to display emotion or register emotion from others. But they do. Kaycee knows enough to know that they do. Her brother feels happy and sad and angry just like anyone else, and even though he's never said it, she knows that he misses her. She used the app when she first moved out, sending a quick message every day.

Hey Theo, hope school was good and Benjamin helped you with your work.

Hey Theo, hope you enjoy soccer today.

Hey Theo, have a good Sunday. I hope Mum makes pancakes.

She understood that her brother either wouldn't reply or he would reply with facts about his latest obsession. Sometimes she would open the app to find endless streams of information on something. For the last six months it's been robots. He's obsessed with robots. And he has told her about them in great detail: who built the first robot, how you build a robot, how advanced they have become. Kaycee doesn't read the long messages properly and then feels guilty because it wouldn't take much to ask him some questions.

But her only thoughts have been about herself lately. By the time she left home she was done with thinking about other people first, with thinking about Theo first. She acknowledges this thought to herself now and feels the overwhelming horror of that idea. How could she have been so self-centred? How could she have ever thought that way? As she sits here by her mother's bed, her mum reminds her of Theo holding on to his knees and rocking away whatever is bothering him. Cecelia has her hands clasped around her knees and her eyes closed as she shuts out her daughter, shuts out the world.

Kaycee can feel that she is on the precipice of losing all of them, her mother, her father and her brother, and she has no idea how she ever imagined that they were not a necessary part of her life.

She was beyond delighted when her little brother had arrived when she was eight years old. She had gone through a period at around five years old of asking her mother for a brother or sister. Everyone she knew had a sibling. She'd had no idea that her mother was struggling to fall pregnant. All she knew was that her mother was irritable a lot and prone to tears. When Theo arrived, Kaycee was so excited she couldn't sleep. But then Theo started crying and he never seemed to stop. Her life went from peaceful and ordered with the attention of two loving parents to chaotic and messy, and she was left feeling ignored for the first time ever. She didn't like that. Not at all.

She loves her little brother. She knows that. She reassures herself of that and has done so every time she feels some sort of resentment towards him because of what his arrival did to all their lives. She loves her brother. But her mother doesn't just love him. She adores him. She thinks about him all the time, every second of the day. Theo seems to be her only reason for getting up in the morning. Sometimes, when she is feeling particularly dramatic, Kaycee believes that her mother wouldn't care if she just disappeared. She knows that this is not the truth, but she also knows that her mother will not survive losing Theo.

'You told him to shelter in place,' she says now. 'Every time we came to the cabin you went through the whole thing with him again in case he ran off. You told him to shelter in place,' she says aloud.

Her mother turns over in the bed and stares at Kaycee and then, finally, she nods her head.

'What happened in the cabin, Mum?' Kaycee asks even though the sergeant said she shouldn't.

Her mother shakes her head, tears slipping down her cheeks, and she closes her eyes again.

'You can't remember, can you?' Kaycee says suddenly, a horrifying realisation dawning on her.

Her mother nods her head, her eyes still closed.

'Did you hurt Dad?' Kaycee whispers. 'Did you hurt my dad?' she says, aware that she sounds five years old.

Her mother shakes her head, and then she turns away again. Kaycee has to take a deep breath in as she tries to suppress the urge to shake the truth out of her mother, to scream and shout and demand that she tell her what happened. 'I'm scared, Mum,' she whispers, and her mother nods her head again.

'We're both scared,' Kaycee says for her.

CHAPTER FOURTEEN

Theo

I open my eyes. The rain is still dripping down. *Drip, drip, swish, swish.* I like the rain. It makes all the other sounds go away. I like the rain but not the booms of thunder, not the lightning, not the hail. Too much noise then. Every sound I hear is loud, loud, and I hear all the sounds at once.

On Mondays at school we do a special game called 'Out in the World', and we all go out to another classroom but it doesn't look like a classroom on Mondays. Sometimes it looks like a place where people get coffee and lunch called a café, sometimes it looks like the office where I go to see Dr Lisa. Dr Lisa has long, straight black hair and she is small. She has a big smile and she shows me cards so I can learn when people are happy or sad. 'What do you think this person is feeling, Theo?' she asked me the last time I went to see her, and she showed me a picture of a man with his eyes close together and his teeth showing. 'Happy,' I signed but that was wrong. The man was angry, and when she explained, I looked again and I could see that he looked like a growling dog. Now I know that a growling dog face means someone is angry.

Last Monday when we did 'Out in the World', the classroom looked like a café and we all had to sit down at tables and wait to get some chocolate milk. I liked it but it wasn't like a real café where Mum gets coffee. In a real café, there is noise, noise, noise. In a real café, I can hear the coffee machine – *hiss, skitter-scatter-roar.*

I can hear people laugh and talk and breathe and sip and chew and… a real café is too much. Too much. I hear all the noises all the time. If there is too much noise, I have to cover my ears and close my eyes and go into my bubble. But sometimes that doesn't help. When the loud booms of thunder came, it was too much and I couldn't go into my bubble.

Saggy skin, blue eyes held me tight, tight. Rose, her name is Rose like a flower. Rose held me tight. Mum holds me tight. Dad holds me tight. Kaycee holds me tight and Benjamin at school. Benjamin holds me tight and says, 'Hey, dude, are you having a moment?'

That's what Benjamin calls it when it's too much: 'having a moment'. Benjamin knows about space and about *Star Wars* and about how to build a robot. 'You're going to be a scientist for sure,' Benjamin tells me and then we work on sounds and spelling. I am a good speller. I am good at numbers. I am good at thinking and I am going to be a scientist like Kaycee. I am not good at life because life is too much.

I am safe on the floor here under the table. I am safe under the blankets with only the *swish, drip* sound of the rain. I can stay here forever. But I have to pee.

I crawl out of the safe blankets and stand up.

She is on the couch. She is watching me with blue, blue eyes.

'Do you need the bathroom?' she asks.

I nod. I can nod. I can sign. I can shake my head. But I can't make the words come out of my mouth. I can make sounds but the words are stuck inside. Inside I answer her. *My name is Theo. My dad said, 'Run.' I like toast. I need the bathroom.* But the words don't want to be in the air.

She shows me where the bathroom is and then she closes the door.

I look around the small room. There is a toilet and a shower and a mirror on the wall. Everything is pink. Pink tiles and a pink basin and a pink toilet. I have never seen a pink toilet. I don't like pink. Pink is too light for me. I like heavy colours like blue and black. I don't want to stay in this pink bathroom because it might float away but I need to pee. I really need to pee. The full-up feeling in my head is here again. I want to lie down on the floor and bang my head but I can't lie down on the pink floor. I will float away. I feel the air in my lungs getting faster and faster. 'Put the brakes on, dude,' I hear Benjamin say. Benjamin says that I am like a car. I like cars. Benjamin says that sometimes I am going too fast, speeding towards a wall, and I need to put the brakes on so I don't have to bang my head. I lift my foot and then I push it down into the floor. I push hard. My lungs get slower. I have put the brakes on. I can stay in this bathroom and use the toilet to pee.

I use the toilet quickly. I push the flush and then I wash my hands. I wash four times in a row. 'Wash your hands, Theo. Always wash your hands.' Mum likes it when my hands are clean. I don't look in the mirror above the pink basin. Theo doesn't live here. I can't see him here.

When I come out, Rose is standing at the stove. 'Eat,' I sign so she will know that food is what I want.

'Eat,' she agrees, 'but I don't know what to feed you.'

'Toast,' I sign because toast will crunch and then there are no other sounds.

She makes more toast and then I eat. When I don't want to eat anymore, I look around the room. I want my iPad. I want my mum. I want my dad. I want my sister. I want *Bob the Builder* and the cabin. The cabin is safe. The cabin is quiet. The cabin is a good space.

I need to get back to the cabin. But first I need help. If I don't get help, I can't go back. It is bad at the cabin now. The cabin wants to be a bad space. If I get help, I can make it a good space again.

I tell her. I brush my chest and then bend my hand at the knuckles and touch my other hand and then bring it back to my chest. 'I need help,' I sign. Blue eyes look at me. I sign it again. 'I need help.'

'It's been so long,' she says. 'Do it again.'

'I need help,' I sign.

She shakes her head. 'I don't understand but I'm going to guess – you're alone so you need me to help you?'

I nod my head.

'Can you write?' she asks and I nod my head.

She gives me a pen. Plastic, slippery, black. No rubber to rest my fingers. I need rubber. I hold the pen and rock and rock. I need the rubber grip or the words won't come, but there is no rubber grip.

'I need help,' I tell her but I can't explain the rubber grip. I hold the pen and I rock and rock.

'I don't know what else you need,' she says. 'You have a pen and you can write on this paper – see here. Why won't you write?'

Pen, slippery, plastic. I need my rubber grip. I rock and rock. I feel my head fill up with anger. 'Put the brakes on, dude,' I hear Benjamin say but I can't. It is too late. The pink is too light, the pen is too slippery.

'This little light of mine,' she sings, making some of the too much go away. 'I'm going to let it shine. This little light of mine. I'm going to let it shine. This little light of mine. I'm going to let it shine, let it shine, let it shine, let it shine.'

The full-up feeling leaves my head and I push down on the floor to put the brakes on. 'Try, Theo, you can try something new and it will be fine. Just try, Theo.' Kaycee says that to me all the time when she is home but she is not home now, not home. Kaycee is at university and she doesn't come to see me. Dr Lisa asked me if I missed Kaycee. To miss someone is to be sorry they are not there. I miss Kaycee helping me try new things. She helped me try mango. Mango is yellow-orange and sweet but the cubes were slimy in my mouth. I tried to eat it but I had to spit it out. 'At least you tried,' Kaycee said. 'I'm proud of you for trying.' I will try this pen so I can tell Kaycee and she will be proud.

Putting the slippery plastic pen on the paper, I write.

Dad is hurt. Mum is loud. Fight. The cabin is not a safe space now. There was

But I don't know how to write the word. My brain can't find it.

There was

I write again.

There was

CHAPTER FIFTEEN

Rose

Rose looks down at the words the boy, Theo, has written on the paper. They don't explain much but she can almost feel the fear in his jerky handwriting.

She only started singing because she needed help from somewhere, and as the rain poured down and they were cut off from everything else, she hoped that at least the Lord was listening. It seemed like he was as the boy stopped his rocking and wrote, but Rose has no idea what to do with what he has said. If she takes him back, will he be afraid of his father? Of his mother? Who hurt who in that cabin? What was there? What does that mean?

She gets up and turns on the radio but it is only static now. That happens sometimes in storms.

'I don't need that rubbish,' she has always said to William about a mobile phone but the truth is she is afraid of having to learn to use it. A body and a brain get old. She doesn't want to have to try and muddle through anything new. But it would have helped now, although it may have been as useless as the radio is. She turns off the radio but the boy stands up, walks over to it and turns it on again. He turns it up loud, so loud that it's irritating, but Rose just lets it be. There must be a reason why he likes the noise and she knows from experience that there is no sense in fighting him.

There will be people out searching, even in the pelting rain. Lionel ran off quite often when he was little and Rose and Mary would have to go out and look for him. No one in town wanted to help. They were all afraid of actually finding him. She knows that once the search starts up again, it will take them a day or so to get to her cabin, but even in the rain there will be those determined to keep looking. No one likes the thought of someone lost in the bush, where you can lose your senses after a day or two of looking at the same thing with no concrete way forward. This boy isn't the first one to be lost in the bush. She has woken up on many a morning to look outside and see the orange high-visibility vests of the SES volunteers weaving their way through the green shades of the bush. Until they get here, she will just have to manage him. She walks over to the radio, turning it down a little, just a little. He doesn't react, for which she is grateful. He is sitting at the table, holding the pen, drawing black lines, one after the other.

She has made him another piece of toast because she has no idea what else to feed him. She could cut up some vegetables and put them on a plate, she supposes; but Lionel was very particular about food. If he saw a carrot, he had a fit. Wouldn't even look at it, never mind try to eat it. Some things almost seemed to hurt his eyes.

Now that she's learned a bit about it, she understands that Lionel didn't see or hear the world like other people. In a room full of things to look at, he saw everything at once. In a room full of people talking, he heard everything at once. At least that's what Rose thinks it must have felt like. She feels an ache in her heart whenever she thinks of Lionel and what he must have suffered, even now after all these years. They treated him like he wasn't a person but he was. He was her brother and she loved him.

It's probably easier with this boy because he can write. Lionel never learned. 'It's funny to think that I miss him, isn't it, Mary?' she says to her sister's picture. 'I mean he drove us all mad but I was sad to see him go.' She shudders when she thinks about the place they took him to. They had no choice by then or he would have stayed with them forever.

'It was nearly impossible to deal with him after Mum died, wasn't it, Mary?' Rose remembers the shock of her mother's early death, the loss of their family's guiding light. It had felt like an unnecessary dose of cruelty on top of everything else. She and Mary had clung to each other the night Dot died, tears flowing. Lionel kept signing, 'Mum,' wanting her calm presence. Mary and Rose had no idea how to explain it to him, and that was the worst thing of all.

Lionel was fourteen at the time. Tall and strong and would only listen to his mother, who was no longer there. He loved his sisters – they could tell that he loved them – but when he got frustrated, he simply couldn't help himself.

Rose watches the boy chew his way through another piece of toast as she remembers her mother's funeral. The whole town was there to pay their respects to Dot, who had worked in the pub ever since their father had run off to go and live in the big city. She was tough and strong and she never drank more than a glass of lemonade, and somehow, despite all the odds stacked against her, she managed to provide for all three of them. Mary and Rose did the bulk of caring for Lionel at night, but at least their mother was home during the day so they could go to school.

With each passing year, Lionel got bigger and more difficult. Rose knew Dot couldn't manage on her own anymore so she left school to stay home and help her mother. Mary had always been a better student.

Some days were harder than others. When Lionel was little, he would take off all his clothes and run away, but a naked grown boy running down the street was not appreciated. It took all three of them to wrestle him back home and get him dressed. He would howl and bang his head, desperate to be allowed out again.

When Dot died, breaking all their hearts, Mary started talking about becoming a teacher. 'I can't stay here and just do this. If I can get my diploma, I can work at the school and help you, but I need to be able to go and get my diploma.'

'I'll take care of Lionel,' said Rose. 'I'll be with him until you're finished.'

'Rose, love, listen to me,' said Mary, and she put her hands on her sister's shoulders. 'You're just a little thing. It's hard enough with the two of us. He's already fractured your wrist and we're both covered in bruises.'

'He doesn't mean to,' Rose said, looking into her sister's eyes that were as blue as her own.

'Of course he doesn't mean to, of course not. But he keeps hurting us, and if I leave, he'll hurt you badly. We have to think about putting him somewhere. He needs to be with people who can deal with him.'

'Mum didn't want that,' Rose replied, fresh tears for the loss falling. It felt like they would never stop.

Mary sighed, all her despair contained in the simple rush of air. She looked over at Lionel and swiped at her own tears. 'I'm nearly twenty-four and you're eighteen. We've done nothing but this our whole lives. It's almost too late for me to have a family if I don't get married soon, and there is no way either of us can think about bringing someone home with Lionel here. I love him, I do, of course I do, but he's too much for us.'

Rose looked at her brother, rocking in the corner, holding on to the scraggly stuffed dog that they had to sneak away to wash as he slept. 'Mum would hate us for it,' she said in a whisper.

'Mum would understand. I've found a place, Rose. The people seem okay. It's in Sydney and they have others there like him.'

'You've already decided,' said Rose, anger rising inside her.

'I have,' said Mary, 'and I'm the older sister. And you know that Mum said I'm in charge when she's not here. She's not here, Rose, and nothing will bring her back. I have to do what's right for both of us.' Her sister's voice was firm and Rose felt the anger drift away. Mary had made the choice for them both.

Rose went to bed that night and cried in her sleep, but she knows now that some of those tears were tears of relief. Her body ached from fighting her brother. Waking up each morning to the turmoil of taking care of him got more and more difficult. And she hated herself for thinking that.

She gives herself a little shake. She has learned, over the years, that looking back and regret only lead to maudlin thoughts, and maudlin thoughts lead to her taking to her bed for days. 'No use pretending that your life is not your life,' her mother used to say. 'Just get out of bed and get on with it.' And her mother had, but after Lionel went away and after what happened to Rose then, sometimes she simply needed a few days in bed to try to come to grips with what her life was. It used to worry Mary something awful, and even though it doesn't happen very often now, when it does, William and Nancy fret over her as well. When it happens, Rose just wants to be left alone, but at the same time, it's nice to know they're there. She can feel a little of the heavy tiredness creeping over her now, the lethargy that forces her into her bed, but she can't let it take hold. Now she has this boy to care for.

Rose has no idea what else to ask Theo, what to ask him so that she can help. He needs to be with his parents, that's for sure, but it doesn't look like anyone will be here anytime soon. And what if his parents are not good people? Rose has known a few in her time who show one face to the world and another to those who get in their way. Are Theo's parents like that? Is the father someone who hurts him? Is the mother?

She tunes back into the sound of the rain dancing on the roof. In the corner she notices a small continuous drip where the force of the storm has broken through, and she hurries to get a bucket. It's only a small leak so she knows it will be fine for a few days. She wishes the downpour would stop so she could leave the cabin and find one of the searchers. She has no idea if the boy would follow her. It's a treacherous path down to the road, especially after this weather. Rose hasn't really left the cabin for months. She does go for a bit of a tramp in the bush every day, when it's not raining, but she only walks around the edges of her cabin, so she wouldn't really consider it as leaving the place. Her legs are easily tired out these days. 'You should join the seniors' gym in town, Rose,' William said the last time they had her over for dinner. 'As if,' Rose snorted as she imagined herself in one of those outfits women wear to the gym, trying to twist herself into unbecoming positions.

William brings a few days' worth of newspapers every time he comes over so Rose knows what's going on in the world. It's a place she's happy to read about but not necessarily live in, not after everything that happened to her. But right now, for the first time in her life, she wishes the world would come to her door. That one of the searchers would appear. She would be relieved to release the boy off into the safety of an SES volunteer or someone else. The truth is she's a little scared. She remembers when Lionel had a meltdown, picking up everything he could touch in the kitchen and throwing it at the wall, at her, at Mary. By the end they hadn't a glass left and Mary had a large cut on her cheek. Theo doesn't seem like he would do something like that, but the thing is, Rose has no idea about him at all. The fact that he is calm and quiet now is a blessing but she knows that can change with the wind.

'This little light of mine,' sings Rose because she needs more help than the Lord has ever given her, but she feels sure he's up to the task. She turns the radio down again so she can hear herself singing.

Clasping her hands together, she sings to the Lord because he hears her songs as prayers, she knows he does.

Outside, the rain is a sheet of noise, drowning out any other sound, and Rose is struck by how calm the boy looks, almost dreamy. Lionel used to look like that during a rainstorm if there was no thunder or lightning. He used to look exactly like that.

Taking care of Lionel was like having her own child to look after. Mary had the blessing of William and Nancy but Rose never received such blessings.

'It does me no good to think about that now, Mary, does it?' she says as she rubs at her sore knees, trying to soothe away the encroaching memories. She might have had a different life but she didn't, and thinking about the past never leads to anything good, unless it is about happy times like Mary's wedding to Bart and the pretty dress they bought her and then the arrival of Nancy and William.

'You could find a fella and get married,' Mary said again and again over the years but Rose knew that wasn't going to happen. She wouldn't let it.

She contented herself with visiting Lionel at the care home they ended up sending him to, where her brother got thinner and thinner, his eyes glazing over. 'Are you giving him enough food?' she asked the tall nurse in charge of Lionel's ward. 'We give him food,' she replied, her voice scratchy with cigarette smoke, 'but he throws it against the wall.'

'But if you make sure there are no bright colours and nothing touches, he will eat,' Rose said.

'We've got a lot here to take care of, missy. I can't be making sure he gets what he wants every day.'

Rose took him chocolates whenever she went. He liked chocolates. He would shove them into his mouth quickly and then laugh and flap his hands with joy.

Once she arrived to find he'd been tied to his bed. 'What has he done?' she asked. She tried not to shout, not to tear the nurse's grey hair from her large head as she asked, knowing that she needed to be polite, knowing that if she upset those in charge of his care, they were capable of great cruelty. She had seen other patients tied to their beds, staring at the wall, their bodies thin and wasted away.

'He wouldn't have a bath and he kept flailing about when we tried to get him in and he hit one of the nurses.'

Rose knew he only did that sort of thing when he was very distressed. 'He didn't mean it, surely you understand that?' she asked.

'I can't have my staff attacked.' The nurse pursed her thin lips with distaste.

'He's a human being, you know,' said Rose softly.

'He's really just an animal in human form,' said the nurse. 'He doesn't understand so he has to be trained.'

Rose couldn't help her tears. 'You shouldn't be here taking care of these people,' she spat.

'As if you would want to do it, dearie. As if you could stand to be spat at and pissed on and spend your days cleaning shit off walls. You come and do this if you're so high and mighty.'

Rose left, her body trembling with anger. She couldn't let this go on; she wouldn't.

'I'll have him come and live with me,' she told Mary after that. 'They're killing him over there. They treat him like an animal.'

'Oh, Rose, love, you can't take care of him. He'll hurt you. Didn't he lash out last week when you asked them to take the restraints off?'

Rose rubbed at the black and blue bruise on her cheek. 'He didn't mean to.'

'He's better off where he is, Rose, believe me.'

As the years passed, eventually it was easier for Rose to stay away from Lionel. It broke her heart to see him. He got worse and worse. He wouldn't even sign anymore. He barely noticed she was there. Sometimes when she walked in, he was calm, almost peaceful, but then her visit would stir him up. He would stare at her and he would flap and stamp and then he would resort to banging his head. Rose hated that her visits distressed him. She understood he was trying to communicate with her, to tell her of his distress, and each time she left, the guilt would lodge inside her. She often had to visit the nearest bathroom, her breakfast or lunch coming up again.

'Stop bringing him the chocolates,' the nurse told her. 'He's better if you stay away.'

She always needed a day or two in bed after a visit, her mind filled with angry black thoughts at the world.

The less she visited, the less he knew her. Sometimes he would keep his face turned away from her, and she couldn't help her tears.

She stayed in the cottage, isolated and alone, missing her brother when she wasn't distracted at work in the haberdashery shop with old Mrs Townsend, who napped behind the counter most of the day.

Theo comes to stand in front of her, pulling her away from the past… He moves his hands and she watches.

She wipes at her cheeks. It amazes her that she can still cry for her brother after all these years. She hadn't been there at the end. She hadn't even known he was sick. It was Mary who got a call because Rose didn't have a telephone then. 'They say it was pneumonia, love,' said her sister when she came round to tell her. 'They said it was peaceful at the end.' Rose thought she would never stop crying. It wasn't that he was gone – she was almost glad for him that he was out of his misery. It was that he had died alone with no kind touch. Sometimes he would let her give him a very tight hug and she knows that at the end she could have done that for him.

She sighs, turning her attention to Theo. He looks so well-cared for. He can read and write and she knows that he has parents who love him, no matter what happened in the cabin. She tries to concentrate on what the boy is asking her for.

'I don't understand,' she says and he does it again.

Something clicks inside her brain. 'Oh,' she says, 'you want me to sing?'

He nods and smiles and jumps up and down, his hands flapping.

'Okay, okay. I'll sing,' she says and she reaches for the only song she really loves. 'This little light of mine…'

The boy sits on the floor, his hands around his knees, his body calm. Rose takes advantage of this to get off her chair and crouch down, look at his feet. She keeps singing, knowing that the Lord is helping her. Theo lets her clean his wounds. He doesn't flinch when she pulls a long sliver of wood out of one foot. She knows that sometimes Lionel didn't seem to feel pain either. It didn't make him any less human though. In fact, in Rose's opinion, it made him more. He was too good for this world, and her only real wish is that the good Lord had taken him back to live with him sooner. It comforts her sometimes to think about Lionel up in heaven, speaking and laughing. She keeps singing as she cleans Theo's wounds, and as long as she sings, he lets her help.

CHAPTER SIXTEEN

Monday

Cecelia

Cecelia is somewhere between asleep and awake. A half-dream runs through her brain, a blur of images and colours.

If she tunes into it, she can hear the endless gushing rain outside. *Find somewhere safe and warm. Shelter in place, Theo. Do you remember how we talked about what shelter in place means? It means that you find somewhere you feel safe, out of the rain and the wind. If you get lost, shelter in place and wait. I will find you. Dad will find you. We will come and find you.*

But they have not come to find him, and she feels the anguish of that inside her. He must be scared and sad. He relies on routine to keep him safe, to make him feel secure. From the time of his diagnosis, Cecelia has been aware that he needs every day to be just the same as the day before, and the day before that, in order for him to cope. She cannot imagine how upended his world must feel right now. With a racing heart, she imagines him lying on the ground somewhere, banging his head to try and soothe the struggle his body is having. He would hurt himself. She bites down on her lips but the pain barely registers in her half-awake state. It has been two nights. That much she knows. In her dream state she tries to scream but nothing comes out of her mouth.

She hears someone enter the room but she keeps her eyes closed. She's awake now but she doesn't want to look at anyone. It's Annie, the nurse. She wears a particular kind of floral perfume that Cecelia recognises. She feigns sleep as Annie takes her temperature, checks her blood pressure, squeezes her shoulder and says, 'Breakfast will be along soon.' She leaves, leaving Cecelia locked inside herself. *Where is Theo?*

Even now, years later, she still feels the clench of her stomach, the physical shock recognition of what she already knew on the day he was finally – at two, nearly three years old – diagnosed as being on the spectrum. That overwhelming, sinking, horrified feeling. She understood that everything in her life would exist in before and after. Before he was diagnosed and after. Before he was diagnosed there was still hope that she was just imagining it, that she was overthinking, that he was just different. But afterwards she was locked into the world of autism, and because she hadn't really understood what that meant or what was possible, she had felt a little like the Theo she had given birth to was gone. The hopes and dreams she'd had for him were gone. Theo was gone and in his place was autistic Theo – an entirely different person even though he was exactly the same child he had been the day before.

'What? Why?' she wanted to scream. She had known it was coming, had prayed it wasn't, had been relieved when it was confirmed, had been devastated when it was confirmed.

Once Nick acknowledged that he thought there might be something wrong, that she wasn't imagining that Theo was behind his peers and his lack of speech wasn't just because children develop at different rates, she threw herself into finding out what was wrong with her little boy. She sat through endless appointments with her paediatrician, an occupational therapist, a developmental psychologist, a family therapist and finally a psychologist who specialised in autism.

'It looks like it's what we thought it was,' Theo's paediatrician, Alison, said as Cecelia and Nick sat in her office, a file the thickness of a brick on the desk in front of them. Her gaze was filled not with sympathy but rather with obvious empathy. Cecelia knew that Alison had a child on the spectrum. All through the months of appointments Alison had reassured Cecelia that her son, Ian, was a wonderful young man, studying at university and managing to fit into society with the tools he had been given from an early diagnosis.

Cecelia felt she had talked non-stop for months to everyone who saw and interacted with Theo, but finally, with the result clear and obvious, she had run out of words.

'It's good that we found out early,' Nick said.

'Absolutely,' agreed Alison. 'There is so much you can do to help him, you wouldn't believe. I've put together a pack of information. There are groups you can join and associations. There is so much you can do these days.'

Cecelia watched them speak, watched their mouths move, but she couldn't hear them properly. *Autistic. Autistic. Autistic. Autistic.* The word kept repeating in her head as she tried to take in what she was being told. She knew that in movies there were clear moments when everything changed in a character's world. It was when they opened the door they shouldn't have opened or went off with the wrong person or crossed the street at the wrong time. And in movies, you can usually see when that is coming. There is a change in the music, a shift in tone, and you want to shout out, 'Don't do that, go there, touch that.' But in life, people rarely see huge, life-changing moments for what they are. It is only in retrospect that you can see how one single event has impacted everything. Cecelia liked it that way. But sitting in Alison's office she was aware that the air conditioner was a little too cold, that outside it was a warm, humid December day, that Nick was wearing a touch too much aftershave, that Alison had not one but two pencils stuck in her hair, and that right then, right there, her life had changed forever. A bomb had dropped right in front of her, exploding, and she was alive to feel the effects. She wasn't entirely sure she still wanted to be alive.

It took her a few days of digesting before she knew which way to turn. The words 'why me?', 'why us?', 'why him?' were a song on repeat in her head. After everything it had taken to have him, it now seemed as though they didn't have him at all. She hated herself for not simply accepting him, for not embracing him for who he was, for being horribly disappointed as she went through lists of all the things he would never be able to do.

'You should see someone to discuss how you feel,' said Nick when she told him just a little of what she was thinking. She kept quiet after that, tortured herself as she went on being a mother as though nothing had changed.

In the end it was Kaycee who gave her the most hope. She was ten years old and flinging herself at life, at the top of her classes and one of the best netball players at school. She played the violin and she liked to sing and dance. She had become somewhat distant since her little brother had arrived and taken over the house, but she still took the time to play with him – if what Theo did could be called playing. What he mostly enjoyed doing was lining up his selection of matchbox cars. He only liked them in the colour blue. He would line up all twenty of them and then return them to their box and then line them up again. If Kaycee sat next to him, he sometimes allowed her to take the next car out of the box and place it carefully in the line.

Three days after she had been told that Theo was autistic, Cecelia was standing in the kitchen, supposedly chopping up vegetables for a salad but in reality just watching her children.

'See, Theo, I'll put this one here,' said Kaycee, holding a little blue toy car. 'I like this one, it's a Ferrari – a Ferrari goes so fast.'

Cecelia paused with her knife on the edge of an overripe red tomato. 'I don't think he understands it's a different kind of car,' she said to Kaycee. They had explained Theo's diagnosis to her. 'I think he just sees a blue car.'

'I don't think so, Mum. I think he knows it's a Ferrari. Dad tells him the names of the cars all the time.'

'Oh, Kaycee, love, I wish that were true but I don't think it's the case.' She tried not to let the despair she was feeling make her voice wobble but it did, and she hastily dropped the knife and wiped away a tear. She didn't want to cry in front of her children.

Theo had lined up all the cars again by this time, and Kaycee said, 'Which one is the Ferrari, Theo?'

Theo rarely responded to questions, which was why the first person to test him had been an audiologist. Cecelia had been worried he couldn't hear.

Theo touched a finger to the blue Ferrari.

'Good job, Theo,' said Kaycee. She put her hands together as though she was clapping but she didn't make a sound, already knowing that a noise like that startled her brother.

'Probably just luck,' said Cecelia. She hated the way she sounded, as though she had given up already, but she was fighting that feeling every day, lying in bed all night questioning what kind of a life Theo would have. She hadn't really slept since his diagnosis.

'Which one is the Jeep, Theo?' said Kaycee.

Cecelia held her breath, ready to comfort her daughter when the little boy looked off into the distance or picked up the cars and put them back in their box again. But Theo touched the blue Jeep. Cecelia gasped.

'Which one is the Porsche, Theo?'

Theo touched the blue Porsche.

'Which one is the Volvo, Theo?'

Theo touched the blue Volvo.

'Which one is the BMW, Theo?'

Theo touched the blue BMW. Kaycee went through all twenty cars. She did it twice and Theo got every one of them right.

'He's not stupid, Mum. His brain just works differently. He knows stuff, and even if he doesn't speak, that doesn't mean he can't understand.'

Kaycee wasn't able to understand why her mother had grabbed her in a hard hug and why she was crying. Her daughter had given Cecelia hope, and from that moment on, Cecelia looked forward to the wonderful boy Theo would become.

Are you sheltering in place, my little light? Are you safe? Please be safe. I don't know what happened or what you saw. But please be safe.

Now, she feels the hands on her. She feels the anger in that cabin. Her heart races inside her chest as the knife flashes, large and sharp, a smooth blade with a pointed end. Her fault. It was her fault.

Slowly, the memory unfurls. Nick was so angry. 'I can't take this anymore. I just can't! You're not the woman I married. I've lost you. There are other people in your life, Cecelia – you don't want to see that.'

'Oh, please, as if I'm the only one whose mind is occupied with other things. As long as you don't have to think about anything but your precious work, you're fine. You'd rather be at work, wouldn't you? You'd rather be saving lives, Mr Big-Time Surgeon. Well, there are people here now who need you.'

'There are people who need you, Cecelia. Our daughter has always needed you. Why do you think she's living at university? It's not because of Theo. It's because of you, not Theo, not me, but you! Nothing is more important than what you want and what you need.'

'I have Theo to take care of!' she exclaimed furiously.

'He doesn't need your endless care anymore! That's what bothers you the most. He doesn't need you anymore!'

The slam of the cabin door. The anger. The smile. The hands.

Where is Theo? She sees his white-blonde curls and his bright blue eyes. 'Sing, Mama, sing,' his hands say, and she sings.

The gush of the rain, the knife, the blood, the hands. The anger.

'You invited me here, Cecelia. This is what you want! You know that.'

She can hear the words but she has no idea who is saying them. But she knows that they confused her. Is it Nick? She told him she wanted to go to the cabin even though he said they should leave it this year. 'Please, Nick, please come with us.' She had imagined… She has no idea what she thought would happen. The magic in their marriage, the things that have kept them together, their love for each other all seem to have disappeared. Each year she hoped that the cabin would bring them close together again.

She wants to open her mouth and scream and scream but he took the words. *Who took the words?* She opens her mouth, hoping to produce sound as she touches her hand to her throat the way Theo's speech therapist gets him to do when they are practising sounds. She makes a deep, low sound, a rumble in her throat. She is capable of sound so she should be capable of speech, but when she opens her mouth, something dark and scary keeps her silent. She can speak but she mustn't speak. A terrible fear makes her clutch at her hospital gown. She rubs her hands together, feeling tears gather and fall. She mustn't speak or something awful will happen.

'Sing, Mum, sing.' She looks at the window, the glass opaque with rain, and she sees her son there, watches his hands move. 'Sing.'

And even though she cannot sing the words, she feels she hears them. *This little light of mine, I'm going to let it shine. This little light of mine.* The song repeats in her head and the words calm her. Finally, she sleeps.

CHAPTER SEVENTEEN

Kaycee

Kaycee watches the solid sheet of rain through the window of her mother's hospital room. Her father is recovering from surgery but she is still not allowed to see him. The risk of infection is too great and they have no idea if he will survive or not. The knife pierced a corner of his heart.

The surgeons reported this to her earlier this morning as they updated her on his condition. They were both older men and looked worn out by the long surgery. They had found her in the café, sipping a can of Diet Coke because water wasn't helping the gritty feeling on her tongue. 'I'm sorry,' Kaycee mumbled, feeling guilty about not being at her mother's bedside, about the Diet Coke, about everything.

'It went well,' said one of the doctors, 'but the next twenty-four hours are crucial.' And then he told her about just how much damage the knife had done. Kaycee felt a short, sharp pain on the left side of her chest as she imagined what her father must have felt.

They allowed Kaycee to stand outside the room he was in, to stare at his inert body through the glass, her palm leaving its warm imprint for a moment. There was little to see except for her father's dark hair, greying at the sides, his chest rising and falling on a machine's command, his mouth held open by the force of a tube. Thin lines of plastic snaked into both hands, delivering what he needed. His bulk was concealed by a hospital sheet and his exposed chest hurt her with its vulnerable nakedness.

'Oh, Dad,' she whispered, wishing she could be near him to comfort him as he has done for her whole life. She thought about her four-year-old self falling off the trampoline in the backyard and coming into the house, holding her arm to show him. He had held it so gently, spoken so softly as he touched and moved it, that even though the sharp pain of a broken bone shot through her small body, she hadn't been frightened or worried. He had been there and he was a doctor and he could make everything better.

Looking at her father's body lying still in the bed, she prayed that the doctors who had operated on him were also able to make everything better like he did. And then a nurse told her she had to leave. She had been allowed to get as close to her father as was possible right then.

'According to the surgeon, it would have taken a great deal of strength to drive the knife in that far,' Constable Emmerson told her when he looked in on her in her mother's room an hour later.

'So obviously my mother couldn't have done that. I mean look at how small she is. My father is a big man. She couldn't have hurt him.'

'Look, Kaycee,' the constable said with another one of his soft sighs that were really beginning to irritate her, 'we don't know what was going on between them. Sometimes, if a person is angry enough or hurt enough, they can do things they wouldn't normally be able to do. Dr Greenblatt has told me that your mother has a large bruise on her side and one on her arm, and while we don't know how they happened, they could have come from her getting hit and probably grabbed. I think you need to consider this as a possibility. We think we know the people we love but sometimes we don't know them that well at all. You've been staying on campus. You may not know how far the situation between the two of them has deteriorated.'

'You have no idea about my parents' marriage either.'

'Maybe not, Kaycee, but I do know marriage can be difficult.'

'My mother did not hurt my father,' Kaycee said through gritted teeth. 'Why are you so keen to shift the blame onto her? Maybe you should be out looking for someone else.'

'I don't think that's necessary,' the constable said, and he gave Kaycee a small, sad smile.

Kaycee turned away from him and went back to looking at her silent mother.

She is completely, totally exhausted. Last night Jonah had finally been able to persuade her to leave the hospital. 'You need to just rest for a few hours or you won't be any good to anyone.'

'But my father is in surgery and Theo is still out there and if I stay maybe she'll talk to me,' she replied, the words rushing out of her.

'Your dad will be in for hours and they won't let you see him because they're worried about infection. Your mother is asleep and there are people looking for Theo. I've been looking all day and I can tell you that there is a whole new group who have just begun. Let's go back to the motel and get just a few hours of sleep, please.'

There is something about Jonah that makes Kaycee trust him. Maybe because he is studying to be a doctor like her father, or maybe it's the way he listens when she speaks and then answers her as if he's really thought about what she's said. Or maybe it's the way he speaks to everyone else with a certain quiet authority, as though he understands how to exist in the world even though he is just a young man. Kaycee feels like she is ten years old most of the time, just bumbling through her days, messing up everything as she goes.

'Tell me about your family,' she said to him as they lay next to each other on the motel bed, still dressed, ready to race back to the hospital at a moment's notice.

'My family?' he said. 'Why?'

Kaycee wanted to grab his hand in that moment but she stopped herself. She felt perfectly natural and safe next to him and she understood that he would watch over her. She didn't know why he was staying but she was afraid to express her gratitude, as though saying something might make him change his mind. He seemed to want to do nothing more than help and offer support. Kaycee was unused to that in a man other than her father.

'I don't know. I just don't want to think for a few minutes so you talk and I'll listen.'

'We could watch television.'

'No… I don't want to have to see the news again.'

News reporters and their vans had flooded the town, and there were people walking around with mobile phones, filming the searchers and doing interviews. If she stood by the window in her mother's room, Kaycee could look down at the hospital car park when the rain lightened for a moment and see two news vans, perched there like vultures, waiting to catch a glimpse of her. Kaycee saw a short interview with the pretty young woman who had stumbled into the cabin looking for help.

'I thought it wasn't real,' the woman named Amber said. 'I couldn't believe what I was seeing and she was just… She didn't say anything at all and I… Can I stop, please? I can't talk about this,' she said, her voice shuddering. Kaycee felt a stab of sympathy for the young woman.

'Please don't speak to the press,' Constable Emmerson told her. 'This is an ongoing investigation and we don't want to muddy the waters before we understand exactly what happened.'

The news is always on in her mother's hospital room, muted and repetitive with the description of Theo running underneath. 'He would have been wearing blue tracksuit pants and a blue jumper,' Kaycee told Constable Emmerson so he could update the searchers.

'How do you know?' the police officer asked.

'All his clothes are blue and he only wears tracksuit pants in winter and shorts in summer. Trust me – he is in blue.' The line of text with Theo's description was updated to include the fact that he was wearing blue.

Staring at the ceiling of the motel room, she took a deep breath as she remembered her brother telling her that blue was his favourite colour. Sometimes it seemed that Theo had a deeper connection to himself and the universe, that he was seeing and feeling things no one else knew were there. The idea of him being out there surrounded by bush, wet and cold, terrified her.

She imagined him in the rain, felt a shiver of his obvious fear in her own body, and she knew that she wouldn't be able to rest if she allowed the terrifying images to continue to assault her.

'Please,' she said to Jonah.

'Um, okay,' Jonah said, settling his head on the pillow next to her. 'I have two brothers who are both doctors. Brian is a paediatrician and Liam is in general practice. My mother is also a paediatrician and my dad is an engineer. He kind of held the home front together while she worked because his work was more flexible. He's the one who taught me to cook.'

'You can cook?' Kaycee asked as she yawned. She felt her body relaxing, almost sinking into the mattress. The sound of constant rain was soothing in the warm motel room with its slightly antiseptic smell.

'I can keep people fed with a few really good dishes. I like it. It's calming. It requires absolute concentration to get right, so while I'm doing it, it's all I think about.'

'What dishes can you make?' she murmured, her brain feeling as though it was slowing down.

'I make a good roast lamb with rosemary and garlic, and I make a brilliant spaghetti, although Liam will tell you his is better.'

Kaycee laughed a little and then she turned on her side and rested her head on Jonah's shoulder, sleep claiming her.

Five hours later she woke to find Jonah's arm draped over her hip as he slept. She wished she could stay there forever but she dragged herself out of bed and showered before returning to the hospital, to sit in this room with her silent mother. Kaycee doesn't believe that her mum is sleeping.

'You know Theo is still missing,' Kaycee says and she sees her mother's eyes flicker under her eyelids. That's the only indication she gives that she has heard what her daughter has said.

The psychiatrist, an older woman with her grey hair cut into a neat bob, has been by to speak to Kaycee. 'Sometimes immense trauma can cause someone to shut down. We don't know what happened but it's not that she doesn't want to tell us. It's that she can't. I have a feeling that she will be able to speak to us soon, but until then, keep talking to her. Remind her about your brother and just keep talking.'

The rain is preventing them from searching for Theo properly. On the wall the television set is still turned to the news channel, and Kaycee only turns the volume up whenever the weather is discussed. She tries not to look when the reports on her family appear. She has seen the same thing enough times by now. They have gotten hold of a picture of her parents at a hospital Christmas party from two years ago. Her father is tall and dignified in his tuxedo and her mother is stunning in a long black slip dress, a dusting of freckles on her shoulders. Both of their smiles are wide but Kaycee knows that before they left for the party, they had a massive fight. Her mother had been giving her a list of instructions on how to babysit Theo, and her father had grown angry with her endless repetition. 'Kaycee knows Theo as well as we do, Cecelia. Why are you making such a big deal of this?' her father had said.

'I'm just making sure she understands his new triggers,' her mum had replied. 'She hasn't been alone with him for a while.'

'Because you make it so difficult for her when she is.'

'I do not do that. I have a responsibility to make sure Theo is kept to his routine.'

'Theo will be fine! Kaycee will be fine! If you don't want to go with me, just say so. I can go alone.'

'Don't be ridiculous, Nick.'

'You're being ridiculous!'

Kaycee had remained quiet on the sofa as she watched her parents. Their arguments were so commonplace by then that she wasn't really bothered. Theo had his earphones on, immersed in a game on his iPad. When her parents finally left, she took her brother to the kitchen and made cupcakes with him, something he loved doing. He liked to be told how many times to stir the batter in the bowl and then he would sit on the floor in the kitchen, in front of the warm oven, and watch them bake. She knew exactly how to take care of her little brother but her mother never trusted anyone but herself. Sometimes Kaycee felt like her mum didn't want to share Theo with his father and sister.

Now, Kaycee sees the weatherman appear on the news and she takes the remote and turns up the sound. 'The rain is set to stay,' the smiling weatherman says. 'It is caused by an east coast low that is sitting above the NSW mountain region. Flood warnings are in place for all low-lying areas with all catchment areas expecting a month's worth of rain over the next few days.'

Kaycee rubs her hands together, worry twisting inside her. Theo can swim but he isn't strong enough to fight the debris and chaos that floodwater drags in.

'Do you remember when Theo was born, Mum?' says Kaycee, turning away from the TV. She remembers that her little brother arrived in a rainstorm, wind whipping the trees sideways and darkness settling over the city at three in the afternoon.

Kaycee was eight years old then and she knows that when her mother's labour started, she had been sitting on the pale grey fabric sofa in the family room, staring out of the window as nature vented its fury. She remembers feeling safe and warm inside her house, knowing that her mum was there and that they didn't have to leave until the storm abated.

Her mother was lying down because her back was sore. She thought she'd pulled a muscle but she was in labour, three weeks early.

'We need to go to the hospital, sweetheart,' Cecelia said, coming into the family room, her face pale.

'Is your back really, really sore?' Kaycee asked.

'No, I think the baby is coming – well, I know he is, my water just broke. I've called Daddy and he's going to meet us there.'

'But it's raining outside.'

'I know but the baby is more important than rain, and I have to be in a hospital so there are doctors to help us if he needs it.'

Kaycee willingly helped her mother get her things together, excitement rippling through her. They knew the baby was a boy, and while Kaycee had wanted a sister, she had made peace with the fact that she was getting a brother. Any sibling was better than none and she would finally be like all her friends.

Now Kaycee knows that on that day, the day her baby brother arrived, she was the most important thing in her parents' lives for the very last time. Once he was born, Theo took over the house, and then as he grew, he took over everything else. It wasn't his fault, of course it wasn't, but it was the truth.

Even now, eleven years later, Kaycee can still remember the struggle her mother had to get Theo to simply sleep for a few hours. 'You were never like this,' her mother tearfully said to Kaycee many times.

He was a difficult baby. He didn't like to sleep except in forty-minute blocks and he screamed for hours when he got the chance. Her mother grew old and tired-looking: her lovely white-blonde hair developed grey reminders of her lack of sleep, and her brown eyes seemed dull. She hadn't started dying it black then and she was ghost-pale.

Her parents tried everything but it was a chance discovery that changed things for them.

One evening when Theo was around six months old, Kaycee was watching television. The volume was on loud even though her mother had begged her to turn it down. By then Kaycee was sick of her little brother and what he had done to her peaceful life. He didn't smile or play or sleep and he screamed all the time. It was nothing like she had expected. Her friends told stories of cute things their sibling said or did but Kaycee had nothing to tell beyond that he cried a lot. She hadn't had a friend over to her house for six months because her mum couldn't get herself together enough to arrange something and because she was afraid that if someone did come over, they would see just how awful Theo was. 'We'll have a girls' day soon,' her mother told her every few days, but Kaycee had a feeling that soon was never going to become now.

The afternoon they worked out how to get Theo to sleep, her mother had been rocking him in her arms for an hour already. He was still crying and Kaycee couldn't take the noise anymore. She turned on the television, finding a music channel and switching it up as high as it could go.

'Kaycee,' shouted her mother, 'turn that down. I'm trying to get Theo to sleep.'

'You're always trying to get Theo to sleep. I'm listening to my music!' 'Break your Heart' by Taio Cruz reverberated around the family room.

'Please, Kaycee!' screamed her mother, her rocking becoming more desperate. Her father was at work, on call at the hospital. Before Theo arrived, he would come home when he was on call, knowing that they lived close enough to work that he could get there quickly. But ever since Theo was born and the crying began, he slept over at the hospital. He was responsible for other people's lives and couldn't function on no sleep as her mother was managing – or not managing – to do. Kaycee slept with her earphones in her ears so she wouldn't have to hear her brother cry all night long.

'If you don't turn that off, you'll be in your room for the rest of the day with no devices!' yelled her mother.

'Fine,' snarled Kaycee, and she pressed a button on the remote, changing the channel to a mess of static.

And suddenly Theo stopped crying. Kaycee grabbed for the remote to silence the noise but her mother shouted, 'No, wait!'

Her brother's eyes blinked, his stare became fixed and finally he drifted off to sleep. Kaycee and her mother stared at him, a bomb that might go off at any moment. Her mum walked slowly over to the cot they had set up in the family room and gently placed Theo inside it. Kaycee held her breath and she knew her mother was doing the same thing. Miraculously, Theo stayed asleep. They had tried everything with him, including sleep machines that made the static noise, but it had never occurred to anyone that the noise needed to be really, really loud.

Her mother placed the baby monitor in position so she could watch Theo on the camera and she held her finger to her lips, reaching out for Kaycee. Together they crept to her parents' bedroom at the other end of the house. Theo stayed asleep. After that, no machine ever made the noise loud enough, so her mother found an old television to put in Theo's room, permanently soothing him to sleep through the night. The sound doesn't have to be as loud anymore but Kaycee still struggled to sleep when she first left home, used to the background noise that had been part of her life for years and years.

His crying and his inability to sleep were the first signs that there was something different about her brother.

Kaycee had been a late talker and so her parents never worried too much when Theo didn't speak, choosing to communicate in grunts and throwing tantrums that embarrassed them all if they were out in public and he couldn't communicate his wishes.

Her father was a typical doctor when it came to his own children. If nothing seemed broken and there was no great loss of blood, he wasn't concerned. But one afternoon her father stopped being so blasé.

A Sunday family outing was the catalyst for the journey towards Theo's diagnosis. From the moment they arrived in the park he was difficult. Her mother usually took Theo to their local one, where there were only a few pieces of play equipment surrounded by a strong black metal gate, and which was usually empty during the week. Theo liked that park and he would toddle around, touching equipment until he felt ready to go on the swing or the slide. Her mother thought the bigger park on that day would be more exciting. But Theo looked terrified. He didn't want to be out, he didn't want to be put down, clinging to her mother – a koala who wouldn't let go. And when she finally prised him off her, he sat rigid in front of the bench, bobbing his head up and down. After fifteen minutes her parents gave up and the family returned to the car.

'I think,' her mother said softly as they drove home, 'that there's something… wrong with him.'

Her father was silent. Kaycee was playing a game on her iPod touch but she was listening to her parents speak.

'I know I've said it before but I need you to hear me, Nick,' her mum carried on. 'There is something going on.'

'I agree,' said her father finally. 'I've been watching him and you're right. I think it may be autism.'

'What?'

Now when Kaycee thinks about this conversation, she realises that what her mother actually wanted was for her father to dismiss her fears. He was a doctor, a heart surgeon, and if he dismissed her fears, she could too. But he didn't.

Theo was nearly three by the time they had a definitive diagnosis.

'What does that mean?' she asked them after they had explained it all to her.

'It means that his brain doesn't work the same way yours does,' said her father. 'He's what we call neurodiverse.'

'But will he learn to talk?'

'We don't know,' said her mother, biting down on her lip.

'Will he be able to go to my school?'

'We're not sure,' said her father.

'Will he grow up and get a job and have friends?'

'We have no real idea right now,' said her mother.

'Then what do you know?' Kaycee shouted.

Her mother burst into tears, leaving the room, and Kaycee realised then that everything was uncertain. She tried over the next few days to spend more time with her little brother, to try and see if there was anything actually going on inside his head. She was used to him ignoring her, used to him lining up his blue cars for hours, used to the way he stared off into the distance if she asked him something, but she felt that there was more to Theo than that. She needed there to be more to him than that. Now she recognises that what she felt then was embarrassment, as though Theo's diagnosis was something to be ashamed of. None of her friends had a brother or sister who was autistic. She was only eleven years old, and now she can look back at that child and forgive her for the way she was feeling. She didn't understand but she wanted him to be more than just his label.

Getting him to identify the cars he played with was a first step. She remembers holding her breath after she asked him to identify each one. She remembers her mother's hug as she grasped her tight. She remembers feeling that she had somehow solved the problem of Theo. But she hadn't because Theo is not a problem. He's just Theo.

Her mother became an autism expert. She missed Kaycee's soccer games and school parent–teacher meetings and she never knew if her daughter had homework, if she was fighting with friends, when she got her first kiss. Her mother became an advocate for Theo and his needs and she seemed to simply stop seeing Kaycee.

Things got better when Theo learned to communicate. The whole family learned to sign, then Theo learned to write and he started attending a school where they declared him 'clever'. And her mother finally lifted her head, but when she looked at her fifteen-year-old daughter, Kaycee didn't want to be seen anymore.

'It's too late for you to mother me,' Kaycee said on the phone only last week when her mother asked if she was eating healthy food.

'You seem to be losing weight, sweetheart,' she said.

Her mother was right. Alcohol was full of calories, but if you existed on crackers and coffee when you weren't drinking, you lost weight.

Now, as the rain drones on, the sound starting to make Kaycee a little crazy, she realises that she's hungry. She hasn't felt real hunger for a long time. She wants a drink, quite desperately, but she knows that she needs to stay away from all that. She thinks she might stay away from it forever now, and she knows that means staying away from Adam as well. He hasn't called her at all, hasn't even sent a text asking if everything is okay. He may not have watched the news but the story would definitely have flashed up on an internet site, and she knows he's pretty much glued to his phone. She fights the urge to send him a message telling him that he should have, at least, tried to make contact. She knows there's no point in doing that. Adam doesn't care about her and he never has. As she thinks this, her phone pings with a text and she looks down. It's from Jonah.

A whole busload of new volunteers just arrived. They're sending me back to the motel to get something to eat and rest. Can I bring you something to eat?

She replies:

Thanks, I'm fine. You rest.

She cannot help her smile. Kind – Jonah is so kind.

She leans forward, touching her mother's hand. 'You have to start talking, Mum. You need to tell everyone what happened. Do you know where Theo is? Do you have an idea of where they should look? Is there someplace he liked to go?'

She has a sudden image of her little brother, alone and cold and scared, running through the bush, and she shudders. He wouldn't have understood what happened in that cabin. She doesn't understand it. Did it all just become too much for her mother?

Her mother is not a violent woman and her father is not a violent man – none of it, none of the police officer's accusations, makes sense. Her mother wouldn't have the strength to hurt her father that badly. Only her parents and Theo were in the cabin, so how did her father get hurt? She thinks about her brother, about how sometimes when it's all too much he lashes out at one of them, not meaning to hurt but hurting anyway. But Theo wouldn't touch a knife. He's been told by their mother that knives are sharp and dangerous and not something that he is allowed to touch. He definitely wouldn't have gone near it.

Until two days ago, the cabin was a safe space for Theo. The first time they went he was four years old and her mother had laid down a trail of blue jelly beans – Theo's reward for behaving – to the front door. The whole family explored outside, waiting for Theo, until it grew colder and darker and her father lit the fire inside in the beautiful old stone fireplace and began roasting marshmallows with Kaycee.

Theo had been standing by the car all that time, one hand on the door handle, holding on to something familiar.

'What do I do if he won't come in?' her mother said as she unpacked groceries into the fridge.

'He'll come,' replied her father as he turned the steel skewer filled with marshmallows over the fire, the sweet charred smell filling the cabin and making Kaycee's mouth water.

Finally, as the temperature dropped, Theo entered the cabin, drawn by the smell, and once he had explored the place three times while his mother explained what would happen that night and in the days that followed, he decided that he liked it. After that, he always asked when it would be time to go to the cabin. He liked the long walks, even though they were the same walks they went on every time, and he liked going out on a small boat with their father to go fishing. He never touched a pole but he would lie with one hand in the cold water, humming tonelessly to himself as the boat bobbed on the river and their father finally got to relax and have some time off.

Outside, the rain slows to a drizzle and Kaycee is filled with the hope that the storm may be abating, regardless of what the weatherman said, but in only seconds it returns full force, lashing the window as though the sky merely paused for a breath before resuming its deluge.

She thinks of her skinny brother, wet and shivering, and she feels sick to her stomach. He can communicate but he can't explain more than simple things, and even though he is able to understand highly scientific ideas, emotions seem beyond him. He has flashcards on the phone he usually carries, where he can look up how a person is feeling depending on the way their face looks, but she knows he doesn't have that right now.

'Are you sad?' he asked her using sign language when he found her crying at sixteen because Charles, her first real boyfriend, had broken up with her.

She smiled and nodded.

He assumed a smile meant she was fine. 'Not feeling it anymore?' he said, pushing back his messy hair.

'Still sad,' she said.

'Why?' He seemed perplexed.

'Because Charles broke up with me. And I really liked him.'

'My truck broke and Dad fixed it.'

'Dad can't fix this,' she told him.

Kaycee loves him for how he views the world. She knows that she loves him, she does. No matter what has happened. She knows from attending family picnics held by the Autism Association that they are lucky with Theo. Once he learned to sign and to read and write, he had fewer meltdowns. And that made everyone's life easier. Kaycee had assumed that when her brother became easier to deal with, her mother would finally have time for her, but when she did finally have time, it was too late. You can't catch up on seven or eight years of mothering. Kaycee felt safer taking care of her own emotional needs. She knew that her mum's attention would always be drawn to Theo first.

'You know what I've never forgiven you for?' Kaycee says now to her mother, the memory of the incident pushing at her. Guilt gnaws at her as she says this. She is supposed to be encouraging her mum to speak by telling her things that make her feel safe and loved. Now is not the time to bring up old pain, but Kaycee knows that if she were not sitting right here, right now, she would never say what she's about to say.

'Graduation,' she says to her silent mother, whose eyes remain stubbornly closed. 'You told me that Theo really wanted to come and I begged you to leave him with someone. All I wanted was one day that was about me but you said he had to be there, that we had to be a family. I knew the clapping would be too much for him. I think you knew it too. Why would you have done that, Mum? You had to take him out and you missed my speech. I know Dad and Gran were there but you missed it.' Two teachers had to help her mother remove Theo from the hall because he was kicking and hitting, not caring who or what he hit. Kaycee sat on the stage, her face flaming as other students cast sympathetic glances her way. Once Theo was born, once he was diagnosed, she stopped being just Kaycee. She will always be Kaycee with the autistic brother.

Kaycee watches her mother breathe in and out, knowing that she has more questions than could ever be answered. She thought her parents were, if not happy, at least accepting of each other and their marriage. What could have happened to send her mother over the edge? Her father is not a small man. It would have taken a lot of strength to overpower him. Her mother doesn't look strong enough, not lying there in the hospital bed, pale and drawn. And what about the bruises on her mother's body? Did her father hit her mother? It seems an impossible thing. He is a surgeon. He uses his hands to heal not hurt.

But anger can do strange things to people as Constable Emmerson said. Before she left, they hadn't been able to make it through a family dinner without her parents sniping at each other. Kaycee had a feeling that the news of their divorce would come sooner rather than later but this violence is something she cannot understand or believe.

There is a soft knock at her mother's hospital door.

'Come in,' she calls, and Sergeant Peterson walks in.

'Hey, Kaycee, do you think you can take a look at something for me?'

Kaycee nods as she takes in the man's slightly pale face. He is holding his phone and Kaycee grabs her mother's hand and squeezes it.

The sergeant looks at her, gives his head a little shake, and then he turns the phone to Kaycee so she can see a picture on the screen.

'We found this in the cabin. We have a forensic team looking through things, obviously. I just want to know if you knew about this.' It's a photo of a wad of formal-looking papers and

Kaycee struggles to see what it actually is. 'I don't know what I'm looking at.'

The sergeant touches his screen, blowing up the top heading, and Kaycee reads the words: 'Family Court of Australia'. Underneath, it says 'Federal Circuit Court of Australia', and then on the right-hand side, in bold black lettering: 'Application for Divorce Kit'.

'An application for divorce,' she says, understanding settling on her like a fine black dust. 'I didn't know,' she says because even though she suspected, she didn't know. 'Where... where did you find it?'

'At the bottom of your father's suitcase.'

Kaycee looks at her mother, who opens her eyes and stares at her. 'Did you... did you know, Mum?'

Her mother looks at the sergeant and then she shakes her head, a tear tracing its way down her cheek.

'Right, then,' says the sergeant, and he gives a quick nod in Cecelia's direction. 'We haven't found Theo yet but we have a lot of people looking, even with the rain. We'll find him, Cecelia, don't worry.' He leaves the room.

'Oh, Mum,' whispers Kaycee, 'I'm so sorry.' Why would her father have taken it to the cabin? Had things really gotten so bad he couldn't wait until after the holiday, or did he want to do it at the cabin so they were away from the distractions of work and home?

Cecelia opens her mouth and for a moment Kaycee is certain that she is going to speak, but then she closes it again and stares out of the window. Her hand lets go of Kaycee's and together they listen to the drone of the rain.

Her mother looks like a child, bewildered by what has happened to her. She looks like Kaycee feels, just like Kaycee feels.

CHAPTER EIGHTEEN
Theo

It rains. It rains. It rains. Rose talks and talks. 'I remember,' she says. 'I think…' she says. 'What should we do?' she asks. The rain makes her words soft in my ears so I don't mind if she talks. She talks to someone named Mary and to 'the lord'. I can't see Mary and I can't see the lord. I looked in the bathroom but they aren't there.

I want Mum. I want Dad. I want Kaycee. I want my blue blanket but the rain means we can't go out. The rain means we have to stay here. The rain has made this place a bubble with only Rose and me inside it.

I am playing with the forks. Sixteen silver forks. They are lined up straight. They are one centimetre apart. I make sure they are straight. I make sure they are even. One fork is bent. I don't like bent. It makes things not straight and not even. I pick up the fork and throw it across the room.

'Yes, well, I feel a bit like that sometimes,' she says. She does not say, 'No, Theo,' or, 'Control yourself, Theo,' or, 'Pick that up, Theo,' or, 'That's not how we treat things we are playing with, Theo.' I stand up and go and pick up the bent fork. I put it back into place in the line. The line is better with sixteen. I like sixteen. The forks live in the drawer where the knives and spoons are. I take out the knives to line them up. Some have stains on them, brown rust that I scrape off. I line them up. At home I line up my blue cars from biggest to smallest, from fastest to slowest, from one to twenty. I line them up and they are even, exactly one centimetre apart.

Rose brings the spoons. 'Let's put these in a row as well, shall we?'

There are fourteen spoons. There should be sixteen. It is not even. It is not right. I feel hot inside me. There should be sixteen. There are sixteen forks and sixteen knives and there should be sixteen spoons. I feel the anger coming. I hold my hands by my ears. It is too much, too much, I want to lie down and bang my head.

'Just wait,' she says calmly and she takes away two forks and two knives. Now there are fourteen forks and fourteen knives and fourteen spoons and I feel the anger woosh out of my mouth. I don't need to bang my head.

'Can you tell me what happened with your mum and dad?' she says.

I look in her eyes but then I can't look at her. Blue eyes, crooked teeth, saggy skin. Blue eyes, crooked teeth, saggy skin. Blueeyescrookedteethsaggyskinblueeyescrookedteethsaggyskinblue-eyescrookedteethsaggyskin.

Too much. Too many pictures.

I close my eyes. Dark. Safe. Calm.

'Sometimes it's easier to say something if you don't look at a person. I know when I had to confess to Mary what had happened, I couldn't look at her. I knew she wouldn't judge me, not Mary, but I knew she would be disappointed in me. It was my fault. I should have kept myself safe.'

I don't understand her words. Not all of them. But I keep my eyes closed. Her voice is low and crackly. I don't mind the sound in my ears.

I don't want to think about the cabin, about Mum, about Dad, about the knife and the blood. I push my hands over my ears. Dark, safe, calm.

'This little light of mine,' she sings loudly and I take my hands away from my ears. I am Mum's little light. 'Run,' said Dad. 'Get help.'

She can help. Can she help? What is help? Who is help? Maybe Rose is help.

I stand up and I go to the table where the paper and the pen are, and I try to tell her. She comes to sit next to me.

I write the words:

Fight, angry, shout.

'I understand,' she says. 'There was a fight.'
I nod.
I sign, 'Scared.'
'Who was scared? You?'
I nod.
'Was your mum scared?'
I nod.
'Did your dad make you scared?'
I look at her. I write:

There was

'There was what? A fight?'
I shake my head.
'There was a knife?'
I shake my head.
'There was… I don't know… There was someone? I can't guess, Theo.'

I nod my head and nod my head. There was someone. There was.

'Someone? Who?' she asks and she sits closer and looks down at the paper so she can see the someone.

I write down something. I write down a name, a name I think is right.

'Who's that?' she asks.

I tap the name with my pencil. I don't know how to spell it. I make a sign, a sign that tells her who it is.

'It looks like…' she says. 'Do it again?'

I make the sign again.

'But that's… Oh, oh no.' Her mouth falls open. I think about my pictures. An open mouth means surprise. I don't like surprises but some people do. I don't think Rose likes this surprise.

She tells me a name. It is the right name and I nod my head. Now she knows. Now she will be help. Rose will be help. Rose knows who there was. Rose knows who was there.

'Is that who scared you?' she asks.

I nod.

'Is that who hurt your dad?'

I nod.

'Oh Lord, oh Mary, what on earth am I going to do now?' she says. She's talking to Mary again. Who's Mary? 'How am I going to keep him safe? How will I get him back to his parents?'

I go back to the floor while Rose talks to Mary and 'the lord'. I don't know if they are help. I don't know if Rose is help. I line up the spoons, I line up the forks, I line up the knives and the rain makes all the other sounds go away.

I am in my bubble with Rose. Rose can help. I listen to the rain and wait. I wait for Rose to help.

CHAPTER NINETEEN

Rose

Rose watches as Theo goes back to rearranging the forks and knives and spoons. He has told her what he needs to and now he has removed himself from the information, protecting himself from what he has seen and heard, arranging the cutlery into a square or a circle before returning them to their neat rows.

She looks down at what he tried to write. It's clear now that she understands. She remembers the sign. But she doesn't want it to be true. She wants the boy to have made a mistake but she knows that that's not what has happened. He sees the world in black and white. There are no shades of grey and he wouldn't say something that wasn't true. She's read that in one of the books William gave her.

The world can be a terrible place. People can seem one thing but be another. It's why she stays up here in this cabin, away from everything and everyone for most of her time. Rose runs her hands over her face, trying to rub away the memory as she takes deep breaths and concentrates on the dripping sound coming from one of the broken gutters over the porch, but memory is stubborn and will not be denied. It was sixty-three years ago and yet it could have happened yesterday. She cannot forget the smile, the leer, the hands, her cries. It was her fault. It was definitely her fault.

She was twenty-two years old but she might as well have been fourteen. She had never been out in the world before without her sister for protection or her brother to take care of. She thought he was being kind. She was flattered by the attention. It was her fault.

'Nobody knows what happened but me and you, Mary, and you're gone so I should be able to take that secret to my final resting place. But somehow it feels connected... It must be connected. Perhaps that's why this little boy was sent to me, Mary – perhaps the Lord knows it's time for the story to come out.' The guilt and shame should not be her burden and yet they are. Back then, it was a woman's responsibility to keep herself safe. 'Mum always taught us that men were lustful creatures who would have you as soon as look at you, didn't she? They couldn't be held accountable for anything they did because they were men. It's funny that, isn't it? We say they're incapable of controlling themselves and then we let them control everything else. Things are different now and that's good. You just wait; women will be running everything soon.' That thought is comforting to Rose but the past is sticky and holds on to her. 'Let me walk you home,' he said. 'Not safe for a young girl on her own.'

She trusted him because she had never known not to trust him. He was young, good-looking, married. That was the important thing – he was married. A married man was safe, wasn't he? 'Ah, Mary, I was so naïve, wasn't I?'

She sees herself as she was then, at only twenty-two with her perfectly curled hair, its ends flipped outwards and sprayed stiff, and her big blue eyes that she outlined in thick black pencil.

'You look lovely,' her sister said. They were getting ready at Mary's house to dance the night away at the church social. Mary was dressed like their mother would have been in a long sensible dress, that ended at her ankles. Mary was already married with William and Nancy and saw no need to dress up. She was more concerned about leaving the children with a young babysitter, who giggled too much but loved babies.

Rose had dragged out her one special purchase from Sydney. The dress was butter yellow and cinched at the waist, the neckline wide, leaving her shoulders almost bare, just like the dress her cousin Sarah had. Mary had told her to take a few days in Sydney with Sarah after they left Lionel at the institution, where the staff assured them they would take wonderful care of him. 'Cheer yourself up,' said Mary, 'stay a few days with Sarah.' Rose had been waiting for the right time to wear it, to show the whole town her modern, pretty dress.

'I like it but I'm not sure what everyone else at the dance will say,' Mary said.

'I imagine they'll ask if I want to dance. A whole lot of farm boys have come in for tonight. I might just snare myself a husband,' giggled Rose.

'Off you go, Rose,' her sister said, 'dance the night away. Bart and I will be along soon.'

She drew looks from the first moment she walked into the church hall. Orange and yellow streamers hung in chains on the walls and from the roof, and there were matching small balloons on the tables scattered around, where people could sit after choosing something to eat from the laden table where cakes and scones and sausage rolls were piled high. Hanging from the roof, a glitter ball twirled and sparkled.

Rose smiled at everyone but no one asked her to dance. The boys stayed away, just looking, and then asked the other girls in their sensible long dresses for a dance.

Finding herself standing in a corner, Rose clutched a glass of strange-tasting punch. She stared down at her yellow shoes, hating that she had made so much effort for people who wouldn't appreciate it and wishing she was back in Sydney with her cousin.

'It's because you're too pretty with those blue eyes and that tiny waist,' she heard and she looked up. He had broad shoulders and a strong jaw and his dark hair was cut short and neat. He had lovely jade-green eyes and he was smiling down at Rose kindly. Rose knew that he had a wife but no children, something everyone in the town had already remarked on. 'Apparently they've already been married for five years,' Mary had told her. 'There is obviously some sort of problem, poor woman.'

'I may just go home,' said Rose, not wanting the man to feel sorry for her.

'I can walk you part of the way,' he replied. 'I wouldn't want a lovely young lady like you out in the streets on her own at night.'

Rose giggled and took another sip of the punch. It was making her head feel light on her neck. 'I'll be fine, but thanks.'

'Now I insist,' he said, taking her elbow gently in his big hand and guiding her out of the hall where couples were laughing and dancing to 'Jailhouse Rock' by Elvis Presley, arms flapping and legs jumping. The summer air was heavy on Rose's bare shoulders and she took a deep breath. 'I think there was alcohol in that punch,' she said.

'I think there was.' He grinned, his teeth white in the pale-yellow streetlights. She felt a small stab of jealousy that he was the husband of someone else.

'Don't you have to stay?' she asked.

'I won't be long. You don't live far.'

'I'm staying with Mary tonight. But how do you know where I live?'

He smiled. 'I know where you live, pretty Rosie. I know most things around here. I even know about secret places.'

'What secret places? I've lived here my whole life and there are no secret places.'

The street was silent and she was glad she didn't have to make her way back through the bush in the summer heat, fearful of treading on a snake out to catch an unsuspecting mouse.

'Ah, now, there you're wrong.' He stopped walking and looked at his watch. 'If we're quick, I can show you a little hut that used to belong to Ned Kelly, the famous bushranger.'

'Really? I didn't know about that. How come I've never heard about it?'

He tapped the side of his nose. 'It's a secret,' and then he laughed, amused by his own joke.

Rose smiled and looked up into the sky, carpeted in a thousand stars. Suddenly the night seemed full of interesting possibility, even if no one had loved her new dress. They walked slowly, not touching. He was a married man after all. Rose felt perfectly safe. He pulled a torch out of a loop on his belt and shone it on the ground, lighting the way for their footsteps.

At the end of the road he turned left, grabbing her hand after her shoe slipped on a loose stone and pulling her along behind him up a dirt road. Rose went willingly, the sound of the cicadas drowning out their footsteps in the dark bush.

'I think we should go back. The snakes will be out now. They always are in summer.'

'Never mind, Rosie, I'll protect you.'

Rose giggled again.

'Here, look, here it is.' He stopped in front of a shack that to Rose looked like it was being held together with mud and hope. 'Doesn't look like much,' she said. The air was a blanket of warmth but Rose shivered. She wanted to go home now. She looked around her, trying to work out where she was in relation to Mary's home, but it was dark except for the beam from his torch. The bush rustled and chirruped as if to remind her that this was no place for her to be at night.

'Wait until you see inside.'

He pushed open the door and Rose was hit with the acrid, musty smell of something dead. There was a single cot with a grey mattress on top of it and a potbelly stove in the corner. 'I don't believe Ned Kelly lived here,' Rose said as she looked around.

'Ah, well, maybe not… But how about a kiss?' he said, swinging the beam of his torch to her face, blinding her a little.

'You're married!' she shrieked, stunned that such a thing could be asked by a married man.

'She doesn't mind. Come on, pretty Rosie, give me a kiss.' The torch beam moved to his face, large and leering, his lips grotesquely puckered.

'No!' She stepped back. 'I'm going home!'

'No, you're not,' he said and his voice was deep and threatening, his eyes black in the gloom of the hut as he lowered the beam.

Rose took another step back. She knew the open door was behind her and she knew that she could make it out. She would have to run in the dark and her shoes would be ruined but she had to go. 'No,' she said firmly but he grabbed her arm, pulled her back forcefully and pushed her onto the bed.

Rose felt her underwear rip, heard the torch falling on the floor. He was not kind. He was large and strong and he smelled of beer. She shut her eyes so she didn't see, held her breath so she couldn't smell, and she tried to hear only the cicadas and not his grunting. The pain that came made her bite her lip. It was not possible that it was happening. It was just not possible.

Afterwards he led her down to the main road and told her not to tell.

'The memory is so clear, Mary. I'm sure I've forgotten more things than I remember but I can never forget that night. He took everything from me, Mary. He took it all.'

Rose looks at Theo. She remembers that there were these long calm stretches with Lionel as well. He would get immersed in something and it would keep him so quiet, you could almost believe he wasn't there. She chuckles as she remembers her brother lining up his collection of dead cockroaches. It was a strange habit but he liked to gather them and then line them all up, neat and tidy, before putting them back in the box again and taking them out.

'Disgusting,' said her sister but Rose didn't mind as long as it kept him quiet.

'What do I do now, Mary?' she says. 'This rain isn't letting up any time soon, and when it does, what if the wrong person comes up to the cabin to find him? What then?' She picks up the frame containing her sister's picture. It is worn smooth at the sides where she always holds it. 'What should I do?'

She takes a deep breath and hears her sister's voice. 'All right,' she replies, nodding her head.

She goes over to where Theo is and taps him on the shoulder. He reels back but she puts her hands up. 'I need to take you to your mum and dad,' she says and he stands up.

'Mum,' he signs, and she says, 'Yes.'

'Dad,' he signs, and she says, 'Yes.'

'But first you need a raincoat. I know you won't want to wear it but you must, and some shoes. If you don't have shoes we can't go to Mum and Dad.' She says the words firmly, letting him know there is no choice, and something must click because he nods his head.

He puts on the long Driza-Bone that belonged to her father. The khaki-coloured raincoat is cracked with age and wear. Rose has always wondered why he left it when he ran off but she's grateful to have it. For a few years, it smelled slightly of beer and pipe smoke, and Rose used to hold it to her nose and imagine a different father for their family.

Rose can see how Theo wants to shrink from the feel of it, can see the battle going on inside his head. 'It's all right, lad. It's only for a bit of time and then you can take it off. But it's cold and wet and I can't have you getting sick. The good Lord sent you to me and I must keep you safe.'

She hauls out some old boots that William leaves at the cabin for when he does odd jobs around the place and finds some socks.

'Put those on,' she says but he shakes his head. 'If you don't, your feet will get hurt. You won't be able to walk,' she pleads, but he shakes his head and she can see the panic there. If she pushes, he will have a fit. She sighs. She is more tired than she can ever remember feeling. She is too old to be walking in the gushing rain with a shoeless child but she needs to get him into town. More than anything, this is what she needs to do.

'Come on, Rose, you can do this,' she says to herself. She stands up, gets herself ready with her coat and floppy yellow rain hat and boots.

In the mirror near the front door, she catches a glimpse of herself and allows herself a small laugh at the incongruous vison there. The large grey raincoat hangs down to her ankles and the brim of the yellow hat slopes over her eyes. From a distance all anyone would see would be a walking coat and hat. 'I'll frighten a few people away in this get-up, Mary,' she says.

She will not bother with an umbrella. The wind will take it and gift it to the trees anyway. 'Right, let's go,' she says. She opens the door and the rushing sound of the rain washes over her. She can see that the water has gouged out channels in the earth, creating giant puddles and mini streams everywhere. Sticks and stones and sand rush down pathways mixed with water.

Taking a deep breath, she holds out her hand. 'You need to help me, lad. I'm old,' she says, and Theo steps forward and grasps her hand and she feels the tense determination in his fingers. Holding her hand is not a feeling he likes but he understands she needs his help.

'Good lad,' she says, raising her voice above the downpour, and together they begin their journey.

CHAPTER TWENTY

Cecelia

Cecelia's eyes are closed as she prays, *Please, God, if you're there, if you're listening, please keep him safe. Keep my little boy safe. Keep my little light safe.*

A swish of air tells her the door has opened, that Kaycee is returning – but it's not Kaycee. Kaycee is a wisp of air entering the room, the overly sweet smell of the motel shampoo she is using to wash her hair and her obvious disappointment from the way she slumps in the chair next to Cecelia's bed. This is not Kaycee.

'Listen to me,' whispers a voice but Cecelia keeps her eyes closed. She recognises that voice. She recognises his smell. It's a chemical deodorant smell that cannot mask the underlying stench of sweat. She can feel her heart beating, hear the sound in her ears.

'You listen carefully. You keep quiet about all this or I promise you that you'll be sorry.'

The words are hissed. The anger is a feeling in the room, thick in the air. She cannot look at him. She simply cannot. *Where is Theo? He is safer out there than in here. If he stays lost, then he will not be found by the wrong person.*

He leans over her, the smell filling her nostrils, and inside her the glass shatters, the memory rushing out in fragments. Nothing is clear; she cannot find the whole story but everything is terrifying. The overwhelming feeling is one of fear but there are other feelings as well: guilt, shame, horror.

A moment in the cabin returns, the words he uttered: 'It's not like your kid will say anything. The boy can't speak. This will be the one time his silence is a good thing.' And then he laughed. His smell has brought the words back, offensive and harsh and something she never wants to experience again.

It's her fault, she tells herself. It's definitely her fault. She allowed it to happen, put it into play earlier that day.

She only stopped in at the bar on Saturday afternoon to grab a drink, a quiet drink alone, just her and her thoughts. Inside she made straight for the large fireplace, for a soft leather chair with her wine glass in her hand, enjoying the crisp taste of Chardonnay as she stared into the dancing flames. She felt the muscles in her neck loosen as she idly looked around the bar.

'Hey, Cecelia, welcome back,' he said when he entered. 'What are you doing in here in the middle of the day?' He was a friend – not a close friend but someone she easily greeted and spent a little time with. It never occurred to her to look at him any other way. Just an old friend.

'Oh, hey. I'm supposed to be grocery shopping but Nick has Theo. They've gone fishing – well, Nick fishes and Theo keeps him company – so I'm treating myself to a wine in the middle of the afternoon. I'm on holiday after all,' and she laughed. She remembers she laughed. Is that when it happened? Is that when she changed in his mind from friend to… what? Victim? This thought sickens her. She had let her guard down.

'Well, I stopped by for a late lunch so I'll join you for a drink. What's been happening?' he asked.

'You know, the usual. Theo is at school five days now so I have more time but I'm doing some work for the Autism Association, some marketing and stuff like that.'

'Ah yeah, Theo, I remember Theo – he uses… um, sign language, right?'

'Right.' She smiled.

'Sounds like you're busy – good for you.'

One wine turned into two and all the while her phone had stayed silent, meaning that Theo and Nick were still out on the water. She didn't want to return to the cabin, where the minute she and her husband set eyes on each other another argument would begin. Instead, she wanted to stay in the bar – just a little while. As she sipped her wine and laughed at his jokes, she knows that, in her head, she was testing out ways to tell Nick that they needed help, that they were too far gone. She was rehearsing what to say to make him stay, to keep him coming home night after night so that it would not just be her and Theo alone. She knew that Nick was right about Theo not needing her as much anymore. It was a truth she didn't want to chew over. For nearly nine years her whole life had been dedicated to her autistic son. These days she had no friends, only acquaintances she had met through the Autism Association. She had no life beyond caring for Theo and thinking about Theo and running her day so that Theo would always have his routine. She knew that the goal of every parent was to raise their child so that one day they would be able to live with a certain amount of independence. She was one of the lucky ones. She wouldn't have to be consumed with caring for Theo forever. But she had no idea of who she was without that. No idea and no concept of how to find her way back to the woman she had been before. She sipped at her wine as the thoughts swirled around and around in her head, a constant chatter behind the conversation they were having.

Outside, the weather was clear and cool, autumn leaves littering the pavements, and inside the bar a fire burned in the large stone fireplace. The smell of cooking burgers drifted out of the kitchen. An hour passed and Cecelia found herself buzzing a little, just chatting and laughing. Did she laugh too loudly, talk too much? He is a good-looking man with beautiful eyes. She knows that she leaned forward and touched his hand once, twice, maybe more.

She knows they parted with a hug. She knows she thought it was nothing more than an enjoyable afternoon between two people who had known each other for years. But now she knows that he thought it was more than that.

It was her fault.

Now, she holds her breath, not wanting to smell him, not wanting to touch him, hoping he will just leave.

But he doesn't. 'I'll find that kid of yours first, believe me,' he spits. 'And if I don't, I'll still get to him first. You don't want me to have to find a way to stop him from telling anyone what happened.' He laughs bitterly. 'Not that he could.'

Cecelia opens her eyes and looks at him, feels hate radiating from inside her. She opens her mouth to scream but nothing comes out. Her whole body is shaking. He leans even closer.

'That's right, you just keep it all inside. This rain is making the search harder. A tourist got lost in a rainstorm like this about five years ago. By the time he was found… well, he needed a really long stay in hospital and he was a grown man. I hope nothing happens to Theo out there. I really hope he's okay.'

Cecelia feels chills run up and down her skin. She sits up. She has to get out of here. She has to go and find her son.

'No,' he says, the eyes she thought attractive now obviously cruel and small, 'you stay right here.' He holds up his hand and she shrinks in the bed.

He smirks and turns around and is gone in a moment. Cecelia watches the door, her heart pounding, waiting for him to return, but when the door to her room swings open again, it is her daughter who walks in.

CHAPTER TWENTY-ONE

Kaycee

'What's wrong, Mum?' Kaycee asks. Her mother is pale, her stare focused on Kaycee, her fingers entwined.

Her mother shakes her head but her hands unfurl, her fingers relaxing against the rough white hospital blanket. Her inability to explain what happened is obviously taking its toll. If they could only find Theo, it would help. Kaycee is sure it would help.

'I wish I could figure out where he would be, Mum. I wish I knew him better.' Kaycee feels tears on her cheeks as she understands that her withdrawal from her family has given her nothing and taken everything.

She had been so determined to show them that she didn't need them, that she was just fine without them.

She arrived at university resolved to just be Kaycee, not Kaycee the girl with the autistic brother, and it actually worked for a few months. She would go home on the weekend, but every time she turned up her mother seemed surprised to see her. Once Theo started going to school full-time, her mum became very involved in all things autism. She took charge of the association's website and she organised a charity event every year. She had a Facebook page where she shared tips for parents who had just found out their children were on the spectrum. Every time Kaycee looked at her, she was furiously typing a reply to a concerned parent or on the phone speaking to another member of the association or she was helping Theo with a school project or dealing with one of his therapists. Theo needed her less and less, and Kaycee assumed that her mother would be happy about this. But instead, it seemed that her mother was desperately filling every hour of every day and nothing was making her happy. Kaycee doubted she understood how to just be content anymore.

So Kaycee simply stopped going home, preferring to lose herself in the quiet university and the bar where she and her boyfriend drank away every Saturday night. Gone boyfriend now. Kaycee shakes her head as she thinks about the pile of assignments that she has to get done over the next month. She's let everything go to hell and she knows it.

There is a knock at the door and she stands up to open it.

'Hello, Kaycee, I thought I would just give you another update on your father,' says Dr Greenblatt, the resident doctor in the hospital.

Her mother's fingers lace themselves together again and she sits up and moves in her bed as if trying to get away from the doctor and – Kaycee assumes – the news he may be bringing.

'I think he's doing well. He hasn't woken up yet but I'm hopeful that the surgeons managed a good repair and he should recover. There are no guarantees, which I'm sure you understand.' The doctor gives her a reassuring smile. 'He's a strong man, so things are looking positive.'

'Okay,' says Kaycee although she has meant to say, 'Thank you.'

The doctor casts a quick glance at her mother, who is looking at him, her brown eyes wide. Her concentrated silence is disconcerting and the doctor clears his throat.

'When can I see him? Not just look at him but actually sit next to him?'

'I promise that will be soon. We just want to make sure he's over the dangerous hours after a surgery. Your mother hasn't spoken, has she? She hasn't said anything?'

'No, no, not yet.'

'My wife wanted to know if you needed anything,' he says and he smiles. He has a kind smile, concerned.

'No... but thank you.'

'Your mother and my wife catch up sometimes when they come down for the holidays. She'd love to come and visit... when everyone is up to it.'

'Oh,' says Kaycee, unsure what to say to this. She looks at her mother, who is staring at the doctor.

'I'll leave you,' he says.

Her mother turns her head away, studying the sheet of rain.

Kaycee rubs at a dull ache in her neck. She can't handle this. She cannot pretend to be an adult anymore. She wants to go back to her bedroom at home and curl up under the duvet. The doctor gives her a nod before leaving Kaycee and Cecelia alone again.

'I don't think I want to live at university anymore,' she says.

Her mother turns her head, meeting her daughter's gaze. A tear slips down the side of her face.

'Oh, Mum, what happened?' Kaycee asks for what feels like the millionth time but all she gets in response is her mother's silence.

'Was he wearing shoes when he ran?' she asks, even though she knows the answer, and for a moment she believes that her mother will simply not reply, just the way she has not replied to anything Kaycee has said. But this time, although her mother doesn't speak, she does shake her head.

Kaycee stands up and takes her mother's hand. She feels her heart beat faster with the possibility that Cecelia might be ready to communicate.

'Was what happened to Dad an accident?'

Her mother shakes her head. A heaviness settles in Kaycee's stomach. She has been holding out a small hope that what happened was an accident. An accident could be explained.

'Did you... did you hurt Dad?' Kaycee whispers, and she is beyond relieved when her mother shakes her head again. And then she thinks about the only other person in the cabin but that's impossible. She takes a deep breath and asks the question because it needs to be asked.

'Was it Theo, Mum? Did Theo somehow hurt Dad?'

Her mother shakes her head again, hard, and her eyes fill with tears.

'I didn't think so,' says Kaycee adamantly. Theo would never hurt anyone. He has lashed out during a meltdown once or twice but he has never deliberately hurt anyone.

'Do you know who hurt him?'

Her mother wipes her tears off her cheek and Kaycee finds herself holding her breath. Does her mother know? If what happened was so traumatic she cannot access the memory, then perhaps she has no idea. Kaycee prepares herself for another shake of the head from her mother. It would leave her right back where they started.

But slowly and carefully, her eyes focused on her daughter, her mother nods.

'You know? You actually know who it was?'

Her mother nods again.

'Okay, can you tell me? Can you tell me so I can tell the police?'

Her mother lifts her hands, covering her face, and her shoulders begin to shake as she silently weeps for all the things she doesn't seem to be able to say.

Kaycee leans forward and wraps her arms around her mother, feels her tears wet her own cheeks. She holds on tightly, as tightly as Theo likes to be held. She has not hugged her mother for years and the feeling of having her arms around her is strange but also familiar.

'Why can't you tell me what happened?' she asks.

Her mother opens her mouth but nothing comes out, and then she forms her hand into a fist and bites down on her fingers in what Kaycee can clearly see is a silent scream.

'Do you actually know what happened?' she asks.

Her mother shakes her head and Kaycee realises that this has been the problem all along. Her mother knows who hurt her father but she doesn't know what happened and so she cannot talk about it. The story is trapped somewhere inside her and Kaycee has no idea how to help her get it out.

CHAPTER TWENTY-TWO

Theo

The coat is heavy and the coat smells strange to my nose. I want to rip it off my shoulders. The rain is rushing, gushing, loud, loud, loud. Her hand is tight. Her skin is rough. My ears are full of whooshing rain. The rain, her hand, her skin, the coat. The rain, her hand, her skin, the coat. My head is full. My head is full of too much. It is too much but her hand is tight. She does not let go. She is old. I cannot let go. I can be her light as well. I can be a little light for her, for Rose.

I want Mum. I want Dad. I want Kaycee but Kaycee is at university. I want help. Rose is help.

'You're a good lad,' she shouts, 'you're helping me walk.'

I am help. I am Theo and I am help.

'Thanks for helping me, Theo,' Kaycee said when I lifted her suitcase into the car so she could go away. Kaycee went away to be somewhere else. Kaycee wanted to be away. I tell Kaycee about robots and Benjamin on the messaging app and she sends me a smiley face. I like it when she sends me a smiley face.

'I'll come back and visit every week,' she said but she didn't come back and visit. There is a space where Kaycee used to be inside me. Inside me there is Mum and Dad and Kaycee and Benjamin. But now Kaycee is not there. Kaycee liked to help me line up my cars and Kaycee knew I needed my pencil grip and Kaycee knew how to cut up carrots and sing 'This Little Light of Mine'. But now there is a Kaycee space inside me and in our house.

Kaycee said I was help. I can be help for Rose while we walk. Rose will tell someone about who was there.

A man was there. The man who shouted. The man who had an angry face. I know angry. I have a picture to show me angry. The man was angry but I was scared. I know scared because Benjamin showed me scared. He put a rubber spider on the floor and then he jumped on a chair and said, 'I'm scared, Theo. I'm scared of the spider.' I know scared. The man made me scared and I took the knife. 'These are very sharp, Theo. Don't touch knives. Knives can hurt people. Don't touch them.'

But I wanted the man to be scared too. I wanted him to stop what he was doing. If I see a spider and I am scared, I stop what I am doing and run away. I wanted him to run away but there are no spiders in the cabin. The knife was on the counter, shiny and smooth. I picked up the knife to make him stop, to make him run away.

The man shouted. Mum shouted and Dad shouted and then Dad said, 'Run, Theo, get help.'

The rain is on my face and in my hair and down my jumper. The rain is cold and wet and soft and hard. The rain is in the trees and in the sky and on the ground. The rain is everywhere, and in the middle of the rain is me and Rose. Me and Rose and we are going for help.

CHAPTER TWENTY-THREE

Rose

It is hard going. The wind pushes her one way and the ground threatens to go out from under her. Her foot slips on the mud and she is only able to right herself because Theo is holding her hand. He's strong but Rose imagines that she's not very heavy.

She used to be quite stout when she was younger, but the flesh on her bones has melted away with the years even if the memories have stubbornly remained. She bends over slightly to catch her breath and then nods at Theo that she's ready to continue.

She remembers running down this hill one night in the slight chill of the autumn air to Mary's house, terrified of what she'd just realised. She stumbled over rocks and tree roots, twisting her ankle as the wind pushed her along, but nothing could stop her desperate dash to her sister's house.

'Two months,' she burst out as she flung open Mary's back door.

'You were just here for dinner, Rose. Why are you back? What's two months mean?'

'My… I've missed two in a row,' she cried, her hand clutching at her stomach.

'Oh Rose, Rose, what have you done?' said Mary, a motherly frown on her face.

'It was done to me,' Rose remembers sobbing. Her sister made tea and they sat by the fire as Rose revealed the secret she had tried to bury somewhere inside her, not knowing that the secret was busy growing there, determined to come out.

Mary poured Rose a cup of tea and handed her a slice of fruit cake. 'You get that into you,' she said. 'You've had a shock and need something sweet. Take a bite and swallow and calm down.'

Taking a bite of the tart cake, Rose swallowed her tears with the chewy sultanas as she arranged the story in her head. Her sister listened, her arms folded across her chest, her face growing pale. Through her tears, Rose recounted the terrible night in summer when the heat was heavy in the air and she thought her life was only just beginning.

'We'll get him arrested,' Mary fumed when she was done. Her sister stood up and paced her small living room back and forth as she vented.

'As if,' Rose said. 'No one will believe me. He told me I wanted it. I went with him, Mary. I went willingly. I thought he was just going to walk me home. But what do I do now? What do I do now?'

Her sister stopped her pacing, squared her shoulders, determined. 'I'll speak to him,' she said. They both stared into the flames of the fire as Mary hatched a plan. William and Nancy had been put to bed. William was only just two and Nancy was a tiny baby. Mary was still recovering from the birth and Rose came over every day after work to help tidy the house and get the children ready for bed.

'You believe me, don't you, Mary?' Rose pleaded. 'I never would have done such a thing and he's married, a married man.'

'Obviously you didn't want it. You're a good girl. I know that.'

Rose finished her tea, grateful for her sister's unwavering faith in her. But the shame of what she had allowed to happen filled her up and the cake was no longer appetising. She had wanted to put it behind her, to never think of the thing that had happened again, but here it was, forcing its way into her life.

'Bart,' Mary called to her husband.

'Oh please, please don't tell him,' Rose said, unable to bear the idea of gentle giant Bart hearing what had been done to his sister-in-law. He didn't call her Rose; he called her Rosy, because of her cheeks, and they had always had an easy friendship.

'I'm not telling him, Rose. Bart… Rose and I are going for a little walk. Listen for the kids, would you?'

'It's a bit cold for a walk, isn't it?' Bart called from the bedroom.

'Never you mind,' said Mary and off they went, the two of them.

Rose knows that she shivered inside her warm coat all the way to his house. She knew it was fear. She dreaded what he would say.

'Maybe you should talk to him alone,' Rose said.

'Oh no, I'll tell him what's what in front of his wife. Lettie needs to know what kind of a person she is married to.' Mary was so determined, so sure of herself. Rose felt ten years old again and in awe of her older sister.

Theo holds on tight, taking slow steps forward along with her. She doesn't like to think about what is happening to his feet on the ground that is covered in mud and sharp stones but he seems steadier because of a lack of shoes. She is looking down and she watches his toes grip the mud, squelching it and getting purchase.

They make their way down the hill that her home rests on, the water streaming down their faces. Rose can feel it inside her clothes, dribbling down the back of her neck and coming up over the top of her boots and into her socks. She might as well have left the coat and hat behind. They do nothing in the determined storm.

Rose feels her age in her bones, in her ankles especially as she tries to navigate the muddy ground where channels have opened up and a puddle could be ankle deep. She holds Theo's hand tightly, grateful that he doesn't pull away although she knows he must want to. There is no opportunity for talking as Rose feels her breath begin to come in pants. Despite the cold she can feel that she is sweating inside her coat.

She looks up and can see that the main road is only a few hundred metres away. As soon as they get to the tarred road it will be fine. Rose has walked that road almost daily for decades and she could make her way to town with her eyes closed although it seems easier these days to just let William bring her what she needs.

'There,' she points and shouts so that Theo understands that this is where they are heading. She looks back down at the ground just in time to see a brown snake slither away, out of the way of her booted foot. It shouldn't be out in the cold but the rain must have disturbed its home. She knows it's just looking for somewhere safe. She shivers. If she'd have stood on it, who knows what would have happened.

She peers forward, and as she does, a bush turkey makes its screaming, flapping way across her path. She feels her ankle twist and her body collapses, hitting the ground as her hand wrenches away from Theo's. She feels her wrist go as she reaches forward to brace herself and then she lies still in a heap in the mud. A strong, throbbing pain spreads through her whole being.

The relentless rain pounds on her head and her body, soaking every inch of her. She turns a little and feels that she may have cracked a rib, the pain slicing through her side, stealing her air. 'Oh,' she gasps. She looks at Theo, who is staring at her, his blue eyes wide with horror.

'It's all right,' she shouts above the rain, 'just help me up.'

But Theo doesn't seem to understand or he is too panicked to understand. He looks around and then he turns in a circle in the rain and he starts to flap his arms. Rose knows she has lost him. He needs time to calm himself on his own and there is no doubt that the noise of the rain and the feeling of the coat on his body and the mud on his feet are all proving too much for him.

'All right, lad,' she says, but not loud enough for him to hear. It's difficult to breathe. She turns on her side again, the pain carving its way through her body. 'Oh, Mary, help me,' she whispers. She pulls her body forward using the arm that doesn't have what she is sure is a broken wrist, sliding forward in the mud. She looks up. A few metres away is an enormous Blue Mountains ash tree, its brown-grey bark stripped away to reveal a white trunk underneath, and if she can just get herself to its giant trunk, she can wait there for help. Its sparse autumn leaves will not offer much shelter but it's better than nothing.

Oh, Mary, help me. You have got to get together with the Lord and help me. I can't die out here in the rain and leave this lad all alone. Please, Mary, you're up there with him, I know you are. Put in a good word for your sister.

Rose looks up again and is surprised to find that she is nearly at the tree. Her body is just pain, in her ankle, in her wrist, on her side. She looks back behind her and sees that even though he is flapping his arms, Theo is actually following her. If he were any other child, she would be able to tell him what to do to help her.

'If he were any other kid, I would want to come home instead of going to the pub,' she hears her father saying to her mother about Lionel, watching him rock back and forth, his eyes focused on the chipped, cream-coloured paint on the wall.

'But he's not any other child,' her mother hissed at him, 'he's my child and the Lord gave him to me because he knew I would love him with everything that I had. That's what you should be doing.'

'We'll get there, lad,' Rose says now to Theo, and she looks forward again. It only takes a few more pulls and she can reach out and touch the rough trunk. Despite the cold, the bark feels warm and welcoming. Rose uses the last bits of her strength to haul herself up so that she can lean against the tree. She is soaked to the bone and shivering. Pain is everywhere and she can feel that her heart rate is getting faster and faster. She is breathing in little pants and she is afraid that she may not survive for much longer if she doesn't get help.

She looks at Theo, who seems stunned into calm. He is not flapping or keening. He is simply staring at her, his bright blue eyes the only colour in the grey landscape.

'You need to get help for me, Theo,' she gasps. 'Get help.'

He stares at her, unmoving. Rose wants to cry.

'Please, Theo.' She lifts her hands and even though every movement is agony she signs, 'Get help.'

Theo looks at her, his mouth working but no sound coming out, and then finally, as the rain intensifies beyond what Rose would have thought possible even after having lived in the mountains all her life, she sees his hands move and he signs the word 'help'.

'Yes,' she says, tears mixing with the rain. She feels so powerless. 'Get help.' She points at the road that she can just see. 'There,' she shouts, 'get help.'

The little boy looks at her for a moment longer and then he turns, running off to the right. It's the wrong way unless he turns left again. A terrible despair weighs down on Rose. It has all been for nothing. He is going the wrong way. Rose doesn't have it in her to shout. She feels that she cannot really breathe. 'Now, now, darling,' she hears Mary say. 'What's wrong? Come on, you can tell me, you can tell your sister.'

Rose closes her eyes and she hears the hymn her mother sang, the hymn she has been singing to Theo. 'This little light of mine, I'm going to let it shine.' She smiles because for just a moment, the pain disappears and she feels her sister right there beside her.

CHAPTER TWENTY-FOUR

Cecelia

Cecelia is dreaming. She is running after Theo in the rain. She has to jump over rocks and fallen tree branches and her feet slip in the mud as she runs. Theo keeps looking back at her and smiling his beautiful, rarely seen, perfect smile. She can feel her heart racing and her lungs burning but she knows she has to keep running. She stops and bends over to try to catch her breath in the pummelling rain, and when she looks up Theo is far ahead of her and she knows that she will never be able to catch him. Her son cups his hands over his mouth and through the rain, as clearly as if he'd used a megaphone, Theo shouts, 'Come on, Mum! You have to hurry or I won't…' His voice fades. He sounds as she has always imagined he would sound, a clear light voice with a hint of the man he will one day become, and joy and gratitude fill her up because he has finally let go of his silence.

Cecelia opens her eyes, gasping, in shock. The light is on in her room. Outside, the rain is steady and the clock on the wall tells her it's nearly 4 p.m.

Theo doesn't speak. *Where is Theo and what was he trying to tell me?*

'Theo,' she says but she cannot make a sound. She turns on her side and gives in to silent tears because she is sure that those were the first and last words she will ever hear from her son.

The voice and the smell come back to her. She knows who hurt Nick. She knows but if she tells anyone, if the words come out… how will she keep Theo safe? Because Theo knows the truth. Cecelia closes her eyes, trying to see exactly what happened and how it happened. If she can find the story, the whole story, then maybe she will be able to speak, and she can tell Kaycee and Kaycee can tell… Who could her daughter tell? Cecelia has no idea who to trust. If he finds Theo, if anyone finds Theo, if Theo is found, then what will happen to him?

She is so helpless here in this bed without Nick. She sits up and looks at her hand where the drip is attached. She prods at the needle, flinching at the sharp pain it causes. She could pull it out, could get out of this bed and leave to try and find her son. But she has no clothes here and no phone. They have taken everything away as evidence. Evidence of what? She watches the continuous, melodious rain and tries to find the thread of the story. She was in the cabin. Theo was in the cabin, in his room. He was on his iPad. Nick had gone for a walk. To clear his head. That's what he said when they were done throwing the same old words at each other. 'We need to talk properly, Cecelia.' But she was busy cleaning up from lunch and avoiding the discussion. She knew they needed to have it but she was still trying to work out how to introduce the idea of counselling.

Nick was evidently also trying to work out how to introduce an idea, but it was the idea of divorce. They found the papers in his suitcase. She would like to brand him as cruel because he brought them on holiday but something tells her he felt he had no choice. Perhaps she would have agreed to a separation at least if he had said something two days ago but not now. Now she knows that if her husband survives, if her son is found, if they are somehow allowed to go on being a family, she will fight to keep them together.

But in order to do that she needs the full story of what happened and not just the fragments of words, the smell, the fear. She chews on her lip. Nick went for a walk and she and Theo were alone in the cabin as the sky darkened to bring the rainstorm that was meant to keep them all trapped in the cabin for days.

A knock at her hospital room door startles her out of her thoughts. 'Just checking in,' says Constable Emmerson. He holds the door open and studies her. 'I wanted to let you know that we have at least a hundred and fifty people searching now. We'll find him, sooner rather than later, I think,' he says quietly with a smile. When she nods her head, he returns the gesture and closes the door. Cecelia returns to her memory of the cabin.

There was a knock at the door and he was standing there. And then? That's where she gets stuck. She cannot understand why she can't get further than this. There is a feeling of terror, an image of a smile, of hands and the words, 'You want this.' But the rest is hidden in a fog.

CHAPTER TWENTY-FIVE

Kaycee

Kaycee is sitting in the hospital café. Her head is on her hands, a cup of coffee growing cold on the table. Outside, the grey day is giving way to a black night. It's only four in the afternoon but the day seems eager to be done. The rain has not stopped and will not for hours yet.

She feels someone sit down at the table and she lifts her head. It's Jonah and she can see his clothing is damp even though he must have been wearing a coat. He is shivering slightly.

'Have…' she begins, hopeful, desperate.

'I'm sorry, Kace, we haven't found him.'

'He's been outside in the rain for two nights already,' replies Kaycee. 'He's strong but he's not that strong. I don't know if he would think to drink the rainwater. I don't know if he would be trying to find somewhere with people. He could have fallen and hit his head on a rock. He could have cut his feet and be bleeding somewhere in the bush. He's suffering. I can feel he's suffering and I just don't know… I don't…' She runs out of words as her tears start to flow.

'Hey, hey,' says Jonah and he puts his arms around her. She can smell the rain on his jumper and it's cold against her cheek, but she wraps her arms around him, needing something to hang on to.

'I'm so… so afraid I'll never see him again.'

Jonah lets go and looks at her. 'We'll find him, Kaycee. There are so many people looking, you wouldn't believe.' His tone is firm, his voice certain. He believes what he's saying.

'But it's so cold and he wasn't wearing shoes and people die in the bush, Jonah. They die!'

'I know, I know, but you have to hang on to the idea that he would be somewhere out of the rain. I think they haven't found him because he's hidden somewhere, which means he's safe and out of the weather. I think that's why we can't get to him. He's hiding, Kaycee, I'm sure of it.'

Kaycee takes a sip of her cold coffee as she considers this. He would be hiding because once an idea is planted in his head, he doesn't let go. The idea of sheltering in place has been repeated to him over and over again, and he would be doing just that. 'He's sheltering in place,' she says. 'You're right, that's what he's doing.' She attempts certainty, but she can't really feel it.

'I found some messages from him on my phone, from weeks ago. We talk to each other on WhatsApp. I haven't checked it for a while. But I looked at it today and I've missed three messages from him. And he's just… he's just telling me about his day at school and his teacher, Benjamin, and about a robot they're building together and it's nothing big but I missed them because I was so absorbed in my own stupid drama and he was reaching out to me and I ignored him. How could I ignore him? He's eleven years old and I just ignored him because I wasn't interested in thinking about anyone but myself. I'm an awful… horrible person… I'm…' She rubs hard at her cheeks, ashamed of her tears because she's meant to be staying strong for all of them.

'Kaycee, listen to me,' says Jonah and she stops talking, taking a deep breath. She knows he's going to tell her that none of that is true and that she's being too hard on herself and she doesn't really want to hear that.

'No doubt you could be a better big sister,' he says instead, shocking her with his honesty, 'especially to a kid like Theo. But now all that matters is that he's found safe and well. But when we do find him, remember this, just a little of this feeling, and be a better big sister.'

Kaycee looks at Jonah, looks into his deep green eyes, and sees absolute sincerity there. He's not letting her get away with how she's been behaving but his words have given her hope. She can be a better future version of herself.

'I'll be a better big sister,' she agrees, a small smile replacing the tears at the thought.

He smiles back at her and then he runs his hands through his hair, small droplets of rain landing on the table. Kaycee runs her arm through them, wiping them away with her jumper.

'Have you seen your dad?'

'No,' she shakes her head, 'they said soon.'

'Infection is a big issue so they'll keep everyone away until they know he's through the worst.'

'I feel like he may have the key to understanding all of this.'

'He may, but you have to give him time. Bodies need time to heal. I may go back to the motel and grab a shower before I head out again.' He stands up.

'Jonah…' she says and he stops moving and looks down at her. 'Why have you stayed?' she asks, her voice small. She ducks her head a little, prepared for him to tell her that he's doing it for altruistic reasons, because he likes to help people.

'Isn't it obvious? I've stayed for you, Kaycee, for you. I mean, I've stayed to help because people need help and it's what I want to do, but I've stayed for you. I've been watching you for months with that idiot and I could never understand why you would be doing that to yourself. I understand a little better now. And now that I do, I'm not going anywhere.'

He leaves the café and Kaycee tries to process what he's said, but her brain is a whirl of thoughts and fears that are holding her hostage. What will happen to her family if her brother isn't found? If her father doesn't live? If her mother can never speak? She cannot think beyond the next five minutes.

She takes a deep breath and lets it out slowly. Jonah is here for her and that's something in her world that is no longer in chaos. She can begin with one certainty and move from there.

She looks at her messages from Theo again and then she types a reply.

Hey, Theo. It sounds like you're having a good time at school. I also think Benjamin is cool. I like the picture of the robot. It's going to be excellent. Maybe it can help me clean my room. Miss you, buddy. See you soon.

CHAPTER TWENTY-SIX

Theo

'Run,' said Dad. 'Get help.'

Rose was help but now she needs help. Benjamin taught me about the word 'need'. I need food and water to live. I need clothes to keep warm when it's cold. I need a bed to sleep in. I need shoes to wear in the street but I don't want shoes. I don't like shoes. Now I need to find help for Rose.

I start to run. She is on the ground. She cannot walk. She cannot help. So I have to help. I run one way and then I turn around. There are trees and bush and rain and trees and bush and rain and there is brown and green and red and yellow and brown and green and red and yellow. Too much. It is too much. I want to lie on the floor, get the too much out. But there is only rain. I cannot lie on the floor in the rain. I run and I run. I have to run. I turn around. I need to run to help. Where is help? Rose pointed at the road. I need to run to the road for help.

I search and search and then the rain takes a breath before it coughs more water and I spot the road. I must run to the road. I must run to help. But the man. What if the man is on the road? I cannot see the man, the angry man. I sit on the ground and I put my hands over my ears, close my eyes. It is too much. I rock and I rock. The rain comes down on my head. The long coat smells funny. It touches my skin and it is like an electric current running along my arms. Benjamin said we need an electric current to make the robot work but I am not a robot and I don't like it. It hurts, it hurts. I stand up and take off the coat and then I am in the rain and the water is on me and inside me and I am wet, wet, but it is better than the electric coat. I look around me and I see all the trees and the rain and the bush and the grass and the plants and the mud and the stones and the sticks and the rocks and it is too much. A noise comes out of my mouth. It is loud and strong and it is the too much noise. I can't lie on the ground and bang my head. I can't make my bubble where it is quiet but I can make the sound.

The noise keeps coming and then I hear Benjamin's voice even though he is not here now. Benjamin is at school or at his house where he lives with his wife who is Tricia and his small brown dog who stands up and dances around when you give him a piece of chicken. Benjamin is not here but I hear his voice in my head above the too much sound. 'Hey, dude, now is not the time to have a moment. We have to finish this first. Sometimes you have to finish stuff and hang on until there's time. We need to finish up our work, okay? No time for a moment now.' Benjamin tells me about time. Sometimes, it's not the time for a moment. I can't have a moment when we are crossing the road or when I am at swimming lessons in the pool. It's not time for a moment then. 'You could get hurt, Theo. Finish crossing the road and then see how you feel.' I can't have a moment now. I need to get help. I close my mouth so the too much sound can't come out and I concentrate. Benjamin says I need to 'concentrate' when I feel like it's too much. 'Concentrate on your breathing, dude. Pretend you're blowing out candles. Your fingers are candles. Blow them out one by one. Each time you blow out a candle, push one finger down. Blow slowly.'

I open my mouth and I blow on my thumb. I blow slowly and then I push it down. Then I blow on the next finger and the next finger, and when I get to five fingers, the too much feeling has gone away, even though I cannot feel my breath on my fingers because of the rain.

I look around me and I see the black road waiting for me. I run towards the road. I have to finish what I need to do. I have to get to the road. I have to be help for Rose.

When I get to the road I trip over a stone and fall. I feel something inside me like anger. I know what anger looks like. In me it feels hot. But I can't stop and I can't have a moment. I need to get up and I need to find help.

'Run,' said Dad, 'get help.'

'Get help,' said Rose.

I see something on the road. I stop. Help. I see help. I think it's help. Is it? It's a man. I see a man. He is far away so I don't know if this is a man who can help or if he is the man that showed me angry, who shouted at Mum and Dad. I don't know if this is the wrong man. I don't want to run. I don't want to go to him. If this is the wrong man, he is not help. He is only angry and shouting, and he will not help. He will hurt. He will hurt me.

CHAPTER TWENTY-SEVEN

Rose

Rose doesn't even feel wet anymore. She doesn't feel cold either. Somehow, she feels warm and safe as the streams of water cascade down from the liquid grey sky. It feels like she has been here a long time, like she has been here forever, sitting under this tree with its rough, grey-white bark.

As she waits in the insistent rain, the past returns to her. The memories will no longer be contained and pushed away. She remembers feeling like she would be pregnant forever all those years ago. She could never have imagined how things would play out once Mary marched to his house, determined to confront him for what he had done to her sister. He opened the door, a grin on his face in expectation of a visiting neighbour, but he soon lost his smile when he saw Rose and Mary standing there.

'You invite us in,' said Mary, her arms crossed, her chin jutting forward, 'and we'll talk about what happened.'

'What are you talking about? What happened when?' he growled.

'Who's there, love?' said his wife, coming to the door. 'Oh, Mary, come in, hello Rose. It's a bit nippy to be out at this time of night. Nothing wrong, is it? You should be home in bed, Mary. Nancy's only a couple of months old – you must be exhausted.'

Lettie had gone grey in her thirties and she'd never coloured her hair. She was thin with a small, pinched face but she was kind to everyone despite her own private pain of childlessness. People whispered and felt sorry for her, married for so long without a child, but Lettie always had a smile for everyone.

Rose remembers the feeling of being in the house with him that night, of the way her skin prickled with fear and something else – disgust, she thought. He was a good-looking man but he wasn't a good man. His smile stopped at his mouth along with his sincerity. His words meant nothing. She had felt safe with him because of what he did for a job, because he was married, but he was in disguise as someone to be trusted. It was a clever disguise.

As Mary talked, everyone else remained silent; only the crackle of the fire and the snap of burning logs added to the conversation. Rose felt the small sitting room with its smart brown sofas fill up with disbelief. She could almost hear the whirring sadness of Lettie's thoughts as the truth spilled out.

Lettie listened, her arms folded across her chest, and every now and again she looked over at her husband, and Rose could see that she knew she was hearing the truth.

He was filled with rage and denial but Mary wouldn't let him get away with it.

'I don't care about that,' she told him. 'What's done is done and here's my sister with a baby on the way and I want to know what you're going to do about that. I'll not have her reputation tarnished in this town because of you.'

Rose felt she would die of shame.

'You wanted it all right, Rose,' he spat, his green eyes dark with menace. 'It was her, Lettie,' he said, turning to his helpless wife, 'her who led me on. I know I made a mistake but it was all her.'

'My sister wouldn't do that,' hissed Mary. 'You forced her! Now what are you going to do about it?'

'What do you want me to do about it?' he roared. 'Your sister is a lying slut.'

'Don't you call my sister names.' Mary was fiercely protective, the mother figure Rose needed.

'Don't you go accusing a man of the law of such a thing.' He thought being the town policeman gave him more rights than other people but Mary was never impressed by anything but kindness. Having Lionel as a brother had taught both sisters to understand that people were all dealing with their own pain.

She and Rose left then with nothing resolved and Rose's cheeks burning red with humiliation in the cold night air. She felt pity for Lettie. They had left her sobbing on her pretty sofa. No one wanted to hear such a thing about the man they loved.

She and Mary went home again, talked in whispers in the front room and tried to figure out what to do.

'There's a place in Sydney you can go – a home. You can have the baby there and then give it up for adoption.'

'But I'll be so far from you, Mary.' Rose heard the pleading in her voice, heard her own desperation not to be sent away from her beloved sister. It felt like a terrible punishment for something done to her, something she had not wanted.

'I'll come and visit, love, I will.'

'You won't, you know you won't! You have Bart to take care of and William and Nancy.'

'There's something else you could do,' her sister replied, glancing away. 'I had a friend from teacher's college and she… Well, it happens, doesn't it? There are people in the city who can get rid of a baby for you.'

'But that's illegal,' Rose whispered, utterly shocked that her sister should know about such things.

'It's up to you,' said Mary softly. 'But you know what will happen if you stay here and have a baby. This is a small town and people won't be kind. You'll always have me but that may not be enough when they sneer in the butchers and Elsie's shop.' She laid a gentle hand across Rose's clenched fist.

'I don't… It's too much to think about, Mary. I'll go now. I need some time,' said Rose, wrenching her hand away, wanting to be alone with the terrible truth of her situation.

'It's cold and dark. Stay here – don't go home.'

'No, I'm off home. I need the walk.'

'Don't leave now, Rose, it's late and it's dangerous.'

Rose turned to her sister, burning with anger. 'And what more could happen to me now, Mary? What more?'

She tramped home in the cold, her torch leading the way in the darkness as she ignored the pitter-patter of fox footsteps in the bush. She was filled up with fury at her own stupidity and she wished, more than anything, for her mother.

It rained that night as well. A light autumn shower that only began as she got back to her cabin.

Rose peers through the rain now, feeling warm in the wind and the cold despite how wet she is. She is alone but her memories have arrived to keep her company, and even if they cause pain, she feels the need, after so many years, to look at them again now.

The constant drumming sound the rain is making doesn't bother her anymore. She is enclosed in a bubble of sorts and she feels quite happy about it. She knows that her body is experiencing pain, in her ankle and her wrist and her side, but she is separated from it. It's there but she can manage. *I should get up*, she thinks. *I should get up and walk back to the cabin.* But she knows that her body is not willing to do that, a thought that she's at peace with.

Everything comes to an end, no matter how you think about it. Rose squints up at the sky as the water pushes her yellow hat more firmly onto her head. Perhaps this is her end and that's fine.

The wind whips up, strong enough to lift some sodden brown leaves by Rose's feet, shifting them along into a puddle.

It is possible that the rain is the last thing she will see, and she would have preferred it to be the sunshine. A blue sky on a cold autumn day is the most beautiful thing. She will miss that. She turns her head slightly and sees Lionel sitting next to her.

'Hello, Rose,' he says.

'Lionel, you can talk!' She smiles and she would like to reach out to him but she doesn't feel she can move.

'Here I can. I wanted to be with you, Rose. We both wanted to be with you.'

Rose moves a little and sees that Mary is here as well. 'It's fine, love,' her sister says. 'We're both here now and it's fine.'

Rose feels she has been given a gift, the gift of her brother and sister right next to her. She is filled with the warmth of their presence. 'I've missed you both so much. I'm glad to see you both and that's the truth. Are you happy up there? Are you both okay?'

'We're fine, Rose,' says Lionel, 'and it's beautiful here. You wouldn't believe how beautiful it is. It's everything Mum told us it would be.'

Rose thinks about how her mother described heaven to them when they were little. 'A garden, filled with every flower of every colour in the world. The sun is always shining and there is only happiness and peace.'

'And ice cream?' ten-year-old Rose asked. 'Will there be ice cream?'

'Absolutely,' her mother replied. 'There will be everything you want so there's never any need to fear it.'

'That sounds wonderful,' Rose says to Mary and Lionel now. 'I can't wait to join you.'

'Will you sing, Rose?' asks Lionel. 'Will you sing for us?'

'I'm a bit tired, Lionel, but I'll do my best.' She takes a deep breath, the pain in her side cutting through her, but she needs to sing for her brother. 'This little light of mine,' she begins, her voice weak and frail, 'I'm going to let it shine…' She closes her eyes and she feels Mary take one of her hands and Lionel take the other and she knows she's the happiest she's been in a long time.

She stops singing but she can still hear the beautiful hymn. It is all around her and she knows she is safe here with her brother and sister, and through the rain, in the distance, she can see a light coming closer.

This little light of mine,
I'm going to let it shine.
This little light of mine,
I'm going to let it shine.
This little light of mine,
I'm going to let it shine,
let it shine, let it shine, let it shine.

CHAPTER TWENTY-EIGHT

William

William stands in the pouring rain, fighting feelings of despair. Even though he is wearing an almost floor-length raincoat, he is completely drenched. His good leather hiking boots squelch and suck with every step and he can feel his wet socks rubbing against his ankles, forming blisters.

They have been looking for the child for two nights and two days and it has not stopped raining for even an hour. He risks a quick look at his watch, seeing that it's 4 p.m. What little light there was is nearly gone. How could the boy live through another night in this?

He has left the car on the road and gotten out to walk because he's sure he will see more that way.

'Time to build an ark,' he joked with Graham this morning as they got ready to leave to join the search party.

He's not sure how the child could have survived being out in the rain this long, although he is eleven so hopefully he's figured out how to find shelter and it's not like he'll go thirsty. 'Come on, old man,' he jollies himself, feeling his legs burn as he makes his way up the road, his head swivelling as he peers through the canvas of rain at the bush, hoping for a glimpse of blue.

William is often involved in searches for people missing in the Blue Mountains and he's never surprised by an early-morning or late-night phone call signalling someone is missing.

'I'm worried about Auntie Rose as well,' William told Graham this morning. 'I need to go and see her. I wish she wasn't so pig-headed about having a mobile phone. The landline is sure to be out of commission for even longer with this weather. It'll take them forever to fix it.' It had been William's plan to ask Sean, who as the highest-ranking police officer in town was coordinating the search, if he could walk in the direction of his aunt's cabin, but he had a feeling that whatever he asked Sean for, the man would deny him. They don't get along. In a way, William feels sorry for him right now. He's looking really rough, the poor bloke, and he doesn't seem to have slept since Theo went missing. His wife, Monica, is keeping busy providing tea and sandwiches to the searchers. The whole town is now involved.

Mount Watson is a peaceful town, only slightly bothered by tourists who swarm in during the school holidays, but to have a missing child and a violent incident in the town is almost too much for the police department to cope with. Constable Emmerson seems confused as to what to do as well, and William knows he is spending most of his time in the hospital, waiting for Theo's mother to speak and explain what happened.

They're also having a bit of trouble keeping the press in line. The journalists have been most intrusive and it doesn't feel like they care about finding the boy at all. They're just salivating for the story about what happened in that cabin. William looks left and, spotting something black, starts towards it but then sees the flash of wings and realises that it's only a bush turkey, probably seeking shelter as well.

He has met the couple from the cabin a few times in the supermarket and the pub. They're friendly enough. William cannot imagine what must have happened for it all to go so wrong. But then no one is ever sure what goes on behind closed doors and all that.

Stopping, William scans the area. The road is quiet so it's possible the searchers have been through here already today. There isn't even a press van around and they're all over the place with camera crews filming everything, plastic protecting their camera lenses. They're doing a good job of making sure that new searchers keep turning up so William supposes he should be grateful. He keeps hoping one of them will stumble across Rose's cabin, trying to get an interview, so at least he could see her on television. The thought of that makes him laugh as he imagines Rose swinging her rake at them.

Now William is only about a kilometre away from Rose's cottage and he can see that the road has been washed away so badly that he will have to take it slowly. There are gaping holes in the old asphalt, which has been unable to sustain the downpour. What look like potholes could actually be quite deep and he doesn't want to step in one and hurt himself.

He stops for a moment, allowing himself the fantasy of a hot shower and a fire and a very, very large glass of some of that expensive red wine he and Graham bought last time they went to the Hunter Valley.

Pulling his phone out of his pocket, he checks it quickly to see if there have been any messages but there's nothing. They haven't found the boy and William cannot help imagining how very scared he must be. He is lost and alone and probably cold and hungry. The poor child.

He looks down at his feet so that he can concentrate on where he's walking, feeling the rain change direction to almost sideways so that it lashes at his cheeks. He knows there are searchers in vehicles going up and down the road and he can't help wishing that he had stayed in his own car. But he knows he can see more on foot. He would have to walk along the dirt road to get to Rose anyway. Even a four-wheel drive would get stuck on the dirt road in weather like this. The wind gets stronger and he looks up at the tall gum trees, seeing them bending slightly.

Hearing an engine behind him, he turns to see it's a police cruiser. The *Bob the Builder* song everyone has been told to play on their phones blares out of the car speakers but the sound is warbled by the rain, the song almost unrecognisable. William lifts his hand and even though the car slows enough so that he can see it's Sean inside, it doesn't stop. As the policeman offers him a wave and drives on without stopping, William mutters, 'You're such a bastard.' He watches the car disappear over the hill. He thinks he's hated Sean since they were at primary school together. Sean grew quickly and was bigger than other children years ahead of him. He had a tendency towards nastiness, picking on smaller kids, even those older than him. Other students initially felt sorry for him. His mother died when he was only little and few could imagine what that would be like. But as Sean took his anger out on those around him, most grew wary of him. William was glad to go off to boarding school for high school. He still found himself dealing with bullies, especially when he didn't fit the norm, but he also found a good group of friends that he's still in contact with today.

He trudges on through the weather, looking left and right all the time.

'Hang in there, mate,' he says, hoping that his message will be carried on the wind to the lost little boy. They have to find him soon or he won't survive. They've never had to deal with a lost child for this many days. William can remember two or three times over his lifetime in Mount Watson when children went missing, and they were always found alive. The young girl who ran away from her parents' cabin was lost overnight but she was found sheltering in a small cave. Would Theo know to take shelter? He thinks about his uncle Lionel, whom he never got to meet. When William was born, Lionel was already in an institution, and he died when William was only five. William remembers his mother and Rose talking about their brother in hushed, sad tones. Only when he was an adult had William understood that Lionel's behaviours could be classified as autism. He shudders to think about the cruelty his uncle would have had to endure at the hands of those in an institution who didn't understand him. 'If you're watching, Uncle

Lionel,' he says, 'watch over this child. His name is Theo and he's like you and he needs some help.' He feels strangely better after he has said this but he's glad he's alone and there is no one else to hear him speaking to the spirit of his dead uncle.

He keeps walking, knowing that at least he will get a cup of tea from Rose and he can stand by her fire and dry off a little before he goes out again. He hates that his aunt won't live in town with him and Graham. She is so incredibly stubborn and for no reason that he can see. They have a garden she could work in and they have a big enough house so that she would have her own little space with a bathroom and kitchenette. Perhaps once he gets to the cabin, he can use this terrible rainstorm to convince her to come into town. He steps gingerly over a large tree branch that has come down in the wind. The noise of the pummelling rain is starting to drive him mad. It's so consistent.

Sighing, he looks up at the road again and nearly falls backwards, taking two slippery steps away from the apparition in front of him. When he regains his balance, his heart thumps in his chest as he stares at the person standing in the middle of the road. He can't see them very well because of the relentless rain but he can see it's a person in a blue jumper that hangs down over their hands, and tracksuit pants, with what looks like muddy bare feet. The skin of their face is almost pure white it's so pale, eyes staring ahead, unblinking despite the rain. William squints through the downfall, sure that he is imagining things. Four in the afternoon is not the right time for seeing ghosts.

The apparition doesn't move and neither does William. He tries to take some deep breaths and he blinks a few more times, hoping that whatever it is will disappear. But it doesn't move. 'I am not going mad,' he says.

'Hello,' he calls over the sound of the rain and then he resists the urge to turn and run when the figure starts to come towards him. 'Hello,' he calls again. 'Are you with the search party?'

The figure doesn't say anything but lifts its arms, and hands appear – small, smooth hands, the hands of a child. All of a sudden William realises he is looking into the glass-blue eyes of Theo Somerton.

'Theo!' he shouts in relief, wondering how the child has survived dressed the way he is. He's not wearing shoes, which William cannot believe. 'We've been looking for you,' he calls to the boy in the hope that he will call back before he remembers that Theo doesn't speak. He doesn't move either, just stares, his hands dancing in the rain.

He takes a deep breath and runs up the road towards the child, who is frozen in place. As he reaches him, he puts out his hand to grab his shoulder but the boy rears back and makes a screeching sound. William stops and remembers that he shouldn't try to touch Theo. He won't want to be touched. He shouldn't have invaded his space.

'Okay,' he says, raising his hands as if to demonstrate that he's not going to try and touch him again. 'Okay, I'm sorry, I'm sorry. I won't touch you, okay?' He shouts a little so he can be heard over the rain. The child is not shivering although he is soaked through. He stands, looking at William as though trying to work out whether he can trust him or not.

The child's eyes are wide and suspicious.

'See,' says William, pushing his hand into his pocket and taking out the chocolate Mars Bar they are all carrying because that is Theo's favourite chocolate. 'I have this for you. If you come with me, you can have it.'

The boy shakes his head and moves his hands again.

'Come on,' says William. He is trying not to shout but the impenetrable noise of the rain makes it impossible.

The child moves his hands again, drops them down by his side and then moves them again. The gestures he is making seem to be repeated and William finally realises he is trying to sign something.

He cannot believe he's been so stupid.

'You're trying to tell me something,' he says excitedly, 'but I don't understand. I don't know sign language.' He shakes his head so the boy understands.

Theo moves his hands again and William can see that it is probably the same word because the pattern is repeated.

'Should I do something?' asks William, frustration making him desperate. 'Do you need something? Do you need help?'

Theo jumps up and down, his hands flapping, and he nods his head.

'Help, you need help,' shouts William, triumphant in his understanding. 'I can help you. I can take you back to town, to your mum and dad. I can help.'

The boy shakes his head, looking almost angry.

'Help,' he signs again.

'I will help,' says William, but the boy stops signing, gesturing for William to come, and then he turns and takes off into the bush. William sees a small trail of blood coming from under one foot. The child is injured but he is moving quickly as though he can't feel it. William wonders again if he's actually following a ghost. *Stop being ridiculous*, he silently berates himself.

'Wait!' shouts William as he starts to run and twists his ankle, meaning he has to hop and run for a short distance until the ankle rights itself. The rain continues to come down as though it will never stop.

William has to keep looking down so he doesn't trip on the holes in the road and the debris from the trees that is strewn everywhere but he keeps glancing up, making sure he can still see the blue jumper the boy is wearing. The child moves quickly but he seems to understand that William is not as fast, and every now and again he stops and waits. William starts to feel a little light-headed. He is not as fit as he once was and the surreal nature of what is happening almost makes him laugh. If not for the clothes he was wearing, William would be certain that the boy wasn't real. His white-blonde hair is long and plastered to his head but his eyes are so bright that every time he looks at William, they seem to shine in the gloom of the afternoon.

When they have gone for what William estimates is only a few hundred metres, Theo suddenly veers off in another direction and William curses his unfit status. He wishes he had already called someone to say he'd found the child but he can't take the chance to stop and use his phone. He doesn't want to lose sight of him and have him disappear again.

He moves through the sodden bush after the boy, stepping in some slick mud puddles that come up over his ankles. He feels a twinge in his knees as they protest but he can't stop.

Finally, the boy stops near a giant Blue Mountains ash tree, its bark white, its outer layer stripped by the wind and the rain. William runs towards him, stopping as he gets closer. The wind finally dies down and the rain slows to a light shower, as if the sky is taking a breath. He stops walking when he sees a bundle of clothing under the tree but he speeds up when he recognises his aunt's floppy yellow rain hat. He can barely believe what he's seeing.

'What?' he says, wondering where the boy got the hat, but then the bundle moves a little and he realises it's Rose. He can't seem to catch his breath and his heart is racing, but ignoring his ankle and his painful knees, William jumps over some tree roots to get to his aunt. 'Auntie Rose,' he says, kneeling in the mud, 'Auntie Rose, are you okay? Oh, God.'

His aunt doesn't move or speak. 'Oh no, no, Auntie Rose!' he shouts and he takes her by her skinny shoulders, gently shaking her.

The rain stops completely and silence descends on the bush. 'Auntie Rose,' moans William. 'Oh, Rose.'

He closes his eyes as tears threaten and then he feels her move a little.

'Hush now, Lionel,' comes his aunt's voice, low and croaky. 'Calm down, love. I've had a fall and broken my ankle… and my… rib… but it's fine. You're with me and it's fine.'

Panic spreads through William. She is delirious. Something is very wrong.

William looks up at the boy, who is jumping up and down and flapping his arms, alarmed.

Pulling at Rose a little, William tries to get her to sit up but her face contorts and she lets out a groan of pain. He realises that he shouldn't lift her, not alone.

'Oh God, I don't know what to do,' he says. Next to him Theo continues to flap his arms.

William looks back at the road. He needs to get an ambulance up here but there's no way they can drive into the bush.

His aunt opens her eyes. 'William?' she says.

'Yes, Rose, it's me.' Relief washes through him with the returning rain. At least she knows him.

'Oh, William. I was with… Did you see Mary? Did you see Lionel?'

'No, Rose… I… Theo, he came and found me.'

Rose looks at the boy. Her voice is just a whisper as though it hurts her to speak. 'Well done, Theo,' she pants, 'you got help.'

The boy moves his hands, and Rose says, 'Yes. You're clever… you're… Oh, the pain… I don't think I can…' She closes her eyes and for a moment William is terrified, fearing that she has actually died. Holding his breath, he puts his hand against her chest and feels it move up and down, and he realises, with a rush of relief, that she's just passed out. Heavy rain rushes down from the sky again and William feels near to tears. He is usually calm in a crisis but, just for a moment, his thoughts are a chaotic whirl. He has no idea what to do.

'I need to call the police and an ambulance,' he says firmly, speaking to himself. Theo flaps his arms but says nothing.

Pulling his phone out of his pocket, he looks up Sean's number. Despite everything, he'll be the best person to call because he can coordinate everything. As he goes to press the number, Rose opens her eyes and grabs his arm tightly, her hand a claw.

'You keep him safe, keep the boy safe. Don't let...' But she closes her eyes again.

He turns to the boy and says, 'I don't think she's going to last much longer out in this weather, Theo. I have a car. I can get my car.' He keeps his sentences simple, making himself clear.

'You,' he points at Theo and then he holds up his hand, palm flat towards Theo, 'wait.'

Theo stops flapping and nods. He crouches down next to Rose.

William sighs with relief. The boy has understood him.

William's ankle protests as he stands up but he draws in a deep breath and starts running.

CHAPTER TWENTY-NINE

Theo

I wait in the falling rain. I am cold. Rose is still but I will wait. It was the right man on the road. He shouted, 'Hello,' and I knew it was not the angry man. He sounded different, and when he ran up to me, I could see he was a different man. He cannot understand my signs like Rose can understand my signs but he understood 'help'. He followed me to Rose and now he can help. I must wait until he comes with his car. Rose called him William. William is the right man to help. I will wait for William and his car.

I wrap my arms around my knees but I can't rock very well in the squishy mud with sharp stones inside it. Rain is in my ears and my eyes but my jumper is too wet to wipe away the rain. Rain is on my cheeks like tears. Rose has rain tears on her cheeks as well but she doesn't try to wipe them away. She is small and crumpled under the tree and her face is strange and grey. Rose is not feeling well. When I am not feeling well, Mum gives me soup and salty crackers. She gives me four salty crackers and a round bowl of chicken soup. I don't have any soup for Rose. I lean forward and I take my wet jumper and wipe the rain tears off her cheeks but they come back. The rain falls from the sky and the tears come back.

I put my arms around my knees and I wait for William to come back. Dad said he would come and find me. Mum said she would come and find me if I got lost. But they haven't come to find me. Maybe William will not come back and it will just be me and Rose with the rain tears on our cheeks.

CHAPTER THIRTY

William

William's knees protest at every rock and stick he runs over, sending twanging pain through his body. The rain pushes down on him, hindering his progress, but he finally makes it to the road, looking frantically up and down to see if another car will materialise. But it is only the empty road, covered in debris from the storm. No one is coming to help him. As he runs towards his car, he pulls his phone out of his pocket. He stops for a moment, checking his level of signal. There is nothing. He lifts the phone to the sky, turns it one way and another, but he cannot find a single bar of signal. It's just him and Theo and Rose.

He shoves the phone back into his pocket and keeps going, his heart thumping, his lungs burning and the ever-present rain smashing into his face.

When he feels as though he may be running forever, he finally spots his car and experiences an overwhelming feeling of love for the old Range Rover.

Inside he turns on the heat and he speeds off up the road, tires screeching, sending mud and sticks everywhere. When he gets to the closest point to where Rose and Theo are, he stops, leaves the keys in the car and dashes towards where he thinks they are.

The sight of his aunt's yellow rain hat through the water dripping onto his face makes him want to cry.

'Well done, Theo,' he says to the boy, who is crouched right next to his aunt, exactly where he left him as though he hasn't moved at all for the last fifteen minutes.

Leaning down, William picks up his aunt. 'I'm going to pick you up now, Auntie Rose, so I can get you to the road,' he says, but she doesn't respond. He thinks she may be unconscious now and he realises that as he lifts her, he may not be doing the best thing for her, but he needs to get her back to the road. *Mum? Uncle Lionel?* he thinks, turning his gaze to the sky. *If you're really here, give me a hand, would you? Help me save her. Help me save them both.*

He braces himself for her weight but he nearly reels backwards because she is so light. Looking at the boy, he sees he's still squatting in the mud, rocking slightly, his gaze distant and unfocused. He cannot leave him here.

Please, please let him follow me. Please. 'Come, Theo,' he says firmly, 'please follow me.'

The rain wears itself down to a drizzle again, which William knows will make it a little easier to get to the car.

Theo doesn't move.

William looks around for a moment, flustered and scared. How on earth will he get the boy to follow him to the road?

'Listen, do you want the chocolate I have in my pocket? Do you want the Mars Bar?' he asks loudly, feeling the need to penetrate the boy's odd stare. 'Do you want it, Theo? Do you want the chocolate?'

The child stops rocking, looking at him, and then slowly, as though he is testing the idea, he nods.

'Okay, then follow me. You have to follow me to the road so I can get Rose help. We have to go and get Rose help.' The boy stands up and makes the sign he first made when he saw William. 'Yes, that's right. We have to get help. Help is on the road. Come with me. Follow me.' He turns around and starts walking, his heart beating in his ear. He wants to cry with desperation. What if the boy doesn't follow him?

But as he walks, listening to his sucking footprints over the thick mud, his feet stumbling over obstacles, he can hear the

child's progress behind him. He's grateful that Rose is unconscious, knowing that if she were awake, she would be in a great
deal of pain. He doesn't want to lose her. It would be as bad as it
was five years ago when he lost his mother. He remembers how
his aunt had sat with his mother at the end and he had known
that even though he and Nancy were grieving, their grief was
nothing compared to Rose's grief. They had been closer than
most sisters are. William doesn't remember a day in his life as
a child that hadn't included Rose. She had held him as a baby
as much as his mother had and he had eaten dinner with her
every night of his life until he went away to boarding school.
His mother and Rose shopped together and cooked together
and visited friends together. When his mother lay dying, he
sat next to her and held her hand when Rose got up to use the
bathroom, and through parched lips that no amount of lip balm
could help, his mother whispered, 'You'll take care of my Rose,
won't you, William?'

'You know I will, Mum, of course I will,' he promised. And he
had. Graham had simply accepted that William's aunt was part
of their lives and they both made sure to check in every day with
her if they could. William lifts his leg high up to step over a tree
branch. *I won't let anything happen to her, Mum. I promise.*

It doesn't take long to get to the road, but by the time they are
there, William feels sick with the mental exhaustion of listening
for the boy and worrying about his aunt.

'In there, Theo,' he says, gesturing to the car with his head.
'Open the door for me.' As he speaks, he wonders exactly how
much the child understands, how much he is taking in, but Theo
quickly opens one of the back doors for him, holding it wide so
William can lay his aunt inside. The rain immediately dampens
the leather and splashes all over the windows.

'Now you, Theo,' he says, 'get in the front.' He tucks a blanket
he keeps in the car around his aunt.

Theo climbs in the front passenger seat and buckles his seatbelt. When all the doors are closed and William is inside, and they are all cocooned in the warm car, the noise of the rain muted, he drops his head onto the steering wheel. 'Thank you, God,' he whispers, 'thank you.'

He looks at Theo, who makes a sign that William doesn't understand, but he assumes the boy is asking for the promised chocolate. Pulling it out of his pocket, he holds it out to the boy, who looks at it but doesn't touch it. William puts the chocolate on the dashboard and concentrates on turning the car around. He hears the child pick it up and the wrapper opening. When he looks over to Theo, he is chewing a huge chunk of the sticky toffee and nougat chocolate. His cheek is bulging and William can see a little colour has returned to his pale face. He is so wet; his clothing is now a second skin, and his hands are blue around the fingertips.

'Rose is my auntie,' William says as he drives. 'She's my aunt. I'm so glad you found me to get help for her.' He feels like he may be talking to himself but he continues. 'Everyone has been looking for you, you know. Your sister came from Sydney to help look but she's at the hospital with your mother, waiting for her to tell everyone what's happened.' William stops speaking, aware that he doesn't know how this child will react to anything at all. He's not sure how much or little he should say. He's not sure if silence would be the better option.

'We'll go straight to the hospital,' says William, needing to keep talking. 'Your sister is there.'

The movement of the windscreen wipers is almost hypnotic and William realises he's exhausted. If he's this tired he cannot imagine how his aunt must be feel. He risks a quick glance at the back seat. Her eyes are closed and her breathing somewhat laboured.

As they make their way down the hill, William presses the screen on his dashboard, praying that his phone will have found a signal. Slowing a little and paying close attention to the road, he searches for Sean Peterson in his phone book. The sergeant should be the first to know. He will be able to call off the search.

'Peterson here,' says Sean, answering the phone immediately.

'Oh, Sean, look, it's William. I have him. I have the boy. He's been with Rose but she fell in the rain, she fell and she's not in a good way. I'm taking her to the hospital.'

'How's the boy?' asks Sean.

'A little shaken up,' replies William, 'but otherwise fine. I think he's been with Rose the last couple of days so at least he hasn't been in the rain. I mean that's what I assume.' He has no idea how his aunt and the boy found each other. The cabin where the family were staying and Rose's cabin are at least fifteen kilometres apart through the bush with no clear path. He has no idea how the child got there.

'I really need to speak to him before he sees his mother,' replies the sergeant. 'He may be able to explain what happened in the cabin.'

William looks over at the boy. He is shaking his head and his hands are moving again. Quick, strong movements repeated over and over.

'Did you hear me, William?' says Sean. 'Drop him here at the station. It's on the way to the hospital. I'll meet you out front.'

William slows down as they reach the town and he looks at the boy again. His hands are moving, he is shaking his head and he looks... terrified.

William has no idea why he is frightened but then Sean shouts, 'Can you hear me, William? Are you there?' as he assumes the line has gone dead. Theo's body startles and he shakes his head again. Theo is afraid of something. William needs to get him to his sister, to someone who understands him.

He is silent for a moment and then he takes a deep breath. 'I understand, Sean, I really do but we're going straight to the hospital. I need to get Rose some help and we can meet you there. I'm also sure that as a minor he can't really have a discussion with you without the presence of an adult, and since he communicates mostly with sign language, it would be better if his sister were there.'

'He can write. I'm sure he can write. And he understands. Don't take him to his sister. I need to speak to him first.'

'Sure,' says William, his tone friendly and easy as suspicion prickles along his spine.

He ends the call and even though he is concentrating on the road, he knows Theo's hands are moving frantically as he tries to explain something to William.

'Listen,' he says, 'I'll take you to your sister. I promise I'll only take you to your sister. But when we get to the hospital, you need to run with me. Run with me and we'll get to your sister. Okay?' He turns and looks at the little boy and slowly, his blue eyes round and fearful, Theo nods.

CHAPTER THIRTY-ONE

Theo

William is the right man. He is not the angry man. He is not the man who shouts, the man who scares me. He is the right man but I heard the wrong man. I heard him and I cannot go to him. He is the wrong man. I need Kaycee and Mum and Dad. I need my blue blanket and Benjamin and home. I cannot go to the wrong man.

CHAPTER THIRTY-TWO

William

They pull into the hospital car park at almost the same time Sean's car does.

'Shit,' mutters William. 'We're going to have to run, Theo,' he says. 'As soon as the car stops, jump out and come with me, run with me, okay?' he says and he sees the child nod. Theo will not find his sister or mother without help, William knows that. He's been to the hospital enough to know how to find the general ward. One of Theo's parents must be there, and if they make enough noise as they run, someone will hear them. He is somehow certain he has to get Theo to his sister before anything else happens.

From the back, Rose moans a little. 'Don't let Sean…' she says and then she falls silent again.

At the hospital entrance, William pulls the parking brake, turns off the engine and sees Sean pull up behind them.

'Now, Theo!' he yells. 'Run!'

He opens his door and Theo does the same. The rain is lighter now and William leaves his door open, knowing one of the nurses will come out to check what's happening. *Stay with her, Mum. Stay with her, Lionel.*

They get to the entrance and William grabs Theo's hand. 'Let's go now!' he calls out.

'Hey,' says Sean through the open window of his police cruiser.

The hospital doors slide open and a nurse comes running out. 'My aunt, my aunt, the car!' William shouts and then, 'Run, Theo,' and together they run.

CHAPTER THIRTY-THREE

Kaycee

Kaycee is resting her head on her mother's bed when she hears shouting. Her mother is deeply asleep. She hasn't eaten breakfast or lunch and the nurse who is taking care of her, Annie, is concerned. Kaycee has spent most of the day coaxing her mother to take small sips of apple juice.

At first, she assumes the shouting is for some kind of emergency but then she hears Sergeant Peterson calling out, 'Stop right now!'

She stands up and stretches before opening the door of her mother's hospital room and peering into the corridor. When she sees what's going on, she steps out, disbelief making her question what she's seeing.

Coming towards her down the corridor is an older man with grey hair and a determined expression. He is jogging along the corridor in a strange kind of limping run, and holding his hand is Theo. Theo never holds hands with anyone, never. Theo is dressed in his blue jumper and blue tracksuit pants but Kaycee can see they are soaking wet. He is also barefoot, his feet covered in mud, and she can see that as he runs, he's leaving a trail of water and blood.

Kaycee opens her mouth but before she can say anything Theo launches himself at her in a hug so tight and so strong that she is slammed up against the wall and the air is pushed out of her lungs. Her clothing is instantly soaked. Even through the jumper she is wearing she can feel that his hands are ice-cold.

'Oof,' she says, and she winds her arms around his shoulders and squeezes as tightly as she can.

'I said stop,' Sergeant Peterson says to the man who was running with Theo. 'Why didn't you stop them, Emmerson?' asks the sergeant. Constable Emmerson is watching Theo, his mouth open as though he cannot believe he is actually there in the flesh. Kaycee understands how he feels. She holds her brother tighter, making sure he's really here.

'Sorry, didn't hear you,' replies the man to the sergeant, and he shrugs his thin shoulders. He is nicely dressed in blue jeans, a dark green jumper and a long raincoat. His grey hair is stuck to his skull, rain dripping off his chin even as his cheeks flush with the effort of his run.

Kaycee looks from one man to the other. It seemed like the policeman was chasing the two of them down the corridor but she can't imagine why.

She holds Theo tightly and for the first time in her whole life, he rests his head against her chest. His skin is cold and her relief at him being safe fills her eyes with tears.

The sergeant puts his hand on Theo's shoulder. 'I need to speak to him right now. He needs to tell me what happened in that cabin.'

Theo shakes his body and makes a keening noise that Kaycee knows is usually a precursor to a meltdown. For some reason, her brother doesn't want this man near him and there is no way he'll go with him.

'I don't think…' she begins, looking down at Theo. He steps back a bit and moves his hands before holding on to her again. Kaycee thinks through what Theo has just signed to her. It doesn't make sense. 'Don't,' he has signed. 'Bad man. Hurt.' Theo seems confused, she thinks, and he may be after all that time in the elements, but something tells her to do as he says.

'Actually,' she says, her voice firm, 'I need to take Theo to see my mother first. And then he needs to get out of these clothes before he gets pneumonia and then he needs to get his feet seen to. You can see they're bleeding. Also, you can't speak to him without me.' She meets the sergeant's eyes and lifts her chin a little. She will not let this man speak to Theo without her. Kaycee has no idea what to make of her brother's message but she needs to protect him. Her mother is mute and traumatised. Her father is hovering between life and death after his surgery. There is no one to take care of Theo but Kaycee and she will do that with everything she has. A fierce feeling of love for her little brother who is still holding on tightly to her sweeps through her body. She will protect him no matter what.

The sergeant pales a little. 'Now listen to me, Kaycee, you can't—'

'Actually, I think she's right,' replies the other man. 'The boy needs to see his mother and you cannot speak to him without a parent or guardian present. I'm William by the way,' he says, turning to Kaycee. 'My aunt Rose is the one who found Theo. She was trying to take him back through the rain because she's off the grid, but she fell. Theo got her help. He's a brave boy.'

It's too much information for Kaycee to digest so she just nods her head and says, 'Thank you… I…'

'I know, a bit much to take in, but we'll speak later. Right now, I need to go and see how Rose is and you need to take Theo to his mother.' He turns and gives the sergeant a hard look before moving away towards the emergency department.

Kaycee lets go of Theo, peeling his arms off her body so she can look at his face. His skin is pale and his ice-blue eyes are filled with confusion. 'Mum,' she says. 'Mum's in here.'

He nods and she glances briefly at the sergeant, who is rubbing his short-bristled, brown and grey hair, his face haggard. Kaycee has no idea why she needs to be wary of him, just that she does. He should be delighted that Theo has been found but that doesn't seem to be the case.

She turns away with Theo, thinking that she can only deal with one thing at a time, and she pulls her brother into the hospital room with her, closing the door firmly behind her, leaving the two policemen outside. In the bed, her mother's eyes are wide, fear and joy and relief all over her face when she sees her son. She sits up, staring at him, and then she opens her mouth, but nothing comes out.

Theo stares back at his mother and then he lifts his hands, signing quickly. He is talking about 'the man' and 'help' and 'Rose'.

'Mum, he's back. You need to talk to him so that he calms down,' Kaycee says. She can see by how quickly Theo's hands are moving that he is growing more and more agitated.

Her mother lifts her hands and Kaycee is hopeful that at least she will sign to Theo. But her hands drift down onto the mattress again.

'Mum, please,' begs Kaycee. 'You have to say something. You have to talk to him.'

But her mother remains mute and still, her gaze fixed on her son.

CHAPTER THIRTY-FOUR

Theo

Mum, Mum, Mum in the bed. Mum has brown eyes and black hair and a small scar next to her eyebrow. Her skin is white, white and her mouth cannot find the words. Mum, Mum, Mum. I want Mum. I want Rice Krispies. I want home and blue blanket and the rocket ship on the ceiling. I want blue walls and soft grey carpet that my fingers can touch when I am sad. Mum is in the bed and her mouth is not moving. I don't know what her eyes are. Are they happy/sad/funny? The walls are white and the smell is sharp and high. There is rain outside. Soft rain. I am wet. There is brown mud on my feet. I want home. Mum opens her mouth. It looks like she has lost the words. I move my hands to sign, 'Mum. I ran. I ran to find help. I got help.' I tell her about Rose and about the man.

Mum lifts her hands up but she doesn't move them. They fall back onto the bed, heavy.

She opens her mouth again but no words come. I can feel the too much feeling coming. I tell her again about the man and help and Rose. But she just looks at me. I see her face, brown eyes, black hair, white skin, small scar, brown eyes, black hair, white skin, small scar. It is too much. I see tears in her eyes. Tears taste like salt. I get tears in my eyes when it is too much and I need to bang my head. Maybe it is too much for Mum because she has lost her words. Maybe she is like me. The words are stuck inside her like they are stuck inside me. But she needs to make the words come out because the man will hurt us. He will hurt me. He hurt dad with the big knife. She needs to make the words come out. Mum needs to sing 'This Little Light of Mine'. I need her to sing to me so that I know I am her light. I need her to sing now or the too much feeling will not go away. I sign that she must sing but she shakes her head. The words are trapped inside.

The door opens and the man comes in. The man who took the knife, the man who hurt Dad, the man I ran from.

'Listen here,' says the man who hurt Dad, 'you don't get to—'

Kaycee starts shouting at the man and the man goes away but the too much feeling is here now. The too much feeling gets bigger and bigger. It's everywhere inside me.

I want to lie down on the floor and bang my head but Mum needs to sing. I am her little light and I got help. I got help just like Dad told me to. I was help for Rose and for Mum and Dad. I got help. I am help.

'Sing, Mum,' I sign again and again and again. But her mouth won't let the words come out. It is too much. I was help but it is too much. I need to lie down on the floor and bang my head so I can make the too much feeling go away. I feel tears in my eyes. Not rain tears, salt tears. Tears taste like salt.

I was scared of the man. I was scared when he took the knife. I was scared when he hurt Dad, and now he is here and I cannot say the words and Mum cannot say the words and I'm scared all the words will disappear and then the man will hurt us all.

CHAPTER THIRTY-FIVE

Cecelia

He is soaking wet, shivering and beautiful. Relief runs through her veins. He is safe. Her little light is here. She watches his hands move as he tells her that he has been with a woman named Rose and explains that he got help. She wants to grab him and hold him to her, crush him in a hug and never let him go, but as his hands move, she sees him becoming more and more agitated. She reaches forward but he moves back. He doesn't want her to hug him, he wants her to speak.

He wants her to sing but she cannot even speak and she cannot think how to explain this to him. She has no idea what he saw at the cabin but she knows she is afraid for him.

The door opens and he comes in, right into the room, into the space where her children are, where her lost boy is found again, and terror prickles at her skin. His grin, his face, the smell. It is all overwhelming and she would like to shut him out, to make herself small, to not be here. She feels the tinted glass return. She cannot speak about what happened. The story must stay buried. He will hurt her children if she tells it. She knows he will hurt them. He hurt her and Nick and now he means to hurt them. Her hands raise themselves and then drift down again. Kaycee yells. She yells and Cecelia hears the strength in her daughter's voice, hears that Kaycee is holding it together when she feels she cannot.

He leaves and her breath rushes out of her in a relieved whoosh of air. She is alone with her two children and the fragments of what happened. Theo is heading for a meltdown. She can see it. She cannot think what to do. The knife and the blood, the iron-scented, deep-red blood that was all over her hands and her clothes, come back to her and she knows she must stay quiet to keep them all safe. That is the only thing she knows for certain.

CHAPTER THIRTY-SIX

Rose

Rose feels like she has emerged from a deep black hole. She has no idea what happened to her. She thinks she may have died and she is afraid to open her eyes. Keeping them closed, she tries to figure out what has happened. She was walking with Theo. She was walking and she tripped and she crawled to the tree and then Mary and Lionel were there. She remembers that. Mary and Lionel were there. Oh, it was wonderful to see them and to hear her dear brother speak. His voice was as she had always imagined it would be, soft and deep, making her face split into a smile. She feels the sorrow of missing them inside her. She hopes that if she opens her eyes, she will see them, but she is afraid that she won't. She is afraid that she is dead and Theo is out in the storm all alone. She was supposed to help him. He came to her for help and she has failed him. She tries to take a deep breath but the pain in her side stops her. It ricochets through her body and she realises that she must be alive. Only living can cause this much pain. The black hole claims her again.

She feels she is awake again, and she pays attention to what she can hear. She can hear the bustle going on around her and she can smell that terrible antiseptic scent she remembers from Mary's last time in the hospital. They are in a hospital. She is not dead. She is alive and consumed by pain. She still doesn't want to open her eyes. After the warmth and peace of being with Lionel and Mary, she's not sure she wants to be here, but here she is. How did she get here? William. He's a good one, that William. She remembers now. He carried her. Did he carry her? He must have. She doesn't remember walking. She doesn't think she was even capable of it.

Theo. She opens her eyes but the light above her burns down into her and she closes them again. *Please, Lord, let him be safe. William will have kept him safe.*

'You rest now, love,' she hears Mary say and she wants to tell her that she can't rest because she has to protect the boy. She has to protect Theo. Sadness fills her up at exactly who she has to protect Theo from, the man that Theo said hurt his father and mother and caused him to run.

Her mind drifts back in time, sixty-three years back, through the decades and the seasons, through the good days and the bad. She remembers her angry walk home the night she and Mary went to his house to confront him, to lay his crime bare before his wife. She remembers how she tossed and turned in bed, sleep an impossible task as she weighed her options and tried to decide what to do. The thought of letting someone take the baby from inside her was beyond horrifying but the thought of being a tainted woman in this small town for the rest of her life was almost worse.

At dawn she heard a kookaburra call, waking her up from a doze, and she got up, determined to make a decision that very day.

She had only just finished a strong cup of tea when there was a knock on the door. Rose hadn't expected Lettie, her eyes filled with something like hope. 'I've talked to him and I've made a decision.' She pushed her thin shoulders back and Rose understood that what had happened had given Lettie some power in her relationship with her overbearing husband.

'I don't want to discuss what happened,' she told Rose. 'I don't want to know what happened and I don't care.' Her chin wobbled a little as she said that, telling Rose that she cared very much indeed, but she wouldn't be the first woman in town to have her man go off with someone else. Men could be bastards with too much beer in them. 'He forced me,' Rose wanted to stamp and shout, but the baby inside her was draining her of any energy she might have had to fight things. There were women in town who got beaten every Saturday night, regular as clockwork, and women who had to live with husbands who went down to Sydney to visit women who accepted money for being with a man. Rose understood that now she had become just another one of those accepting women. Accepting and made powerless by a big man and the baby inside her.

'We'll take the baby once it comes,' said Lettie. 'I'll pretend it's mine. It will be our secret and no one will ever whisper a word, not one word.'

Rose stood in the open doorway, letting in the cold wind but not prepared to allow Lettie into her house.

'It would be a gift, Rose – not to him but to me. It would be a gift.'

Rose studied the small woman, whose pain was written in the lines across her face. She was a good person who had only ever wanted to be a wife and mother, and she had been cursed with a barren womb and a dreadful man by her side. Rose didn't understand how, but she felt a thickness of sorrow for Lettie. It took over the feeling of sorrow she had for herself. Lettie was as trapped as she was, maybe even more so.

Stepping back, Rose finally allowed Lettie inside. She put the kettle on to boil again and together they worked out what to do. Lettie's voice was halting at first, unsure, but as she talked Rose could see her eyes shine a little at the prospect of a child because any child was a blessing no matter how it came. And as she talked it did seem to become possible that the plan would work, until Rose thought about being in the house with him, with the man who had attacked her. What might he do now?

'I can't,' she said, shaking her head as the horror of having to live with him painted a dreadful picture in her mind. 'I just can't. He…'

'Listen,' said Lettie, sitting up straighter, laying her hand on Rose's arm. 'He won't come near you. I've made him promise. I've told him… I won't let him near you and he's agreed. He doesn't want a scandal. He doesn't want his wife to speak against him and I told him I would, I told him.'

'But what if he…' began Rose.

'He won't, Rose. I cannot tell you what goes on between a man and his wife but I can tell you this: he won't come near you, I promise.'

It was all agreed on, and when Rose arrived to stay at their house, Lettie moved into the little back room with her.

Rose could only relax when he was out of the house at work, but as Lettie had promised, he didn't even look in her direction if they found themselves in the same room. When he was out, she and Lettie got along fine, but she saw the woman's shoulders tense as the time drew nearer for him to walk through the door. She didn't like to think about what Lettie's marriage was like before she came. The worst place in the house was the bathroom because in there, Rose couldn't get away from the smell of him. The best place was the little bedroom she shared with Lettie that smelled only of the flowers she brought in for Rose once a week.

Sometimes Rose would be in her bedroom and she would hear them talking. They never argued but they never laughed together either. Rose had spent many nights in Mary and Bart's house and the sound of their laughter through the thin walls is something she has never forgotten. Lettie was not gifted the joy of a marriage like Mary had. Lettie spoke only of the baby to come, only of the things she would do when she was a mother and of the delight the child would bring her. Rose accepted Lettie's joy even though she could not feel it herself. She existed on edge for the months she lived with them, waiting for him to attack again, only relaxing once she and Lettie were together in the back bedroom if he was home. But the time passed as time does and the baby kicked and moved, determined to be allowed to exist.

When she got too big to go out, time began to drift and Rose thought the pregnancy would never end. The only highlight of her day was Mary popping in to bring her little baked treats filled with honey and chocolate.

Rose knows that the town whispered about what was going on. The story she, Mary and Lettie told the gossips in the butchers and at the store was that Rose was helping them because Lettie was pregnant and poorly. Once she started to show and it couldn't be hidden, Rose stopped leaving the house, and they stuffed a pillow under Lettie's dress so she could waddle around town, proudly showing off.

And then in the middle of one night, after she had lived with them for seven months, it was over in a burst of pain and blood.

Because of that, because that was the decision she made, now she is here in the hospital and a family is broken. Theo and his family are suffering because of her child, her only child, the child she gave away to the wrong man. She gave the baby to Lettie, not to Seamus with his constable badge and his evil hands. But the Lord had other ideas.

And now she has to protect Theo from her boy, from her very own child, from the son she left with a violent man. The boy she was forced to give up, the boy who had no choice but to grow up into someone capable of violence. He had no choice with a father like that.

She is aware that Theo could have the story wrong. Between his signing and writing and his understanding of a situation like that, it could all be muddled and Rose could have misunderstood as well. The trouble is she doesn't think that's the case. It makes perfect sense. The apple doesn't fall far from the tree. A violent man could only have raised a violent boy.

The black hole claims her again. All thought disappears.

When she is aware of being awake again, she knows that she's not dead and that she's in a hospital. *Nothing wrong with my brain, Mary – it's just the body that keeps letting me down.* She tries to shift a little to get more comfortable on the hard hospital bed, and as she moves, she realises that her ankle doesn't hurt nearly as much now and that her side is also suddenly not much of a problem. She tries to rotate the wrist she feels is broken but she can't really move it. It's being held stiffly by something. There is some pain but not as much as she thought there would be. She also feels that she is dry and warm.

She opens her eyes.

'Hello, Rose,' says a gentle voice from somewhere. 'You had me a bit worried about you. We've put you into a gown and given you some pain medication. You're going up for an X-ray in a minute and William has gone to get himself some dry clothes from home. He said to tell you he'd be back very soon.' It's a nurse with red-orange hair and wide blue eyes. Her words are slow and loud as though she thinks Rose may be deaf.

'Maisie Stewart,' says Rose and then she coughs. Her throat is dry.

'That's right,' says the nurse and she offers Rose a wide smile. Rose can see some relief in her eyes now. She has proved she hasn't gone doolally as Mary would say. Young people do seem to need you to keep proving that to them.

'I knew your grandmother,' says Rose.

'I know. I saw you at her funeral last year.'

'She was a good one, was Delia.'

Another smile from Maisie. Rose is proving herself very sane and present in the world despite the medication that she must be on. They must have given her a lot of stuff to stop the pain. Rose feels kind of floaty if she thinks about it.

'She was. Now is there anything I can get you?'

'The boy?' says Rose.

'William said to tell you that they got him to his sister and not to worry because she's as much of a tiger as you are. Not sure what that means but he seemed happy.'

'Happy, yes.' Rose smiles and she closes her eyes again.

The last couple of days flash through her mind, and as she drifts off to sleep, she offers up a prayer to the Lord and thanks to her sister for looking after the both of them. She is grateful Mary and Lionel are together and that they're waiting for her. She can look forward to death now the same way she would to a family reunion.

She wakes after a few minutes or hours; she has no idea but she is immediately agitated. She feels clearer and she knows that things are going to get very difficult if what Theo told her is the truth. She wishes it wasn't. But she's sure it is. From what she has read or at least understood, the little boy isn't likely to fake fear or point the finger at someone who doesn't deserve it. He probably wouldn't lie.

When the truth comes out the town will never be the same again, but secrets have a habit of revealing themselves. It doesn't matter how deep you bury them, how well you hide them; they are unearthed and found, and once they are, everything changes.

CHAPTER THIRTY-SEVEN
Kaycee

Kaycee watches Theo's distress mount as he tells his mother to sing and she keeps opening and closing her mouth, a suffocating fish out of water. Whatever happened in that cabin, it has changed her mother. She looks smaller and less formidable every day. Kaycee remembers a time when she thought her parents invincible. That feels like a very long time ago now.

'You need to wait,' she tells Theo, trying to get through to him before the meltdown begins, knowing that it is probably too late. 'Mum's throat is sore. You remember when you had a sore throat and it hurt here,' she touches her throat, hoping that he will understand. But in truth she can't understand why her mother still won't speak. It's been two days since that tourist found her in the cabin and the doctors have said that she is physically fine. Kaycee was sure that Theo being found would lead to loud rejoicing from her mother and yet she is just staring at her son, her hands limp.

'What is wrong with you?' says Kaycee, anger heating up her cheeks, unable to stop herself. 'They've found him and he's here. Speak to him. Can't you see how upset he is?'

Theo's hands dance through the air and then he starts flapping his hands and turning in a circle. Kaycee knows that they are not far from Theo lying on the floor and kicking and screaming a deep, strange, guttural sound that communicates how overwhelmed he is. She doesn't blame him. He's been missing for two days and two nights and who knows what happened to him in that time? How will she ever know for sure what he saw in that cabin? Did Theo watch their mother stab their father? It is ludicrous, just ludicrous.

He is soaking wet and his feet are filthy and likely to get infected but Kaycee knows that if she tries to touch her brother, he will explode in a fury of biting and kicking and screaming. He is too distressed to deal with it now.

'Theo, please,' she says as the door swings open and Dr Greenblatt and Sergeant Peterson come in. She folds her arms. She doesn't want the sergeant in here. There is something about him that bothers her. She doesn't particularly like Constable Emmerson either, who hovers and watches them all. She wishes they would all just give her family some time.

'Oh,' says the doctor as Theo begins to make a grunting sound.

'He's distressed that Mum won't sing to him,' Kaycee explains.

'Well, I need to speak to him now,' says the sergeant.

Kaycee covers her ears with her hands as Theo starts making the sound that she knows is the beginning of a meltdown. Her eyes are burning and she feels like she's been in this hospital room for her whole life instead of just a couple of days.

She looks at the sergeant as she removes her hands, gesturing to her brother. 'Obviously you can't interview him. Can you please just leave it now until he's calm and my mother is better?'

Theo stops turning in a circle and looks straight at Sergeant Peterson. His blue eyes widen, his face pales. He signs to his mother again, over and over, his hands frantic. And then he drops to the floor and the kicking and screaming begin.

'Just get out!' shouts Kaycee, needing to get her brother away from the aghast looks that both the doctor, who should know better, and the sergeant are giving Theo.

'Go, go, go!' shouts Kaycee, and they both leave the room. She catches a small smile on the sergeant's face but she has no idea what there is to smile about. She has never thought much about him but the more time she spends with him, the stranger he seems.

Watching her brother, she knows that there is nothing she can do now but wait it out. Sometimes her mother will crouch down next to him and just be in the space with him but she doesn't feel like that's what Theo wants now. He certainly doesn't want her. He wants his mother to stop lying in the bed as though she has lost the power to even react to what's going on; he wants his mother to sing. Kaycee feels like she's the one who's going insane. Her brother is kicking and screaming, her mother is staring down at her son as though she's never seen him before, and outside this room the weird policeman wants to somehow conduct an interview.

She observes her brother for five minutes, watching the time on her phone. The longest he has ever been like this is half an hour. It was over another child at school biting him. He couldn't take the invasion of his space. Kaycee was at school when it happened but she heard her mother talking to her father that night when she was supposed to be in bed. 'They called me to come in but there was nothing we could do. Eventually Benjamin started talking about calling an ambulance and getting him sedated. But I wouldn't let them. I told them to all leave the classroom and I sang to him for ten minutes and eventually he stopped.'

Kaycee opens her mouth to sing but she knows Theo won't even hear her – she cannot yell the words; it will have no meaning for him. She has no choice – she needs to wait this out.

At the ten-minute mark she starts biting her nails but finally, Theo's kicking slows down, the screaming fades and he lies still on the floor. His face is pushed into the cold grey tiled floor that is now stained with mud and Theo's blood. When he is very still, she knows that she can get closer to him.

Sitting down next to him, she wraps her arms around her knees. She wishes he could understand, that it were possible to just speak to him like any other eleven-year-old, but then she takes a deep breath and releases that desire. Theo is her brother and he is just fine the way he is. She can speak to him as she would to anyone else. How and what he understands is something she will never be quite sure of but no one can ever comprehend how someone else truly experiences the world, regardless of whether they are like Theo or like her.

'I know it's hard, Theo,' she says. 'I know something happened that was terrible and that it's all messed up in your head. I know you've been lost and without Mum or Dad or me for a few days. Everything is very strange and I know that. I know that you just want to shut out the whole world right now and I understand, I really do. But you have to keep it together for me, buddy. You seem scared of the policeman and I don't know why because you usually like police uniforms. Mum won't speak and I don't know how to make her, and I know that I'm so much older than you and you think I can handle the world better than you can but right now, buddy, I'm just not doing very well.' Kaycee gives in to the tears as she sits on the floor next to her silent brother, watched by her silent mother. She doesn't know how she's going to fix any of this. Her father might die, her mother is unreachable, her brother can't tell her what happened and she has no one to turn to who could possibly help.

She rocks herself back and forth, comforted by the motion in the same way that she knows Theo must be comforted by it. And then she starts to sing. Her voice is high, not as deep or as good as her mother's, but she sings so Theo can hear and understand that she is here for him because she *is* here for him. 'This little light of mine, I'm going to let it shine. This little light of mine, I'm going to let it shine. This little light of mine, I'm going to let it shine, let it shine, let it shine, let it shine.'

Her voice catches in her throat as she remembers her mother singing it to her when she was in hospital having her tonsils out. It has always been the comfort song of her family. When Theo has been really distressed, even her father will sing to him. As the words dance on her lips, she feels like her family, her life as she knew it, is over and nothing will ever be the same, and she cannot comprehend how this has happened.

She buries her head in her knees and lets her sorrow go. She's only nineteen. She's not ready to lose her mother and her father, even though she has been pushing them away for so long. She's not ready to grow up and take care of her brother. She needs her family, and as she sobs, she understands that all the drinking and all the partying that she has been doing is because of this one simple thing. She needs her family. And they need her. That has always been the truth. They need her now more than ever.

Next to her she feels Theo get up, and in an uncharacteristic gesture he rests his hand on her head for a moment. She is oddly comforted by the light touch, as though he is telling her that, against all possibility, it will be all right. She stops crying and rubs her hands across her cheek, sniffing and standing up. She goes into the bathroom to get a tissue and blow her nose, and when she comes out, she sees that Theo is sitting on her mother's bed. He is holding his knees and rocking, and her mother has also wrapped her arms around her knees. She is also rocking back and forth a little, as much as she can on the bed. Kaycee looks at her brother and she can see that he looks more like her mother than ever despite their different colouring. They have the same pale skin and the same heart-shaped faces and high cheekbones. Theo is tall but skinny and her mother is small and slim, and she can see that they have the same hands.

Kaycee breathes in the silence, relieved that the meltdown is over. She sits down in the chair next to the bed and sees that the lace on her sneaker is undone. She bends down to tie it and as she does, she hears the song filling the silence in the room. She doesn't look up, not wanting to stop her mother, not wanting her to be silenced by Kaycee's scrutiny. As she listens, she notes that Cecelia's voice is higher than usual, thinner and less in tune, which is odd.

She looks up at her mother but her mouth is closed. Kaycee turns to look at her brother, her hand goes over her mouth, keeping herself from making a sound. He is the one singing. Her non-verbal, autistic brother is rocking, his stare locked on his mother's face, and he is singing. His voice sounds like an out-of-tune instrument – long unused but capable of producing music anyway. She can see the concentration in his face, see that it is taking everything he has to produce words where there were no words before, and she knows instantly that this is Theo's sacrifice. From the look on her mother's face, she understands that this is beyond what Cecelia has ever expected. Theo has sacrificed his silent, safe space for words and noise in order to reach their mother.

Kaycee holds her breath, praying that no one comes in. Although she wishes at the same time that someone else was here to witness this miracle.

And as she watches, her mother joins Theo. Cecelia opens her mouth and finally, the words emerge from her.

'This little light of mine, I'm going to let it shine…'

She joins her son and together, for a minute, they sing the song they both love as Kaycee watches, her tears returning with her mother's voice.

CHAPTER THIRTY-EIGHT

Theo

It's Mum and she has lost her words. She has lost her words that she used to have. So many words. 'What do you want for breakfast, Theo?' 'How are you feeling, Theo?' 'How was school today?' 'Please eat your lunch.' 'Please brush your teeth.' 'It's time for bed now, Theo. Do you want me to read you a story? Shall I sing for you? You want to hear "This Little Light of Mine", don't you? That's my favourite song too – do you know why? Because you are the light in my life, you and your sister. And I want you both to shine. I know it's hard for you sometimes but I'm here and Dad's here and Kaycee too, and you're a light for all of us so we'll help you shine, my darling. We'll help you shine.'

But she can't get the words out anymore. The thing that happened took her words. The cabin, the man, the blood. 'Run, Theo,' said Dad. So, I ran and now Mum can't get the words out. I have to help her. Mum is my light. She sings for me and gives me food and tight hugs and she talks and talks and talks. How will she shine without her words? How will she sing? I look inside myself, inside Theo where the words are, and I close my eyes and I ask them to come. Mum has lost her words so I have to give her mine and the only words that I can give her are the ones that will help her shine. The words don't want to come out, the words are too hard, they will make too much noise, but I have to make them come. 'Try, dude,' Benjamin says when I can't do something.

'Just try, dude.' I can just try. I touch my hand to my throat like my speech therapist says to do. I feel the rumble coming from my stomach. I hear the words in my head. I open my mouth… I open my mouth and the words come, they just come. My voice is strange. My voice is loud and soft and up and down. My voice is light and heavy and too much and not enough. My voice is everything. But I need to give my voice to Mum. I sing and then Mum finds her voice as well and then we sing together because we are both the light for each other. We are the light. When Mum opens her mouth and the words come, I can see the light in her. 'This little light of mine,' we sing. 'I'm going to let it shine.' I smile and Mum smiles and together we sing and we let our lights shine.

CHAPTER THIRTY-NINE
Cecelia

His voice. Cecelia cannot imagine that there could be a more beautiful sound in the world. It is high and reedy because it's never been used this way before but it is more wonderful than she could have imagined. And as his words reach inside her, down into her heart, Cecelia finds herself responding, as though she has never been silent at all.

She listens to the slightly off-key melody they create together, and when he stops, she stops and everything she has been holding back, everything she has been hiding, comes rushing up. She places her hand on her chest, feeling a tingling pain where she knows the knife went into Nick. Nick, her husband and the man she will not let go of. The story is there now, clear and hideous. She knows what happened in the cabin. She turns to her daughter, to her fragile, beautiful daughter. 'I need to see Dad,' she says. 'Can you take me to Dad?'

CHAPTER FORTY

Tuesday

Rose

Rose opens her eyes and looks around the hospital room. William is sitting in a chair next to her bed and Graham is sitting in one by the window. They are both asleep, their bodies at unnatural angles, and she knows that they will both be stiff and sore when they wake up. They are no longer as young as they once were.

Through the window she can see the sky, the blue sky where an autumn sun rises to shine on the drenched earth. The three-day rainstorm is gone. Its memory will linger in the ravaged landscape for a while but eventually it will be forgotten along with other storms that blow in causing chaos and destruction and then disappear. But Rose will never forget because the storm brought Theo to her. Images rush at her. Theo and the rain and the walk and the fall and her collapse and the tree and Mary and Lionel sitting next to her, holding her hand. Had she been dying? Perhaps. Perhaps they were simply a hallucination. Perhaps they were sent by the Lord to get her to hang on. Whatever they were, she is here, alive in this bed, and she got her message across.

'Thank you, Lord,' she whispers.

'Rose,' says William, sitting up in his chair.

'You two shouldn't have stayed. I'm sure I would have been fine.'

'Where else would we have gone? We're family,' says Graham, rubbing his neck.

'Is my ankle broken?'

'Don't you remember the X-ray? The operation? They put a pin in to hold the bone. It will be a long recovery but you'll be fine. You also broke your wrist and you have a cracked rib.' William sounds a little agitated at all the things Rose cannot remember.

She wants to tell him she remembers the important things.

She lifts her arm where there is a heaviness she is not used to, sees the plaster keeping everything stiff.

'I don't remember... It's all a bit muddled, really. But it will come back. You're William and you're Graham and I was with Theo. Don't worry.'

'That's natural,' says William, relief in his voice. 'They'll release you in a few days, when they know you can get yourself moving. They want to send you to rehab but we think it would be better for you to come home with us. We'll get a nurse. We're getting your room ready.'

'I'll be—'

'I'm not even going to argue with you, Auntie Rose. You'll stay with us now. Mum would be horrified if I ever let you go back to that cabin again.'

'Humph,' says Rose. 'Could a body get a drink of water in this place?'

William laughs and stands up, giving her a plastic cup with a straw.

'How's the boy?' asks Rose when her lips and throat feel better.

'Well, now that's an interesting story. Yesterday while you were getting sorted, he talked. Well, not exactly talked.'

Rose nearly chokes on her water. 'Theo doesn't speak.'

'He does now,' says William, stretching backwards to produce a click from his back. 'He sang to his mother... What was the song again?'

'"This Little Light of Mine",' says Rose, and she cannot help her smile at their look of surprise. But really what else could it be? 'It's why he came to me for help, I'm sure. He heard me singing it.'

'Mum used to sing that all the time,' says William.

'We sang it to Lionel. He used to like it. It calmed him. I can't believe Theo sang. Has he said anything else? Has he told them what happened?'

'Not yet. But because he sang, his mother sang. I'm sure she'll explain what happened now.'

Rose nods, knowing what's coming to the man who is responsible, and she is surprised to find a little sadness in her heart for him.

'He's… he's mine, you know,' she says quietly.

'What?' asks William, and she sees a concerned look dart between the two men. She knows they think she must have finally gone completely doolally.

She sighs, not sure if she wants to make this confession now, if there is any need for it to be out in the world, but then she decides that she will not be here on this earth for much longer. Mary knew the truth but she's gone now, and once Rose is gone the secret that is her truth will be buried forever, and maybe if people had known about the father, they would have been wary of the son. It is her story so she should be the one to tell it. She knows that the shame she has carried with her for more than sixty years is not her shame, but rather that of the man who hurt her. In her day she could only view it as her fault. He told her so too. She shudders now as she remembers his words afterwards: 'You're nothing but a slut, Rose Wilson, and if you say one word, I'll tell everyone the truth about you. You're the one who lured me away from my wife with your pretty smiles and words and that dress – what kind of a woman wears a dress like that? It's your fault.'

'It's not my shame and not my fault,' she says now.

William takes her hand. 'What, Rose? What are you talking about?'

Rose feels the tears that she thought she had run out of long ago. She looks at her bedside table where there is a box of tissues, and without asking, William hands her one.

'It's okay, Auntie Rose, you can tell us.'

'We're listening, Rose,' says Graham.

'Sean,' she says.

'Sergeant Peterson? What's he got to do with you?' asks William.

The words are stones in her mouth and she knows the only way to say them is to simply spit them out. 'He's my son.'

'I don't get it. His father was Seamus Peterson.'

'I know who his father was,' says Rose, bitterness rising inside her. Seamus Peterson, who was once a young constable, then a gloating sergeant, and who is now long gone without having paid for his sins.

'But he was married to… um… wasn't her name Lettie? She died when Sean was very young.'

'I know that,' says Rose. 'I've not lost my mind. But some stories stay inside you for so long, it's hard to get them out when you need to.'

'Well, we're here and we're listening. You just take all the time you need.'

Rose gives his hand a squeeze. He's really such a good man. She's safe with him and with Graham, and she can tell the story now. It's the right time. 'When I was twenty-two…' Rose begins.

William and Graham listen, their mouths open in shock as the words tumble out of her, and finally Rose draws a deep breath and gestures to her nephew that she needs another sip of water. The story feels like it happened to someone else, it was so long ago now. Only the smallest slice of pain reminds her that it was done to her, to innocent Rose in her special yellow dress bought in Sydney. After it happened, she ran all the way back home but crept into the cabin quietly, even though she lived there alone, not wanting to take her humiliation back to Mary's home. In the bathroom she scrubbed at her skin with cold water. She balled up the dress and her torn underwear and stuffed them under the house to deal with the next day. She would never again wear the dress, where a spot of blood would always be, dark and sinister against the cheerful yellow of the dress. She buried it instead, knowing that she was burying who she had been along with it.

'You should have reported him,' says William now, rage making his voice high.

Rose is exhausted when her tale is done. She lets her head drop onto her pillow and closes her eyes. 'I should have kept the baby, raised him myself,' she whispers because her voice is tired.

The night he arrived, the night her body opened from the inside out and he slid into the world with his fists clenched and his mouth roaring, she heard Seamus and Lettie fighting for the first time. 'I want her out of my house. She's nothing but a slut! I don't want her around my son,' he raged.

'You leave her be, Seamus. She needs time to recover and she can feed the baby.'

'I don't want her touching my son!' Oh, he was so full of ownership. So proud of himself as though he had meant it to happen all along. Rose felt her hatred of him burning inside her. She wanted to take the baby and run but she couldn't care for a child. Not in this town, and there was nowhere else to go.

Rose hadn't imagined that anything could hurt worse than the pain of forcing a baby into the world but his words cut deep. She got up in the middle of the night, blood seeping between her legs, and she packed quietly. It was summer by then and the night air was warm as Rose crept out into it, breathing in the freedom of being alone and outside, of a body that held nothing but herself. She had missed the winter and spring, locked up inside waiting for the baby. She and Lettie had spent the nights playing card games and backgammon to while away the cold hours.

Lettie would have dinner with Seamus and then bring Rose's food to her room for her. Rose never left the room if Seamus was home unless she had to use the bathroom. Lettie took care to cook things that would tempt Rose to eat in the last month of her pregnancy. She made roast chicken and potatoes and chocolate cake for dessert.

'I'm getting too fat,' Rose told her.

'Rubbish, you're lovely. You should just rest and enjoy this time,' she said and she stared at Rose's ever-expanding stomach with envy.

'Why should I enjoy it?' Rose asked, resentful. 'It's not as if I'll have a baby afterwards and a husband to enjoy it with.'

Lettie sighed. 'I know, I'm sorry, Rose. I wish it was different. I wish I wasn't barren and he hadn't felt the need to go running to another woman. I wish I'd been enough for him and that he'd never had to go and find someone else.'

'Oh, Lettie,' said Rose, 'this is not about you. You can't help nature.'

'I don't like to think of you being sad after it's over, Rose. But you can visit. You can be part of his life and watch him grow.' Lettie always thought the baby was a boy.

'Seamus wouldn't like that.'

Lettie closed her eyes and gave her head a little shake. They were both trapped by the same man who had an important job and who felt the world owed him what he wanted.

'Maybe do something different,' Lettie said. 'Go to Sydney or something and live your life for a bit.'

Rose nodded but she knew she wouldn't. She hadn't seen Lionel for two years by then and she felt cut off from everything she had once been. Inside her the baby moved all night long and Rose tried to feel a little love for it, but the way it had come to be overshadowed everything. She knew that she could have found someone in Sydney to take away the child's life before it had begun to grow when she first found out, but she also knew that she couldn't go against everything she'd been taught by her mother and the priest. Every child was a gift and she knew that. This child would be a gift for Lettie and Seamus, even though that man deserved nothing. She knew that the moment the baby was born, she would go back to her small cabin and she would wrap herself up in nature and the peace it brought.

'We'll give you some money,' Lettie told her.

'I'm not selling my baby, Lettie; I'm giving it to you.'

'It's not for that, Rose. It's so you can have some time to recover. I've talked to Seamus and he knows to put some aside.'

Lettie pushed the money into Rose's hands the night the baby arrived. And Rose took it, knowing that she would need it. Her belly was still big and she knew her breasts would fill up with milk. She had imagined she would stay with Lettie and Seamus for at least a month afterwards. Instead, she found herself out in the street, just after the baby was born, her small suitcase and the fistful of money all she had to take with her.

She thought about going to Mary, whose house was only a few streets away, but quite suddenly she knew she needed to be alone. She walked from town to her cabin, in the dark, feeling her way with knowing feet. She was in terrible pain but she knew she would recover soon enough. She would have to bind her breasts to stop the milk but she didn't care. Each step she took away from town made her feel a little better. Made her feel a little better but also broke another tiny piece off her heart. The further she walked the further away she got from her boy, her own little boy. She had not wanted him, not at all. But when he'd finally emerged from her body into the world, Lettie had given him to her to hold while she cleaned up and Rose had peered down at his tiny face. She had lifted her hand to touch his small, perfect hand and he had grasped her finger and looked at her, the two of them acknowledging who they were to each other.

'I'm sorry about the way you were made,' she had whispered to him when Lettie left the room.

'I think you'll have a nice mother. She's very kind, and she likes to sing and cook. She makes a lovely roast dinner. I'm sorry that I can't love you, that I can't keep you. I'm sorry for all the things I did. But I'm doing what's best for you. Trust me on that,' she had told him, whispering the words into his small ear.

Lettie had whisked him away for a bath too quickly and then Rose had slept, and when she had woken up, she'd heard Seamus hiss the word 'slut' and she had known she couldn't stay in the house. He hadn't spoken to her while she was growing his child but she knew that he would start to look at her in a certain way again. No matter how strong Lettie thought she was, she had a baby to look after and she couldn't protect Rose as well.

So Rose made her lonely walk back to her cabin, leaving her baby behind because she had no choice. She knew that Mary had been by to give the little place a good clean once in a while. There was some tea in the cupboard but not much else. Rose lit the lamps and then looked at herself in the mirror, ignoring her aching body. Her blue eyes were glassy and her beautiful, thick brown hair was threaded with grey. She had no idea when that had happened; it seemed to have come overnight. She was only twenty-three but she knew that she looked like an old woman.

In the morning Mary arrived with groceries, more food than Rose could believe. 'You should have come to me. You need to be taken care of,' her sister scolded.

'I need to be alone now, Mary. Can you just let me be?' Rose replied and her sister held her tight in an understanding hug.

'I'll keep bringing food for a bit, until you're ready to go back to work,' Mary said as she went to leave, and then she stopped. 'He's beautiful, Rose. I stopped by to… Well, I thought you would be there obviously. Lettie showed me. She feels terrible, Rose, but she's… well, she's a mother now and she has to take care of him.'

'I know,' Rose choked because she had only needed to see him once to know that. His eyes were grey but she thought they would turn green like his father's. She would never look into his eyes again. She also understood that she would never be a mother – not to a child from her own body. She had mothered Lionel and she had given birth to this child but she would never merge the two with a child of her own.

What helped afterwards was food. Rose had always been slender but she took to eating like she was fattening herself up for slaughter. She baked sweet things and ate whole cakes by herself. The sweetness stopped her thinking about her boy, even though news reached her anyway. Mary would always update her.

'Lettie's walking up and down main street with him in a pram beaming at everyone. Seamus got so drunk at the pub that he fell asleep in the street. I saw him lying there, Rose, and I walked over, made like I was trying to help, but I gave him a kick. He didn't move, too drunk to feel anything.' Mary pursed her lips in disgust. 'He doesn't deserve his life, he really doesn't. But the baby is lovely. He's got his green eyes but your brown hair. He's sitting up in his pram now, smiling at everyone. He's a happy little chap. You made the right choice.'

'Enough, Mary,' Rose eventually said. 'I don't want to hear about him anymore. I go to work and I go home. I don't want to hear about him.'

'You could leave for a bit, maybe go to Sydney and find someone, start again,' Mary tried.

'I'm done, Mary. I just want to be left alone.'

It was so hard to watch him grow up. No matter how separate she kept herself from the town, there was no way she could avoid seeing him now and again. Before Lettie died, she remembered that everyone talked about what a beautiful child he was with a willing smile. Rose would glimpse them walking sometimes as she made her way to and from the haberdashery store and she could see him smiling and pointing at everything before he learned to speak, chatting away to his mum in baby language with a few words here and there as he got a bit bigger. Rose tried not to feel the pain of his growing up without her in her heart. She'd made the best decision; she knew she had. Lettie got some meat on her bones and she laughed more, joined the church committee and got involved in the life of the little town. But then Lettie got sick. The womb that had refused to bear her any children turned on her and filled up with tumours. In the end, she succumbed when the child was only two. Every day for months after Lettie's funeral, Rose woke up, her fists clenched from agitated sleep, and forced herself to resist the urge to go and claim the little boy as her own. When Seamus started taking him out of the house again, his smile had disappeared and he seemed to grow more sullen with each passing year as his father sank further into his bottle of whisky. He was a mean adolescent and eventually Seamus packed him off to a strict boarding school run by the Christian Brothers. Rose thought she would never see him again but he returned, still filled with anger and obviously, she now realises, violence. But he returned with a badge. The same disguise his father used. The very same.

'Seamus was a terrible man, terrible, and Sean must have suffered being raised by him,' says Rose to William now.

'I don't doubt that,' says William, 'he was a really nasty child. But, Auntie Rose, are you sure that he was involved in what happened at the cabin?'

'It's a bit difficult to work out how he could have been involved,' says Graham. 'I mean, he's a policeman.' Rose can hear the scepticism that Graham is trying to hide. She understands it but she knows the truth.

'Theo told me, and I believe him. Sean was involved. He never would have become a man who could hurt people if I'd raised him.'

'It was a different time,' says William. 'It would have been impossible to raise him by yourself. Oh, Rose, I am so sorry. It

wasn't your fault and it wasn't your shame. What a terrible thing.'
He pats her hands and Rose feels her body warm with relief and
love for the two men who have always been so kind to her. She
feels the story spread itself thin in the room, dissipate a little, let
go of its hold. She may have hidden from life but life has found
her. It has found her in the care she gets from William and Graham
and Nancy and when the Lord sent Theo to her so she could help.

'But what did he do?' asks William. 'What did Sean do?'

'I have some vague idea, but I'm not entirely sure. It's their
story to tell, Theo's and his mum and dad. I need to rest now,
boys, but will you tell me when I wake up? Will you tell me all of
it? And you need to make sure Sean doesn't go near him. I don't
know if his sister and mother will understand. So will you… will
you boys make sure?' she asks urgently. Rose is exhausted down
to her bones but she needs to make sure they understand even if
they are unsure that Sean was involved.

'We'll make sure, Rose,' says Graham. 'You rest and we'll make
sure.'

'We will,' says William, 'and we will tell you everything when
you wake up. All you need to know now is that everyone is safe
and that Theo's father is recovering. You rest now, Rose, rest and
recover.'

Rose feels her eyes closing; secrets are draining and heavy to
hold on to. It's a funny thing to only put down a burden you've
been carrying at eighty-five. But put it down she has, and after
sixty-three years, she feels as though she can finally, truly rest. What
the Lord has planned for her after this she cannot know, but right
now it's enough that she no longer has to carry the burden of her
past into whatever future she has left. It's enough.

CHAPTER FORTY-ONE

Kaycee

Kaycee hands Cecelia the sandwich she got her from the café, watching as she takes a bite.

'Thanks,' her mother says. 'I've never been a fan of hospital food.'

Theo is sitting on her bed, absorbed in a game on his iPad, retrieved from the cabin by Constable Emmerson along with some clothes. Since he sang with his mother he has said, 'Kaycee,' and, 'That man,' and, 'Dad said, "Run."' He said those three things before Kaycee left the hospital last night. She had wanted to touch his mouth while it moved as if to reassure herself that Theo was the one actually speaking. It was a surreal moment, something that she had never imagined would happen, and yet it had. His voice saying her name resounded in her head all night. His voice sounds like her own voice does. She knows it will deepen over time but right now they share the same tones.

'Has he said anything else this morning?' Kaycee asks and her mother shakes her head.

Theo has returned to the silence where he feels comfortable, and both Kaycee and her mother know that badgering him to speak will only keep him silent for longer. Kaycee had been so excited to hear his voice, she had thrown questions at him at first: 'Who am I, Theo? Who is this? What colour is the sky? When did you know you could speak? Say something else?' Her brother had simply stared at her, taking refuge back where he was safe.

'I just saw Dr Greenblatt,' says Kaycee. The doctor had placed a warm hand on Kaycee's arm as they passed each other in the hallway. 'I hope you got some sleep, Kaycee,' he said, his voice filled with concern.

'I did, thank you,' replied Kaycee, grateful that the doctor had sent her home last night. Jonah had been waiting for her in the motel room, clean and dressed after his day in the rain looking for Theo.

'I'm so glad he's safe,' he said, grabbing Kaycee and holding her. Kaycee wrapped her arms around him, feeling the fear of the last couple of days seep away.

'We still don't know what happened,' she said. 'My mum says she's only getting bits and pieces back. She can't remember it all yet. But she wants to see my dad. Dr Greenblatt said that they can speak in the morning.'

'Will Theo be able to help?' Jonah asked. 'He can sign.'

'He can,' agreed Kaycee, 'and the most wonderful thing happened.' She explained about Theo singing.

'Woah,' said Jonah. 'That's just amazing. So can he explain what happened?'

'He may not be able to. I don't know how much he saw and how much he understood of what he saw. He may not want to speak again either. It's all a bit up in the air.' Kaycee frowned as she thought about the idea of her brother talking. She wanted him to be able to explain what happened and at the same time she was scared of him explaining it. What if her mother hurt her father? What did Sergeant Peterson have to do with any of it? The anxiety of what had actually happened made her jittery for the rest of the night until she finally dropped into an exhausted sleep. This morning when she woke up, the churning anxiety was there to greet her.

Theo won't speak to Sergeant Peterson. He is terrified of the man and Kaycee knows there's a reason. She won't let him near her brother. She doesn't know how she will keep the sergeant away, only that she has to.

Her mother won't speak to Sergeant Peterson either.

'Dr Greenblatt told Sergeant Peterson that he can't interview you for a day or so,' she says to her mother now, 'and the psychiatrist agreed with him so we have a little time, but Mum, it's only a little time before you have to speak to him.'

Kaycee watches her mother take small bites of her sandwich and she bites down on all the questions she has running through her mind: *What happened? What happened to Dad? Why did Theo run? Why couldn't you speak? You have to explain.* She knows that she cannot simply fire questions at her mother. Memory is a delicate thing and the brain has a way of trying to protect itself from things it doesn't want to know.

'Hey, Theo,' says Kaycee, turning her attention to her brother. 'I brought you a Mars Bar.'

Her brother looks up at her and then back down at the game he is playing.

'He had three of them yesterday. And he's just had breakfast,' says her mother. 'He'll want it later.'

Kaycee is pleased to see Theo has had his feet bandaged and he is clean and warmly dressed. The cot where he spent the night is folded in the corner of her mother's room.

'Mum, can you explain what happened?' Kaycee asks tentatively. She is wary of sending her mother back into her own mute state.

Cecelia puts down the sandwich, making a face, and Kaycee can see that the food is suddenly unappetising.

'When can I see Dad?' her mother asks.

'He's still in critical condition. The doctor told me that the next twenty-four hours are the most important. They have him on strong medication but they aren't keeping him sedated. They want him to wake up.' Kaycee has still not been allowed to sit next to her father's bed.

'It was my fault,' says her mother as the door opens and Dr Greenblatt walks in without even a knock.

'Your husband is awake and responding well,' he says, smiling. 'We're going to remove the breathing tube now. The police have requested that you do not see him but I thought Kaycee might want to?' The doctor has the grace to look slightly ashamed of having to say this, dropping his head a little.

'But I…' begins her mother.

'It's fine,' says Kaycee. 'I'll go and see him. Mum, after that you're going to have to explain what you meant. I'm going to see Dad and then I'm coming back here and we're going to talk, okay?'

Her mother nods, tears falling off her chin. Kaycee wants to comfort her but she knows she has to see her father.

Following the doctor to the lift, they ride up to the second floor in slow silence. 'Would have been quicker to take the stairs,' mutters the doctor.

Kaycee nods. 'Why is it so slow?'

'It's older than you are,' he says with a sigh.

Her father is still in the critical care ward. His face is pale, his lips white and his blue eyes rimmed with red. His dark hair is plastered to his skull and Kaycee feels the urge to brush it off his face.

But he tries to smile when he sees her. There are two empty beds in the room, both surrounded by machines with screens and tubes coming out of them. Her father is the only patient, the only one hooked up to the heart monitor and attached to an IV pole with not one but two different tubes. The smell of antiseptic is stronger in the room than in the rest of the hospital and it finds its way into her throat, forcing her to cough.

'It may be difficult for him to speak,' says Dr Greenblatt. 'The breathing tube can aggravate the throat.'

'Can I touch him?' asks Kaycee. Her hands are already moving towards her father, who looks smaller in this bed. When she was six years old and tall for her age, he could still lift her into the air without any effort. He doesn't look capable of even lifting his hand now, and Kaycee shudders at how he has been damaged.

'You can give his hand a squeeze. The stab wound to his chest was very deep. He'll be fine but it will take time.'

Kaycee walks over to her father's bed and grabs his hand. She is beyond relieved when she squeezes his hand and he squeezes back. His hand is warm and dry.

'Mum?' he says, his voice a low rasp.

'She's fine. She's in a room downstairs.'

'Theo?' he asks, his eyes panicked.

'He's also fine. He ran off and went missing for a couple of days but they found him. He was with a lady… it's hard to explain.'

'Good boy,' says her father.

'Can you tell me what happened, Dad? I mean it's all so crazy. You nearly… nearly died and Mum hasn't explained and Theo… well, Theo…' Kaycee waves her hand because she cannot think how to explain that Theo can speak. Not now.

'It was my fault,' rasps her father and Kaycee feels her mouth drop open. She has no idea what to think. It cannot be everyone's fault. It cannot be no one's fault either – so whose fault is it?

CHAPTER FORTY-TWO

Theo

I find the wolf. I tame the wolf. He will come and live in my house. I am playing *Minecraft*.

'Theo,' says Mum. I don't want to look at her. I am not listening. I can't listen. I am building a new room in my house. I need to build it and then I will be safe.

'Theo, please, you have to look at me,' says Mum in a soft voice. 'Theo, Theo, put that down.' She sighs heavy breath into the air.

'Theo, you're going to have to tell Kaycee what happened, what you saw. I know you don't want to think about it. I know it was terrible but you have to tell her. I remember it but not... not everyone is going to believe me but they will believe you, Theo, because you saw what happened.'

I feel the word 'no' inside me. I don't want to think about the cabin. I can't. It's too much. I told Rose. Rose knows. I don't want to think about it again. The 'no' rises up into my throat. Before the singing I couldn't get the words out, they were stuck, but now the 'no' wants to come into the air. 'No,' I say. 'No,' I say again. 'No, no, no!' I am loud. My voice is loud. I didn't know my voice could be so loud and so strong.

'Okay, okay, shhh,' says Mum. 'Okay, you don't have to, darling, just play.'

I take my axe and chop down some trees for wood. I am building a new house. 'Chop, chop,' goes my axe and the 'no' falls down, down to my toes.

I am playing *Minecraft* and I can't think about the cabin again. I can't.

CHAPTER FORTY-THREE

Rose

The rain runs down her neck, chilling the skin it touches. It fills her eyes, obscuring her vison as she tries to see the boy. But he is gone. She has lost him. There is only the bush and the grey-brown trees with their long, tangled branches, their limbs drooping in the heavy rain. 'Where are you?' she shouts. She feels herself whirl in circles, faster and faster as she searches for him, her mouth open, the rain drowning out the words, 'I've lost him, I've lost him.'

Rose startles awake, her body rushing up from the dream. Theo found her but there was only one boy she lost. One boy who is now a man who has done something terrible.

She looks at the clock. She's only been asleep for an hour but she needs to know what's happened, what's been told and what's the truth.

A knock at the door makes her sit up in bed. She pulls the sheet up around her chest and says, 'Yes.'

Sean pushes open the door, his entrance forcing Rose to pull the sheet up further.

'I thought I'd check on you. How are you getting on?' His face is a mask of calm, the question friendly.

'I'm… fine,' says Rose, wishing with everything she has that William would return from wherever he's gone.

'I wanted to ask you a few questions about Theo. I know that he can't speak but I thought he might have somehow, I don't know… told you something? You know about what his mother did in that cabin.'

If this were last week, Rose would have smiled kindly. If this were last week, she would have answered his question or at least attempted to. She has always found it strange to be in his presence, to know what he does not and to feel the slight pull towards him, even as she has become aware over the years that he has not grown into a nice man.

But she knows too much now and it saddens her. His calm demeanour and his uniform are concealing the damage that was done to him as a child and the damage he has now inflicted on someone else. She has no idea what actually happened but she knows that she needs to be careful.

'Like you said,' she says slowly, 'he doesn't speak.'

'But he can write – maybe he wrote something.'

'No,' she replies a little too quickly and his green eyes narrow, suspicion flaring.

'You wouldn't be lying to me, would you, Rose? I mean it's not like there's any reason to lie to a policeman, is there? I need to find out what happened in that cabin. If you can help me in any way, you should.'

'I don't know anything,' says Rose, and she is aware of how old she is, how weak she feels.

Sean steps closer to her bed, so close that she can smell something chemical on his face – aftershave, maybe. He has the same face shape as his father, the same colour eyes he did. Now that his hair has turned grey, there is little in his looks to link him to Rose and yet she has to curl her hands tightly in the sheet she is holding to prevent herself from touching his arm.

He smiles slowly. 'I've always looked out for you, you know. It's dangerous for a woman your age to live alone, so I occasionally drive out to your cabin, just to check.'

'I've never seen you.'

'Well, that doesn't mean I haven't been there.'

Rose pulls the sheet up to her chin. 'I'm tired,' she says. 'I need to rest.'

'Listen, Rose…' he begins and she feels the liquid warmth of relief run through her as the door swings open and William is there.

He doesn't give Sean a chance to say anything more.

'My aunt needs to rest. I asked you to give her a few days. The doctor asked you to leave everyone alone for a bit. Please go.'

'I'm going, I'm going,' says Sean, raising his hands.

'He knows something is up,' says Rose when he is gone.

'Hmmm,' says William, 'I didn't know he was back in the hospital. I really hope he stays away from that family.'

'Do you know anything else, William? Has Theo's mother explained?'

'No, the story hasn't come out yet but it will, Auntie Rose. You rest now. Everything will come out soon enough.'

CHAPTER FORTY-FOUR

Cecelia

Cecelia watches her son sitting in the corner of the room, lining up a large collection of straws. Annie brought in a whole lot of them for him. He sits calmly, almost dreamily, lining them up, making them neat, spacing them equally. He lost interest in the game on his iPad.

She wonders, as she has done for just about every day of his life, what he is thinking, what he is feeling. The last few days must have been hideously traumatic for him, and yet to look at him now, showered and dressed in some clothes Constable Emmerson retrieved from the cabin, you would not be able to believe what happened to him. She has no idea how to help him either. It's not like he can go to counselling and explain his feelings. He has not spoken a word since he sang except for 'Mum', 'Kaycee' and 'Dad said, "Run",' and then, finally, 'no'.

Cecelia holds on to the joy of his voice, the joy of the sounds she never thought he would make. She would like to ask him a thousand questions but she is painfully aware that he will not answer any of them. He sang the song because it is part of him, because he has heard it every day of his life. He may have been trying to calm her, to make her feel better because that's the way she uses the song for him sometimes.

She wants to see Nick. She would like to leap out of this bed and run around the hospital until she finds him but she has to keep Theo with her, has to keep him away from Sean Peterson. She keeps glancing at the door, fearful that it will open and he will be standing there. The thought of his smug face, of his leering smile, is disgusting. Dr Greenblatt has assured her he will keep everyone away for another day or two. Constable Emmerson is hovering around outside her room, unwilling to move. She is still a suspect after all.

She has no idea how she's going to explain what happened. Does Nick remember? Does he remember it all? And if he doesn't remember, will Sean Peterson convince everyone she is lying? And then what will happen? What will happen to Theo if she is accused of hurting Nick? Her whole family will fall apart. She needs to talk about what happened but it needs to be at the right time. Mostly she needs to make sure her children are safe and they have a family to come home to.

She wishes for a moment that she had not remembered because it sits inside her now, a heavy sick feeling of shame and guilt. If she goes over it in her head, she still cannot work out why, after seven years of friendship, ever since they first vacationed at the cabins, Sean thought that she was interested in him in a different way. Did she signal it to him? Maybe she did. She had drunk wine with him, laughed with him. Maybe she had even touched his hand. But did that mean he was entitled to touch her? Why would he think that? Why would any man ever think that?

She had not planned on meeting him at the pub, it was an accident. But she had enjoyed talking to him. On the first morning at the cabin, she had understood that the holiday would have none of the magical healing properties she always hoped for. She and Nick would not return home closer and more understanding of each other. Now she knows that he only came because he wanted to give her the divorce papers.

She and Nick argued all the way from Sydney. He had complained about the traffic leaving the city and worried aloud about his patients.

'Can't you just switch off for a few days? This is the one time we get away as a family.'

'We're together as a family every night,' he said, his concentration on the road as he sped up to overtake a truck, forcing her to grab her door handle.

'Every night? That's a joke. You're never home,' she said bitterly as he slowed down. She looked ahead of her, not wanting to see his face.

'When I'm home you ignore me,' he muttered, a repeated grievance, a child's complaint, and Nick was not a child.

She turned to look at him, furious at having to say the same thing again. 'I have Theo to take care of. Why can't you help with that when you're home?' She could have had the conversation, the argument, with herself. She knew what was coming.

'I help as much as you will let me and Theo doesn't even need as much care anymore. You hover over him. You never leave him alone for even a minute and he is fine to sit and play on his iPad sometimes. You could take twenty minutes to have dinner with me.' He didn't raise his voice, but there was irritation and bitterness in his words.

'Any progress Theo has made is because of the work I do with him all day every day when he's not at school.'

'I'm not saying that you haven't done wonders with him.' He sighed and she could hear something worn down, something defeated in his voice. 'I'm saying he's doing better now and we could have some time together when I get home.'

'He doesn't speak yet.'

'But he signs and he writes and he communicates, Cecelia. You're just worried that you'll have nothing to do with yourself.' He was angry again, accusatory again, his voice rising. Their marriage issues were all her fault. She hated it when he started analysing how she felt about her own life. He never asked her; he assumed and was full of judgement.

Cecelia felt a burning rage run through her body when he said that. She feels it now as she thinks about it but she feels it because it's true. When Theo was diagnosed, she was determined to be the best possible mother she could be to an autistic child. There was not a book, an article, a therapy or a person she hadn't read, tried or spoken to. But he is functioning now – more than functioning; he is smart and he can communicate and he is reading and writing far above his grade level. His lack of speech is more his choice, the therapists think, than because he doesn't understand how to speak. But Cecelia has no idea what to do with her life now. What should she do now?

'Quiet,' Cecelia hissed in the car, not wanting him to disturb Theo, who was calmly playing a game in the back seat with his headphones on.

They were both still simmering in their anger as they moved around the cabin, putting things in place.

The argument simply resumed the next morning and then Nick took Theo fishing and she went to get some groceries and she saw the pub and thought, *Why not?*

She anticipated a quiet drink, not a drink with Sean but it was nice to see him nonetheless.

'How are you, Cecelia?' he asked over their second glass of wine and he touched her hand, just lightly. It wasn't the question because it's a question people get asked every day; it was the way he asked it. She felt that he wasn't just making a polite enquiry, wasn't just making conversation, but that he genuinely wanted to know how she was, how she, Cecelia, actually was. And it had been a very long time since anyone had wanted to know that. People wanted to know how Theo and Kaycee and Nick were, how she was going with Theo's therapies, how she was managing to make her life work. But no one ever wanted to know how she actually was, no one that she wasn't paying like she was paying the therapist she saw once a month simply to vent.

She knows now that what she felt as she looked at Sean that afternoon was gratitude and maybe, no definitely, a flicker of attraction. Was it attraction or was it just that someone, anyone, had actually asked about her?

'I'm…' she said, tears filling her eyes that she brushed away quickly, embarrassed to be crying in a public place.

'Oh, sweetheart,' he said. It wasn't an unusual endearment – he often called her sweetheart; he called a lot of women sweetheart.

She returned to the cabin feeling a little lighter, a little better.

'I may have to go back to work,' Nick said as she walked in.

'You're joking,' she whispered, keeping her voice down because Theo was in his room only a few feet away from them and she wanted to scream and shout.

'If I have to go, I have to go.' His phone was clutched in his hand and he waved it at her as if to indicate he had no choice. The phone was in charge of their lives.

'Fine, do whatever you want. You will anyway.' She didn't want to be in the cabin without him but she was tired of trying to keep Nick where he didn't want to be. Her wine-induced good mood evaporated.

Nick's jaw tensed and she saw him biting back his words. 'I'm taking a walk now while I wait for an update, but when I get back, we are going to talk. I can't do this anymore.'

She thinks now about the divorce papers in the bottom of his suitcase. Was he planning how to give them to her on his walk? Was he practising the words to tell her it was officially over?

'Will I get you back, Nick?' she whispers and Theo turns to look at her before returning to his straws. There are four colours – red, blue, yellow and green – and he arranges them in order. Cecelia understands why it would be comforting as she watches his hands move.

When the door to her room swings open, she jumps a little. Sean is waiting to speak to her, she knows he is. He has threatened her and Theo but they should be safe here in the hospital. Surely, they should be safe.

It's not Sean but Kaycee. Her shoulders slump with relief.

'Dad says he won't talk about what happened until you're with him,' she says. 'Dr Greenblatt says it's okay. I have a wheelchair.'

'I can walk,' says Cecelia, sliding her legs out of bed and grabbing a robe Constable Emmerson brought her when he got some things for Theo to wear.

'Come, Theo,' she says. 'We're going to see Dad.' She anticipates resistance from him because he hates to be disturbed but he gathers the straws in his hand and stands up.

'Dad,' he signs and she nods.

There is a flutter of fear in her belly at the thought of seeing Nick in a hospital bed, at the idea of her strong husband hooked up to machines. *He's recovering well. He's recovering well.* She repeats the words the doctor has said in her mind, reassuring herself that he will get better.

Now she needs to see him, to touch him, to talk to him so that they can tell the story and then, hopefully, her whole family will be allowed to go home and recover well.

CHAPTER FORTY-FIVE

Kaycee

Her mother sits down in a chair next to her father's bed and Kaycee holds her breath. What happened in the cabin is her mother's fault. What happened in the cabin is her father's fault. Whose fault is it?

Kaycee turns to look at Constable Emmerson, who insisted he accompany them.

'We wanted to interview your parents separately,' he told her when she emerged from her mother's room with her mum and Theo.

'Where's Sergeant Peterson?' she asked, worried that the man would appear and stop them all. Theo is afraid of him. There must be a reason for that.

'There was a car accident in town he had to go and look into. He doesn't want your parents to speak to each other until they've been interviewed separately. I think he was going to speak to Rose first but he should be here soon.'

Kaycee examined the young constable and decided to take the chance that his general inexperience and the kindness he had shown her family might work in her favour.

'Please, Constable. It will help my brother. It will help us all. My mum needs to see my dad. We all do. I'm asking you to let us be together as a family, even for a few minutes.' She tilted her head and allowed him to see her eyes shining with unshed tears. She wiped her hand across her cheek for effect, hoping that he would believe her. 'You can come with if you want.' She bit down on her lip as she said the words, worried that she should not have made the offer, but surely it was better for the constable to be there?

She glanced at her mother, who gave her a little nod, which Kaycee found reassuring. If her mother had hurt her father, she wouldn't want the policeman there.

Now he is standing a little apart from them, his mobile phone in his hand as he records this meeting.

Kaycee waits for one of her parents to say something, a small part of her expecting another argument to sizzle into the air despite everything that's happened.

Her mother leans forward and grabs her father's hand. 'I thought I'd lost you, my love,' she whispers.

'You could never lose me,' he says, his fingers curling around her mother's hand, and Kaycee understands they are not just talking about his surgery. She smiles and feels herself flush at the sight of her parents holding hands and at the way they are looking at each other, giving her a sudden insight into how they must have been before marriage and children and the world wore them down. She has a feeling of watching something private and personal, and were it not for the circumstances, she would take her brother away so they could be alone. They are talking about their lives, about their marriage – not just the last three days. They are talking about who they are to each other.

Theo is on the floor, arranging the straws he has brought with him, and she goes and sits down next to him, waiting patiently for him to let her in on the game and for her parents to tell their story.

'I shouldn't have had a drink with him,' her mother says.

'I shouldn't have left you,' her father replied.

Kaycee looks up at her parents. 'You need to tell us what happened, Mum.'

CHAPTER FORTY-SIX
Cecelia

The words come slowly. Cecelia feels her cheeks burn with shame that such a thing could have happened to her, that she should have allowed such a thing to happen.

She was surprised when he showed up at the cabin that afternoon. Nick had stormed off and Cecelia was pretty sure they would never come back to the cabin again. It was no longer a peaceful, happy place, just a place where she and Nick were together more so they could fight more.

Sean's timing was strange since they had only just seen each other in the pub, little more than an hour before. Now she thinks that it's possible he had been watching the cabin, waiting for his moment.

'I thought we could pick up where we left off,' he said.

'Oh,' she replied, not understanding. They hadn't left off anywhere. They had finished their drinks and said goodbye. 'I'm fine,' she said, forcing a smile. 'It was just a difficult morning and…' She didn't want him there, didn't want anyone there. She wanted time to herself to work out what she and her husband were going to do. There was something about the way Nick told her they were going to talk that worried her. It felt as though he had come to some conclusion without her. She didn't want him to return from his walk and for them to just resume fighting. They needed a better way forward.

'Come on, Cecelia,' Sean said, 'I know that's not the case. I see the way he treats you. I see that he just doesn't get what you're going through.' His eyes were wide to show his concern but his voice was low, almost seductive. Cecelia felt a tingling of worry. He was behaving strangely.

'Oh, Sean, it's just… you know, marriage.' She waved her hands in the air, hoping that it would end the conversation. He was married after all. She knew that the concern she was feeling was misplaced – he was married. She'd had dinner with him and his wife – a pretty woman, slight with blonde hair. She knew he was just being friendly. But he didn't say goodbye and leave. He stood there, looking at her. 'I really should get dinner on,' she said, needing him out of the cabin.

'Where's Theo?' he asked.

'In his room, headphones on, not interested in anything except the game he's playing.'

'Good,' he said, 'good.' Cecelia nodded as though she agreed, but she took a small step back, away from him. She knows now that instinct was telling her she needed to be further away from him. 'I should—' she began. But she didn't have time to complete her sentence because he stepped forward, right up to her and placed his hands on her cheeks, drawing her to him and pushing himself against her lips.

Cecelia stops talking and looks at her daughter, who is staring up at her, horror etched on her face. Theo is playing with the straws and she hopes he is not really listening, but even if he is, it wouldn't matter. He saw it all. This thought turns her stomach. Her little boy, her angel, her light – how awful for him to have seen what happened.

From the moment Sean's lips met hers, it felt wrong, awful and the slight attraction she had felt over some wine seemed utterly ridiculous. His aftershave was overpowering this close and his skin was scratchy where he had missed a patch of hair when he was shaving. She pulled back immediately. 'Sean, what are you—'

'Come on, Cecelia, I'll bet it's been a while. He barely even looks at you. Theo's in his room, Nick's not here.'

'Look, I'm sorry if I gave you the wrong impression, Sean. Today was just hard and you were kind and...' She apologised and explained, hoping to keep herself safe. It's what women did, what women do.

He grabbed her arm, his fingers digging into the muscle, and she felt a jolt of real fear.

'Sean, what are you doing?' Her voice was suddenly high with fright.

'You're all alike, you know that?' he said, baring his teeth as though he wanted to tear into her skin. 'You want our attention and then you don't want our attention. It's never simple with you women.'

'Look,' she replied, trying to shake his hand off her arm, but he was holding on too tightly. 'Nick will be back soon. You need to just leave. Just leave and we can pretend this never happened.' *This can't be happening*, she thought.

'I don't want to do that, sweetheart.' He smiled unnervingly. 'You've been flirting with me for years. Every time you come here you give me those little looks, those secret smiles. I know you want me. You can drop the coy act.'

Cecelia bristled with anger. 'Just let go of me,' she said firmly. She had to protect herself. How dare he think he could do this?

'No, I know what you want.' He pushed her towards the couch and then shoved her backwards onto it, pulling at her clothing. Cecelia couldn't actually believe that he was doing what he was doing. It was completely surreal.

'Get off me,' she hissed as he pushed his body onto hers, his hands going everywhere and a ragged fingernail scraping her skin.

She didn't want Theo to hear, couldn't risk him coming out of his room. She had no idea how Sean would react to her son. She was conscious that he was in his uniform, that he had a gun on his side. She shoved against him.

'Get off me, get off me,' she said, her voice strangled, her heart racing, fear forcing the air from her lungs.

'What the hell is going on here?' A voice suddenly filled the room and Sean stood up.

Thank you, God. Thank you, God.

'Hey, Nick, just stopped by for a chat,' said Sean to her husband, smoothing his hair.

'That didn't look like a chat.' Nick stood up tall, his shoulders back, his face full of suspicion and anger.

Cecelia stood up, her face flaming, and she pulled at her shirt where some buttons had come away. She moved away from Sean as fast as she could.

Nick moved into the room. 'You're not… What were you doing?' Cecelia could hear him fighting his shock. He looked at Sean and then at Cecelia.

'Your missus and me were just being friendly. You know that women need to be taken care of, Nick, and it doesn't seem to me like you've been taking care of her. She's been giving me signals for years.' He thrust his large belly out and then he stepped forward, a little swagger in his step, as though certain that he was in control right then.

'Liar, you're a liar!' Cecelia shouted. Indignant tears spilled over onto her cheeks. There was no way Nick would believe him, was there? 'Please, Nick, he's lying,' she almost begged.

'I think you're lying, Sean,' said Nick slowly. 'I saw what you were doing. I heard her asking you to get off. I don't know who you think you are but that looked like assault to me.'

'Now just hold on there,' replied Sean, resting his hand on his gun. 'You're getting way ahead of yourself, mate. She wanted it.

She asked for it and then she saw you. I'm sure we can all agree that it's a good thing nothing happened and just move on with our lives. Guess we won't be having any more wine together, hey, Cecelia,' he said to her and then he winked.

'You absolute—' began Cecelia but then she heard a soft grunt and turned. Theo was standing in the kitchen looking at the three of them, holding a knife. None of them had noticed him there. His eyes were wide and panicked. He jutted the knife towards Sean. He had seen something, heard something, and Cecelia knew without a doubt that he was trying to protect her. 'It's okay, Theo,' she said. 'You can put it down. Dad is here now. You can put it down.'

And she had meant those words because no matter what had happened between her and Nick, how complicated things had become, she understood that she was safe when he was there.

'It's fine, mate,' said Nick, 'you can put it down. Everything is fine.'

Both she and Nick began making their way towards Theo, their hands up, ready to grab him or the knife, but Sean moved faster than both of them. And Sean was deeply furious at having been disturbed.

'You little shit.' Sean covered the few steps to Theo in seconds, grabbing his shoulder.

'Eee,' squealed Theo and he lunged at Sean with the knife. Sean grabbed his hair and pulled and then he grabbed the knife and held it above Theo. Nick ran at him, yanking his son and pushing him away. Sean stepped towards Nick, the knife in his hand, and suddenly Nick made a sound, a low grunting sound as he looked down, seeing the knife was inside him. Sean was holding the handle, his mouth a circle of disbelief. A frozen moment of horror passed.

Cecelia was numb as she watched the blood stain Nick's shirt, and then he looked up at her, his mouth slightly open, his confusion obvious. He turned to look at his son as his face paled. 'Run, Theo, get help,' he gasped.

Cecelia felt the protective numbness give way to sensations, sounds, the smell of sweat and blood in the air and she shuddered at where she was and what was happening. She screamed from deep inside herself, filling her own ears with the noise of her distress. Theo took off, out the door.

Although Nick tried to fight back, Sean plunged the knife further, deeper into his chest, and Nick fell over, the blood spreading thickly across his blue shirt, changing the colour slowly as blue and red merged.

As Nick fell, Sean let go of the knife. He looked down at Nick, then he grabbed a tea towel off the counter and hastily wiped the knife handle.

'No!' screamed Cecelia, darting over and dropping to her husband's side. She looked up at Sean. 'Please, no,' she said covering his body with her own, and as she did this, her hand went to the handle of the knife and she pulled it out, dragging a deep wail of pain from Nick. She knows she probably shouldn't have done it but she had needed it out of her husband's body. She held the knife towards Sean, her hand trembling. 'No,' she begged, her hand shaking.

Sean looked around the room, his head swivelling, and then he ran for the door. He stopped before he left the cabin, his face flushed, breathing hard. 'You had better call this in as an accident. You had better keep your mouth shut. I'll find that kid. I'll catch up to him and I'll…' His voice was menacing, filled with evil intent. Nick was still, his eyes closed, his breathing laboured.

In Cecelia's hand, the knife vibrated with the shaking of her body. 'I won't… say anything. Don't hurt Theo. Please, please don't hurt Theo,' she pleaded.

He pointed his finger at her, warning her, and then he was gone.

She heard his car start up and roar away. Silence closed in on the cabin and then there was a rumble of thunder in the distance, the incoming storm threatening.

Nick's eyelids fluttered but didn't open. She could smell the metallic blood on his shirt as it raced across his chest. Her body was heavy. Shock enclosed her in a bubble and she couldn't think, couldn't speak, couldn't move until a policewoman rested her hands on her shoulders and said, 'Let go of it now, let go.'

She knows that someone came into the cabin, a woman. She remembers a scream, remembers staring at a woman's face, but she has no idea who she was or what she was doing there.

She just remembers the bubble feeling, the feeling of being separated from the whole world by a thin pane of tinted glass and needing to remain still and silent. She understood she needed to keep quiet about what had happened to protect her son. It was all that mattered.

She has no idea how Theo managed to reach her, but as he sang, she felt the words rise up inside her and the glass shatter and fall away. You cannot hide from the truth. She can no longer hide from the truth of what she's done to her marriage in her quest to be the perfect mother of an autistic child. She cannot hide from the fact that she pushed her daughter away because she thought she didn't need her as much as her son did. And she can no longer hide from the fact that Theo is going to be fine. He will always be special, always different, but he will be fine. He will be fine and she needs to find herself a life with her husband and children. That's the truth she understands now. The other truth, the truth of what happened in that cabin, needed to be told and she has told it now. She has.

CHAPTER FORTY-SEVEN

Theo

Mum is talking, talking, talking. She has found her words now. She is telling about the bad thing. She is telling about when Dad said, 'Run, Theo, get help.'

I did run. I did get help. I got help. I got Rose. And when Rose fell, I got help for Rose. I am Theo and I am help but I don't listen to the words anymore. Kaycee is watching Mum talk and talk and there are tears on her cheek. Tears mean you are sad. I am not sad because I am here with Mum and Dad and Kaycee.

I am safe and I am quiet inside me and it is not too much right now.

CHAPTER FORTY-EIGHT

Kaycee

Kaycee cannot think how to process what her mother has just said. She stands up because her legs feel like they've fallen asleep. 'Mum… I'm… It wasn't your fault,' she bursts out and she crouches down by her mother's chair. 'There's no way it was your fault.'

Her mother grabs her in a hug that is long and hard.

From the door to her father's room, they hear someone clapping. It's Sean Peterson.

'That was a wonderful story you just told, Cecelia,' he says, his voice flat. 'But of course, you know it's not true.'

'Um, Sergeant, Sergeant, sir, I really think you shouldn't be here,' says Constable Emmerson. His voice wobbles a little at having to speak to his superior in such a way.

Kaycee stands up. 'Get out, get out,' she hisses at him.

'Not until I hear the truth. Your mother is a liar. She and your father are trying to put this on me and I won't have it.' He points his finger at Cecelia, his round face growing red. He sounds so completely certain, so sure of himself, that for a nanosecond Kaycee even wonders if he's telling the truth.

'My mother wouldn't lie,' she says through clenched teeth. 'You need to stay away from them, from all of us.'

'Listen here, girlie,' he replies. 'I'm a police officer and your parents are two damaged individuals in a crap marriage. Just about everyone in town knows that. She asked me to come to the cabin.

She wanted me there and she wanted what happened, and when he caught us, it all went to shit but it had nothing to do with me. I've just been caught in the middle of their sick relationship. She stabbed him because he wanted a divorce and she didn't want to be alone. That's the real truth you need to accept.'

'Look, Sergeant, in light of what's been said, I really think—'

'Shut up, Emmerson. I'm in charge here.'

'You're a liar,' whispers her mother, her hand holding on to her father's.

'You're a liar,' Nick croaks.

'Oh, please, no one is going to believe the two of you,' Sean spits, baring his teeth.

'Theo saw it all,' says Kaycee. 'He can tell us.'

'Him?' The sergeant laughs. 'He can't speak. And I don't care what he does with his hands. He can't explain it at all. You hold on to your silence, boy, that's all that you're good for.'

CHAPTER FORTY-NINE

Theo

I look at the angry, angry man. I know angry. Benjamin showed me a picture. He says I can't speak. He says I must stay silent. I am a silent boy but I am a boy who can communicate. Communicate is when you tell people how you feel and what you think. Benjamin explained communicate to me. It's when you answer questions and talk about yourself. And even if you can't talk, you can still communicate.

I was silent but I could still communicate. But I'm not silent anymore.

I stand up and leave my straws in their neat rows on the ground. I point my finger at the man.

'He hurt Mum and he hurt Dad. He hurt Dad with the knife,' I say and then I sit down again. My voice is strange in my ears but I don't mind.

There is a lot of shouting but I don't listen to the shouting.

I line up the straws again. Red, yellow, blue, green. Red, yellow, blue, green.

CHAPTER FIFTY

Wednesday

Rose

'Sean's been arrested,' says William. 'That constable, the young one, Samuel Emmerson, he was in the room when the Somertons saw each other. They have the whole story. You're not going to believe this… Theo told everyone. He stood up and told them that Sean hurt his mum and dad.'

Rose doesn't try and stop her tears. She is feeling groggy from the pain medication, drifting in and out of sleep. 'It will take quite a few weeks to feel back to normal at your age,' Dr Greenblatt helpfully informed her.

She listens as William tells the story and she does believe it.

Her son will go to prison. He will be there for a very long time. She will most likely be long gone by the time he gets out, and he has no idea that he is hers. He would have become a different man if she had raised him but she had no choice. It's taken such a long time for women to have any choices at all in their lives, and from what she reads and hears on the radio, everyone keeps trying to take those choices away.

'I need to tell him,' murmurs Rose.

'Need to tell him what?' asks William, patting her hand.

'That he's my son,' she says.

'Oh, I don't know, Rose,' replies William.

'I need to tell him. Whatever he's done and whoever he is – he needs to know.'

William gives her a quick kiss on the forehead. 'Whatever you want, Auntie Rose.'

There is a soft knock at the door and William goes to open it.

'Oh,' he says as he sees three members of the Somerton family huddled in a group.

'We want to say thank you,' says the older woman, and Rose lifts herself a little to see them.

'Come in, come in,' she says.

They crowd into the room and Rose studies them, matching Theo's face with that of his sister, who shares his white-blonde hair and blue eyes, and comparing them to their mother, with her dark hair and brown eyes. Theo must look more like his father. Her son looks more like his father and is, sadly, exactly like his father. Rose smiles at the little family.

They are all dressed warmly, Theo in blue, and they are all a little rosy-cheeked as though they have been outside in the cold for a walk. They bring with them the smell of damp earth and autumn air. Theo looks around the room and then he hides behind his mother.

No one quite knows what to say and all the things that need to be said hang in the air, filling up the space. Until finally Rose says, 'You've raised a good lad in Theo.'

'Thank you. I can't… We can't… We can never tell you what it means to us that you helped him,' says the girl because her mother is trying not to cry. 'I'm Kaycee and this is my mum, Cecelia.' Her voice is sure and strong.

'The good Lord sent him to me,' says Rose.

'I was praying for him,' says Cecelia, taking a deep breath, 'praying that he would be safe. But I never thought… Well, he was so lucky to have found you. We were so lucky. I don't think… If anything had happened…' she says, wiping away some more tears.

'Some prayers are answered. Not all but some,' says Rose. 'That's what you need to hold on to now, some prayers are answered. Is your husband…?'

'Doing well,' says the woman with a smile. 'He'll be fine.'

Rose nods her head, satisfied that this little family have not been irreparably damaged by the child she gave birth to. It would have been a heavy load of guilt for her to carry. She will still carry guilt but at least the Somerton family will return home intact. It could so easily have not been the case.

'Come here, Theo, let me look at you, lad.'

Theo steps out from behind his mother. He looks well, warm and dry, still like an angel with his halo of curls.

'You got help,' she signs.

He nods his head and lifts his hands. He signs back, 'I got help.'

'You were very brave,' says Rose.

'I was brave,' he signs. Rose notes that he signs slowly so that she can understand.

'Yes,' Rose nods, 'you're a good lad.'

'You were brave,' he signs.

Rose chuckles. 'Yes, I suppose I was.' She feels Mary's voice in his words. She has been brave enough to finally tell her story and she knows Mary would have been proud.

And then slowly, clearly, his voice light and sweet, Theo says, 'You were help, Rose.'

'Oh, Theo,' says his mother.

'Well done, Theo,' says his sister.

'That's my good lad,' says Rose.

And Theo smiles, a simple, perfect smile as the autumn sunshine touches his curls, his silence gone, along with the rain.

EPILOGUE

Four weeks later

Rose

'I'm fine, William, you can stop fussing and go to work,' huffs Rose.

'Okay, if you're sure…' he says, uncertainty in his voice.

'William, that nice young Maggie will be over soon to help me shower, and I can walk now that I've got the boot. Off you go.' Rose makes a shooing motion with her hand.

He gathers up his things and leaves the house, reluctance in every step. Her nephew is usually home with Rose until Maggie arrives to spend the day with her, but today he has to go in early to catalogue a shipment of books.

'Must be costing a fortune,' Rose said to William and Graham about the nurse coming every day to help her shower and dress and generally keep her company. But she has to admit that she does enjoy chatting with her. Maggie is one of those people born with a sunny disposition and she is happy all the time, filled with joy at the rising sun or at the presence of a rainbow in the sky after a rainstorm.

'The health fund pays some and we are perfectly capable of paying the rest as you know, Rose. Graham has always been a dab hand at stocks, and of course his books sell really well.'

Rose has never really discussed money with William and Graham but they do seem to have a lot of it for a librarian and a historian who writes books. Their house is beautiful with wide timber floors and stonework everywhere, and Rose has her own little space with a bedroom and bathroom and even a small kitchenette where she can make herself a cup of tea if she wants to.

'You're not going back to that cabin, ever,' William said to her at the hospital.

'I'll stay till I'm able to care for myself and then home I go,' Rose snorted.

'We'll see about that,' said William, and Rose knew she was going to have to fight to go home. The thing is, now that she's here, she's not sure she wants to be anywhere else.

As she hears the door close, she picks up the remote and turns on Netflix. William and Graham were very patient about explaining to her how to use the television set in her room and here in the living room. And a whole new world has opened up to Rose. She's obsessed with a series about the queen. 'Let's see what those royals have been up to, Mary,' she says as she clicks through screens.

As the music begins, signalling the start of the next episode, she reminds herself that she needs to get Maggie to post a letter for her. Sean has been denied bail and is being held on remand down in Sydney. She has written to him four times, including today's letter. He hasn't replied to any of them but his wife, Monica, did come by with some fruit and chocolate after Rose got out of the hospital. Nearly the whole town has been by at least once, and Rose was pleased when the visiting died down, but grateful that so many thought to come and see her. The story ran through the town faster than a wildfire, the gossips savouring every detail. But most people have been very kind. William had a wonderful time baking up a storm for everyone, and Rose thinks as many stopped by for his biscuits and cakes as to see her.

'Sean got your letter. He told me that it explained a lot and he's grateful that you wrote,' Monica told her. She was thinner than she'd ever been and Rose felt her heart swell with sympathy for the woman. She is standing by her husband, supporting him when many wouldn't.

'He is a product of his upbringing. It doesn't excuse anything, and he should pay, but he's suffering for it, Rose. He looked a different man when I went to visit. It's not easy for an ex-policeman in jail.'

Rose didn't know what to say to that so she simply patted Monica's hand.

She will keep writing to Sean every now and again. He did a monstrous thing but monsters are made not born, and there is some good in him somewhere. She only hopes he can find it before his life is over.

The programme begins and she smiles. 'Look at that, Mary. I wish you were here, love,' she sighs.

Outside, the wind whips up some brown leaves and Rose feels a little chill in the warm room.

'I know, love, of course you're here. You're always here.'

CECELIA

Cecelia watches Theo rearrange the line of toy cars again. Yesterday she heard him whisper the name of each and every car. He's still shy about using his voice, except for the word 'no'. That's a word he uses with almost frustrating frequency but Cecelia cannot be anything except grateful for every sound he utters.

She is standing in the kitchen preparing dinner for Theo. It's already dark outside and very cold. Winter is really here. Theo is sitting in front of the gas fire, occasionally turning from his line of cars to watch the dancing orange flames.

There is a ping on her phone and she looks down to see a text message from Nick.

Surgery went well. Leaving the hospital now. See you soon xx

She sends him a thumbs up in reply. She knows he was worried about this surgery on a twelve-year-old boy so he will be relieved to have it done, especially since it's only the second surgery he's done since he returned to work. He has healed quickly but held himself back from operating on anyone until he was certain he was ready.

Cecelia would never tell anyone she was grateful for his injury but sometimes she experiences something like gratitude when she thinks about it. The two weeks he spent at home have changed their marriage. It was clear to both of them the day Sean came to the cabin that their marriage was over. But once they returned home with those terrible few days behind them, they both understood that they needed a new way forward. Cecelia found a therapist willing to come to the house, and together she and Nick have cracked open their marriage and stared into the parts they didn't want to see. There have been a lot of tears, from both of them, but sometimes they manage to laugh their way through their twice-weekly sessions. In between they have continued talking, arguing, laughing, loving each other.

Cecelia knows they have been given a second chance. Neither of them wants to waste it. New rules for family time have emerged and Cecelia is looking for work again, just part-time – something to allow her some time away from only thinking about Theo and his needs. She understands that he doesn't need her complete focus anymore. He survived a traumatic event, he understood he needed to get help and he did just that. He is more capable than most children his age, and she knows it's fine to let go – just a little.

It wasn't easy to come to this conclusion and there have been many nights when she has wondered who she will be if she is not defined as Theo's mother, but she's willing to find out now and that's made a huge difference to her relationship with Nick and with Kaycee.

She wipes her hands on a tea towel and starts loading the dishwasher as she thinks about Kaycee's last email. She is thinking about moving back home so she can be around more to help with Theo but also because, Cecelia knows, Jonah still lives at home with his parents, only a suburb away.

'That would be the most wonderful thing in the world,' Cecelia wrote in response to Kaycee's idea. It would be wonderful to have her family all together. Right now, she and her daughter are making time for each other every couple of nights to really talk. Cecelia knows that soon Kaycee will be busy with exams and assignments and they won't speak as much, but they have made a good start on repairing their relationship. Some days Cecelia feels like she's walking around with a roll of duct tape, patching up her family because there are so many cracks that she tried not to see. Most days she is extraordinarily grateful that her family are here to tell the tale. And she is beyond thankful for Rose, who took her little boy in and kept him safe.

Sean's trial is a long time away and she knows that both she and Nick will have to testify. The thought makes her nervous; the idea of seeing him again makes her break into a sweat but it needs to be done. She has refused to allow Theo to appear in court but the public prosecutor has agreed to record his statement; he can speak or use sign language, whichever one he feels most comfortable with on the day. She wonders if Rose will attend the trial although she imagines it would be very painful to look into the eyes of the man she gave birth to, knowing what he did and what he tried to do.

She tries to call Rose once a week, just to see how she is getting on. They don't discuss Sean or the trial or anything that happened during those three days. Cecelia is waiting for the elderly woman to bring it up but perhaps Rose is waiting for the same from her. They are delicately polite with each other. Things are still too raw. Cecelia is sure the conversation will be had during one of their calls but she's happy to let Rose lead the way.

The smell of roast potatoes alerts Cecelia to the fact that Theo's dinner is ready. As she puts everything on the plate, making sure nothing touches, she starts to sing without thinking about it.

'This little light of mine. I'm going to let it shine.'

And from the living room, she hears her son, her little light, hum along for a moment before the cars draw his attention and a new line is begun.

KAYCEE

Kaycee waits outside the lecture hall. Jonah's class will be over in a few minutes and they are going to get something to eat together. She stares down at her phone as she waits, reading through the very long, very complicated message from Theo about exactly how long it took him and Benjamin to take apart an old robot and about all the parts it had. She smiles as she reads. Theo has a lot to say about robots and she imagines a future for him one day at a giant tech company where the fact that he is neurodiverse is an appreciated asset.

The door to the lecture hall next door to Jonah's opens and students stream out, forcing Kaycee to step back. Someone bumps her shoulder and she looks up into Adam's brown eyes. 'Oh, hey... hey,' he says, having the good grace to blush.

'Hey, Adam,' she says and then she smiles because he's not her problem anymore.

'I haven't, um, seen you at the bar... you know.'

'Yeah, I've given that up. It's not really a productive way to spend time. I'm catching up on my work. I can't believe I nearly wasted the whole year. But I'm back on track now.' Adam nods, understanding the implied insult, and then he shrugs and raises his hand in a goodbye and is swept away by the stream of students. Jonah says he's still at the bar every night, a different girl on his arm.

Change is hard, Kaycee knows that. It's hard and you have to commit, but sometimes there is a catalyst that is so huge, it can only be viewed as a message from the universe.

She nearly lost her family. She nearly lost them all because she was so busy trying to lose herself.

She is looking forward to being back at home, to spending time with Theo and her parents, who are just a little bit annoying right now with their endless secret smiles and laughter.

The door to Jonah's lecture hall swings open and she steps aside.

'Hey,' he says when he sees her, his eyes lighting up in a way that she never assumed was possible.

'Hey,' she says. 'Ready?'

'Ready.'

THEO

'Theo,' says Mum, 'it's time to put those toys away and come and get some dinner.'

'No,' I say and Mum laughs.

'I know that's your new favourite word, Theo, but you still have to come and have dinner. Benjamin is coming over to babysit while Dad and I go out, and you won't be allowed to share the cookies with him unless you've eaten dinner.'

I pick up my blue cars and put them in their box. 1, 2, 3, 4, 5, 6, 7, 8, 9, 10. Next row. 1, 2, 3, 4, 5, 6, 7, 8, 9, 10.

I sit at the table where Mum has put dinner. The peas are not touching the chicken and the roast potatoes are not touching the peas and now I can eat. Benjamin is coming. He knows about robots. We will make a robot from the kit Dad bought me. Underneath my blue jumper, I am wearing a red T-shirt. Mum got it for me for 'try something new day'. I don't like red. I only like blue. But the T-shirt has a robot on the front with long metal arms and legs and lots of buttons. Tonight, me and Benjamin are building a robot so I need my robot T-shirt. Benjamin teaches me at school but tonight he is coming here to be with me when Mum and Dad go out on a 'date night'. A date night is when Mum and Dad go out and I need Benjamin to come and stay with me. Fourteen days ago, Kaycee stayed with me. She doesn't like robots but she knows about science. We did an experiment with Coke and Mentos and there was an explosion and Kaycee laughed and I laughed and then she cleaned up the mess.

Kaycee is at university now. Her boyfriend is Jonah and he is going to be a doctor. Dad is a doctor. He says Jonah is a 'brilliant young man'. I eat my peas. There are thirty peas. Mum knows that I like thirty peas. I eat my chicken.

A lady came to visit Mum after school yesterday. Her name was Amber. Amber is a gold colour. Her name is a colour. I liked that her name is a colour. I played *Minecraft* on my iPad and I built a new room for my house.

Amber said, 'I just needed to know you were all okay.'

Mum said, 'We're well. Nick, my husband, is still a little weak but he'll be fine, and he's just… Well, I wanted to thank you.'

Amber said, 'I don't think I was exactly a hero. I was in shock.'

Mum said, 'Anyone would have been.'

Amber sat on the blue sofa and held hands with a man like Kaycee holds hands with Jonah. His name is James. James is not a colour, just a name.

The chicken is crispy and the roast potatoes are warm and salty. I finish my food so that I can have cookies with Benjamin. Benjamin is coming because Mum and Dad are having a date night. They have a date night every two weeks on a Wednesday. Today is Wednesday and this Wednesday was circled in red on the calendar that hangs on the back of the kitchen door. That means that this is a date night for Mum and Dad.

Benjamin will help me write an email to Rose. Rose doesn't have a computer. William has a computer.

His email address is williamrhodes@gmail.com. I will tell Rose about the robot. Rose likes my emails. 'I like your emails,' she wrote. Rose was help. Rose was help until she fell and then I was help. Theo was help and Dad says I am also a 'brilliant young man' like Jonah.

Rose lives with William and Graham. Graham knows about the history of robots in Australia. But he doesn't know about robots now. Benjamin knows about robots now. In eighteen days, we are going to visit Rose and Graham and William for tea. It will be Sunday.

'Good job, Theo,' Mum says because all the dinner is finished. Mum smiles. She is happy. When you smile, you are happy. Except sometimes. The sergeant wasn't happy when he smiled at Mum. He was trying to hurt her but I was help.

'Run,' said Dad, 'get help.' I ran. I found Rose. Rose was help. I got help. I was help and now Mum smiles and Dad smiles and Kaycee smiles and I can make the word 'no' come out of my mouth and the words 'yes' and 'Mum' and 'Dad' and 'Kaycee'. Other words come too.

And when the words come out of my mouth, everyone smiles.

A LETTER FROM NICOLE

Hello,

I would like to thank you for taking the time to read *Bring Him Home*. If you did enjoy it, and want to keep up to date with all my latest releases, just sign up at the following link. Your email address will never be shared and you can unsubscribe at any time.

www.bookouture.com/nicole-trope

It is always difficult to write about a situation that you are only able to view from the outside. It was very important to me when writing about a child on the spectrum that I did as much research as I could so that I would be able to faithfully communicate what it felt like to be a member of a family with a child who is neurodiverse. In all my readings – both those that were written by people who are on the spectrum and those written by people with family members on the spectrum – one idea kept coming up again and again: once you've met one person with autism, you've met one person with autism. There is no way to blanket all those who are on the spectrum with certain behaviours, ideas or opinions. People on the spectrum are as different as people in any situation. Theo is simply Theo, and while many of his behaviours are recognisable as possibly being part of a group of behaviours exhibited on the spectrum, who he is is entirely himself. Theo is just Theo.

I do hope that if you are on the spectrum or if you are raising a child on the spectrum, you feel that I have done justice with this character. I found him fascinating to write and loved the way he thought and how he saw the world.

For Rose, the change in the way society sees children like Theo when compared to how they saw and treated her brother Lionel many decades ago was an important form of closure. We, as a society, know better now and so we do better when accommodating neurodiverse people. We are not perfect, but better.

Despite what this family suffered, I am glad that they managed to find a way forward, together and stronger for the experience.

I see a bright future for both Kaycee and Theo and many happy years ahead for Nick and Cecelia, who nearly lost each other.

If you have enjoyed this novel, it would be lovely if you could take the time to leave a review. I read them all and find it inspiring when readers connect with the characters I write about.

I would also love to hear from you. You can find me on Facebook and Twitter and I'm always happy to connect with readers.

Thanks again for reading.
Nicole x

NicoleTrope

@nicoletrope

ACKNOWLEDGEMENTS

I would like to thank, as usual, Christina Demosthenous for her wonderful editorial advice and her ability to be constantly working but also always available to stressed authors. I am so pleased to be working with her and look forward to each new set of notes and the ideas that she brings to the work.

I would also like to thank Sarah Hardy for all her hard work in spreading the word about this novel. Thanks to the whole team at Bookouture, including Alexandra Holmes and Martina Arzu. Thanks to DeAndra Lupu for another brilliant copy edit, and to the proofreader, Liz Hatherell.

Thanks to my mother, Hilary, for being my first reader and my final reader before the book is sent out into the world.

Thanks also to David, Mikhayla, Isabella and Jacob.

And once again thank you to those who read, review, blog about my work and contact me on Facebook or Twitter to let me know my work moved you. Every review is appreciated and I do read them all.